PRAISE FOR

℘ENUMBRAS

"*Penumbras* is Braden Bell's best writing so far. Adventure, magic, humor, and teen angst can be found on every page. And any book that casts a music teacher as the coolest of them all is a book worth reading. If you liked *The Kindling*, you'll love *Penumbras*."

DENAE HANDY, columnist for *Meridian Magazine*, and blogger of *My Real Life Was Backordered*

"If you love a fast-paced story and magic with a twist, *Penumbras* is your book. Braden Bell captures young love in all its humorous awkwardness and poignantly portrays honor and virtue and the human susceptibility to the ugly subtleties of evil."

M. ANN ROHRER, author of *Mattie*

"Magic and mayhem rock Marion Academy again in Braden Bell's *Middle School Magic: Penumbras*. Their previous battles have made Conner and Lexa Dell and their best friend, Melanie Stephens, stronger and more skillful Magi, but Conner learns that facing the darkness has consequences that can tarnish even the purest of hearts, pulling even the best of friends apart."

LAURIE LEWIS, author of *Awakening Avery*, and the Free Men and Dreamers series

"Braden Bell has done it again! Told with inventive wit and well-informed logic, *Penumbras* is about the unfolding gifts and powers of our young Magi friends. The action begins in paragraph one and never lets up as the battle between the forces of darkness and light continues. This time the struggle is more personal, for Conner must contend with the aftereffects of his imprisonment in the Shadowbox, and he needs the particular gifts of his sister Lexa and his friend Melanie to save him."

—LIZ ADAIR, Whitney Award winner
of *Counting the Cost*

MIDDLE SCHOOL MAGIC

PENUMBRAS

MIDDLE SCHOOL MAGIC

PENUMBRAS

BRADEN BELL

SWEETWATER BOOKS,
AN IMPRINT OF CEDAR FORT, INC.
SPRINGVILLE, UTAH

ISBN 13: 978-1-4621-1220-3

LIBRARY OF CONGRESS CATALOGING-IN-PUBLICATION DATA

Bell, Braden, author.
Penumbras / by Braden Bell.
    pages cm -- (Middle school magic)
  Summary: Just when Conner, Lexa, and Melanie think life is normal again, a dangerous shadow creature begins to hunt them and the three must develop their powers in order to conquer this new peril and protect their school.
  ISBN 978-1-4621-1220-3 (pbk. : alk. paper)
  [1. Magic--Fiction. 2. Monsters--Fiction. 3. Middle schools--Fiction. 4. Schools--Fiction.] I. Title. II. Series: Bell, Braden. Middle school magic.
  PZ7.B3889145Pen 2013
  [Fic]--dc23
                                2013005916

Published by Sweetwater Books, an imprint of Cedar Fort, Inc.
2373 W. 700 S., Springville, UT 84663
Distributed by Cedar Fort, Inc., www.cedarfort.com

Cover design by Angela D. Olsen
Cover design © 2013 by Lyle Mortimer
Typeset and edited by Melissa J. Caldwell

Printed in the United States of America

10 9 8 7 6 5 4 3 2 1

*To my stage managers, the unsung heroes of any production.
You made magic and brought order. Thank you.*

*And to the Harding Academy Class of 2013.
You have touched me deeply, and I am a better person for
having known you.*

Contents

CONTENTS

CONTENTS

CHAPTER 1

SHADOW PUPPETS

CONNER DELL DIDN'T MEAN TO BLOW UP the school bus.

Or the bathrooms.

In fact, he only wanted to go to sleep and possibly dream about Melanie Stephens.

But explosions had a funny way of happening when Conner and his friends were around.

It all started on the annual seventh grade science trip to the Sea Lab at Dauphin Island, Alabama. Fifty-four thirteen-year-olds on a five-day field trip. What could go wrong?

Especially when three of them happened to be Magi.

For a fraction of a second, Conner thought he saw shadows slithering along the base of the cinder-block walls. Tensing, he blinked and looked again.

Nothing. He was alone in the darkness of his dorm room.

Well, except for the presence of his friend and field trip roommate, Pilaf.

Across the room, Pilaf disturbed the darkness by turning on his flashlight and digging through a giant floral print suitcase. Fishing out a book, Pilaf hunched over, tucked the flashlight under his chin, and read.

"What are you reading?" Conner asked.

"Sorry. Did I wake you up?" Pilaf squeaked. "I couldn't sleep. I guess I slept too much on the bus."

"No worries." Conner burrowed into his sleeping bag. He didn't like messing with sheets on these trips. The springs of the ancient bed creaked beneath him. "I'm not sleepy either." *Lexa? Can you hear me?* Conner reached out in his thoughts, wondering if his twin sister was awake in her room on the girls' floor. Head-talking was a cool benefit of being one of the Magi—a secret group of warriors who used the power of Light to battle evil.

No answer from Lexa. Her allergy medicine must have knocked her out.

Melanie? He tried Lexa's best friend, Melanie Stephens—also one of the Magi-in-training. Conner listened for her response, trying to ignore the backflip in his chest that came when he thought of her. No answer. Melanie had taken something for motion sickness on the bus. She must be knocked out too.

Conner jerked up as something skittered across the ceiling right above him. No doubt something was there this time. He grabbed his own flashlight, raking the beam across the ceiling tiles as someone whispered his name.

Co-o-o-o-n-n-e-r-r-r-r-r.

"What?" Conner pointed his flashlight at Pilaf, who

looked up from his book, blinking behind his thick glasses. Pilaf's blinks always reminded Conner of the way a light on a computer blinked when it processed data.

"What?" Pilaf squinted back at him.

"Why did you call me?" Conner asked.

"I didn't." Pilaf looked down at his book.

On edge now, Conner lay back down, scanning the room for more shadowy movement, his fingers ready to snap his flashlight back on at any second.

Co-n-n-e-r-r-r-r-r D-e-l-l-l-l-l.

A whispered, hissing sort of growl sounded in his head as a flicker of movement caught his eye. He whipped his head around in time to see a shadowy tail vanish under Pilaf's bed. Flipping his flashlight on, he investigated the space under the metal frame.

Nothing there.

"What are you doing, Conner?" Pilaf managed to blink and stare at the same time.

Trying to protect you from slithery shadow monsters that could slurp your soul like a slushie, Conner thought. How could he keep the flashlight on without alarming Pilaf? Out loud, he said, "Uh, it's a game. Flashlight tag. You're it." He shined the flashlight at Pilaf.

"How do you play?"

"Well . . . one person's it, and he shines a flashlight all over the room."

"That's all?" Pilaf blinked until Conner wondered if he was broadcasting the telephone book in Morse code. "It seems kind of pointless."

"Uh, yeah." Conner said. "You're right. Lame. How about shadow puppets?" He slipped his hand in front of the flashlight, wiggling his fingers until the shadow resembled a horse.

"Cool!" Pilaf shouted.

A knock at the door interrupted them, and their tired-looking science teacher poked his head in, glaring beneath tousled red hair. "What's going on in here?"

"Sorry, Mr. Keller," Pilaf said. "We slept on the bus ride, so we're not tired. Conner's making shadows with his hands. Look, a horse!"

"Neeeiiiiggghhh." Conner threw in sound effects as a special feature.

Apparently unimpressed with great art, Mr. Keller frowned. "Get some sleep. We have a full day tomorrow."

"Yes, sir." Conner swallowed his depression at the thought of a five-day science class. Five days of plankton, ocean salinity, salt marshes, and beach ecology. Five days of science, 24/7. At least they were close to the beach. That might be fun.

"Do another one," Pilaf whispered as the sound of Mr. Keller's footsteps retreated down the hall.

"Okay, but be quiet this time." Conner opened his fingers, making a snake's mouth, complete with a flickering tongue.

It seemed so real that Conner thought he heard a hiss. Unsettled, he dropped his hands, but the hissing noise continued, twisting into words.

Co-n-n-e-r-r-r-r-r D-e-l-l-l-l-l—

Trying to squash the sound, Conner raised his voice. "Here's another one." He cupped his hands on top of each other, stuck his thumb up, and opened his fingers slightly.

"Wow!" Pilaf yelled. "A wolf!" He giggled as Conner

opened the wolf's mouth and growled. "Little pig, little pig let me come in." Conner prayed that none of the other seventh-grade boys heard he'd been doing Three Little Pigs shadow plays. That would not be cool.

Co-n-n-e-r-r-r-r-r D-e-l-l-l-l-l—

The weird voice became louder. Conner dropped his hands away from the flashlight.

The wolf head stayed there.

Fighting panic, Conner switched the flashlight off, but the wolf head remained, darker than the darkest shadows on the wall.

It stretched and grew bigger, becoming life-size within seconds. It turned and stared at Conner, now a three-dimensional head sticking out of the wall like some kind of freaky hunting souvenir.

The wolf growled, jumped off the wall, and sailed across the room toward Conner.

CHAPTER 2.

School Bus Flambé

CONNER DOVE OFF HIS BED AS THE HUGE shadow-wolf landed and tore into his sleeping bag. He ninja-rolled across the floor as a blizzard of fabric and insulation flew through the air. Between rolls, he noticed Pilaf's praying-mantis eyes stretched even wider than usual, but Conner didn't have time to say anything. He needed to get out of the room and lead the wolf away from Pilaf.

Crab-walking backward, Conner scuttled toward the door as the wolf leaped from the bed to the floor. *Lexa!* he shouted in his head. *Melanie!* No answer. He held up his arm and shot a bolt of red Light at the wolf. He missed, but the wolf slowed to dodge the burst, allowing Conner time to jump up and run out of the room.

He made it three or four yards down the long hall before the shadow-wolf leaped through the thick cinder-block wall and sailed toward him, jaws open. It growled, and now it sounded mad.

Should he fight or run? Fighting an unknown enemy seemed stupid, so Conner ran. He juked to one side and sped up, wishing he'd gone farther in his Magi training. Real Magi could turn into comets and shoot through the air—which would come in handy right now. Unfortunately, Conner, Lexa, and Melanie hadn't learned that yet—only their teachers could do stuff like . . .

Teachers.

Teachers! Duh! Mrs. Sharpe, their history teacher, was one of the Magi and had come to chaperone the trip. She'd know how to handle this thing. Conner thought about sending her a sigil—Magi communicated by sending messages in small pieces of their souls called sigils. But the wolf growled just inches behind him, and he decided that he didn't dare stop, even for a second.

So Conner ran as fast he could, his bare feet slapping the cold tile beneath him. Even though Conner ran at top speed, the wolf gained on him. Growing desperate, he remembered his spring break trip to Disney World two months earlier. Two bad guys, Kyle and Kelli Black, had kidnapped Melanie's younger sister, Madi. Conner had been the only witness, and in an effort to save Madi, he'd managed to move extra fast—not quite comet speed, but much faster than normal.

He really needed that now. So he focused, straining every brain cell, every muscle, in an effort to spark super-speed. The hallway grew fuzzy, as if he were running inside a tunnel made out of red Light. He felt himself accelerate, moving much faster than usual, like one of those cartoon characters whose legs spin in a blur.

Unfortunately, the increased speed reduced his control,

and Conner veered to one side, like a speeding bullet with no ability to steer. As the wall rushed closer and closer, he tried to alter his course but couldn't. Instead, he managed to speed up just enough to shoot through the open bathroom doorway instead of crashing into the wall.

Inside the U-shaped bathroom, he hurtled toward a row of toilet stalls. Gross. With enormous effort, he threw himself to the right, managing to blast into a room full of showers instead.

He shot past the first shower with so much speed that his hand hit the cold-water knob and sliced clean through the pipe. Water spurted out from the pipe behind him as he hit the next knob—and the next. He felt a little heat on his hand, but he went so fast that it didn't hurt. He beheaded the knobs on the next three showers before his mind caught up and pulled his hand in.

Past the showers now, another wall rushed toward him. Using all his strength, he threw himself to the side and managed to fly back through the opening and into the hall.

A hundred yards ahead, Conner saw the doors leading out of the dorm building. He needed to get the wolf away from a building full of unsuspecting, sleeping people. Focusing on the doors, he shot forward like a spitball with a jetpack. Risking a glance over his shoulder, he saw that he'd definitely gained some yardage.

Covering a hundred yards in ten blinks of an eye, he suddenly saw both the locked metal doors and a major flaw in his plan: he wouldn't be able to stop in time.

Bracing for impact with the doors, he threw his arms over his head.

But no crash came.

The air around him grew intensely hot, and Conner hit something that felt like thick, stretchy fabric—as if a trampoline had been stretched across the doorway. For a long second or two, he ran but didn't seem to move forward. The air grew hotter and hotter, and just as the temperature moved from "bake" to "broil," he burst through the doors, and a salty breeze blew into his face.

Outside, Conner crossed the parking lot in three seconds. Steering remained difficult, and the faster he went, the harder it got. So by the time he noticed the back of the school bus rushing closer, he couldn't change direction.

Could he fly, or at least jump, over it? Magi did that, right? He jumped and the ground rushed away from his feet as he soared up past the back emergency door. Unfortunately, his feet didn't quite clear the bus. Instead, they sliced into the metal of the roof.

His momentum carried him forward, but his feet dragged behind, slicing lengthwise through the roof of the bus. His feet and ankles got hot but didn't hurt. Well, it didn't hurt him. The bus on the other hand . . . Mr. Keller was not going to be happy with the Conner-sized gash running down the middle of the roof.

Friction slowed him down, and by the time he'd gone about half the length of the bus, he sensed the wolf getting closer. He looked over his shoulder in time to see it pounce.

Conner ducked, which changed his trajectory, knocking him into a steep dive. Heat engulfed his whole body as he shot down, down through the floor of the bus.

He sniffed. *What is that smell? Oh shoot. Not good. Gas.*

He'd just blasted with super-heated, super-speed through the gas tank.

Fueled by growing panic, he managed to come out of his dive just in time to miss pounding a crater into the asphalt below the bus. He managed some extra speed and raced away from the school bus as an enormous explosion sounded behind him.

Mr. Keller was going to be so mad.

On the bright side, maybe the explosion had killed the shadow-wolf?

He risked another look over his shoulder and saw the creature jump out of the flames around the burning school bus.

A few more steps and sand pushed up between Conner's toes as the waves rolled closer to him. Not wanting to end up somewhere in the Gulf of Mexico, he veered to the left, skidding into a sharp turn just inches before hitting the water. He couldn't believe how difficult it was to steer, and he didn't dare stop.

As he shot along the sand at the edge of the beach, the ocean spray spritzed his face. Next to him, waves washed forward in endless rows, dappled by moonlight and shadows.

Shadows.

Water.

Memories of the Shadowbox rushed over him. After freeing Madi, he'd been captured, and while imprisoned, he'd ruined some experiments being run by Lady Nightwing, the evil, mad-scientist Darkhand. She freaked out and threw him in the Shadowbox, a coffin-shaped device that projected images into Conner's mind, creating some kind of virtual reality where he did terrible things. Things he hadn't told anyone about. Things he couldn't stand to remember.

It had been almost two months, and he thought he had gotten over it, or at least buried it. But now, suppressed memories erupted from an open sewer somewhere in his soul. Sparks of hot guilt flared up, severing his connection to the Light and slamming the brakes on his high speed.

The red Light-tunnel around him collapsed. His feet stopped before his body did, and Conner crashed facedown into the sand, inhaling several lungfuls of beach before his brain told his mouth to shut.

Coughing out sand, he looked over his shoulder and saw the wolf bounding closer.

Time seemed to both slow down and speed up. What did a shadow-wolf do when it got you? Eat your body or maul your spirit? Or both?

He held up his hands, trying to re-open his gateway and connect to the Light, but nothing happened—except that the wolf got closer.

Desperate, Conner tried again. Still nothing.

With the wolf just inches away and adrenaline running a 5K inside of him, Conner tried once more, shoving his hands into the air.

The air crackled and smelled like sulfur as shining, black flames erupted around his hands, twisting into a jet of dark fire that blasted into the wolf's chest, knocking it back several yards.

Black fire?

Badly shaken, Conner looked down at his hands. Tiny

black sparks still flickered along his skin. That meant his worst fears . . .

The wolf growled and jumped back up on its feet. It had grown much bigger. Now the size of a small, really ugly horse, it snapped its teeth, crouched back, and jumped into the air, sailing toward Conner with an open mouth, trailing flecks of shadow saliva.

CHAPTER 3.

LEXA'S DREAM

L EXA DELL ROLLED OVER ON HER COT, aware that she had started to thrash with growing violence as her dreamless, Benadryl-fueled sleep shifted. Moving out of regular slumber, some part of her soul awakened, sensing hidden truths, which her brain translated into vivid visions.

As faces flashed in her mind, she recognized kids her own age. Potential Magi, these kids had been kidnapped and taken to a hidden lab where Lady Nightwing experimented with the energy that was released when their hidden powers Kindled.

Now their faces filled her dreams in flashes and bursts, mixed with images of shadowy creatures that flew through the night, hunting and stalking them.

The dream zoomed in, lurching forward, and Lexa recognized one of the figures—her brother Conner, running for his life, chased by a shadowy monster Lexa couldn't quite see. She tried to get a closer view, but black flames

13

erupted, choking everything else out. Flames twisted and jumped, burning, burning, burning, until the world seemed devoured by black fire.

The flames shrunk, and Lexa saw them reflected in two beetle-black eyes so dark they seemed almost dead. Flickers of hate bubbled up from a twisted soul, giving the only light to the otherwise lifeless eyes. Long strands of greasy, black hair hung across a tight face of pale-gray skin. Cruelty and malice had carved deep lines into the face, making it old before its time.

The Stalker. The vicious Darkhand who had nearly murdered Dr. Timberi and planned painful deaths for Lexa, Melanie, and Conner.

But as Lexa watched, the Stalker morphed, turning from a human monster in a black trench coat to a portly, middle-aged man wearing a sweater vest. Dr. Timberi. Their theater teacher and Magi mentor, who had sacrificed himself to protect Lexa and Melanie.

Black flames burst up, surrounding Dr. Timberi as his expression screamed with agony. He seemed to plead and beg for something. And then he changed into the Stalker again.

The Stalker snarled and vanished into another flurry of faces. Coming strobe-light fast, Lexa could barely register them.

Conner snarling with rage.

Melanie screaming.

And, making a strange cameo appearance in her own dream, Lexa watched herself crying.

Tiny lights everywhere, pushing back against the raging, black flames—

Lexa woke up, gasping for breath on her bed. She'd

almost tied a knot in her sleeping bag from all the twisting.

"Lexa?" From her bed across the dorm room, Melanie mumbled, her words thick from the side effects of motion-sickness medicine. "What's wrong?"

Lexa gathered her long brown hair into a ponytail, giving it an instinctive tug against a rising fear she didn't understand.

"I don't know, Mel. Weird dream. I think something bad's about to happen."

Conner? Lexa opened her thoughts and reached out to her brother. *Conner! Are you okay?* No answer. But she sensed something—fear. And she heard breathless gasps, as if he were running.

"Mel, something's wrong!" Lexa untangled herself from her sheets and called out in her mind. *Mrs. Sharpe! Wake up, please! I think Conner's in trouble.*

Mrs. Sharpe's groggy thoughts answered her a few seconds later. *I'll go check on him. You two stay where you are, just in case.*

"What was your dream, Lex?" Melanie asked.

"Well—" Lexa tried to grab on to the images as they faded away. "I don't remember everything. Black fire and shadows. And the Stalker and Dr. Timberi. And those kids who got kidnapped, I think."

"Was it a regular dream or a vision?"

"Pretty sure it was a vision—like a message from the Light. Pretty sure—but I don't remember that much." She paused. "I think I was maybe crying."

"That's weird," Melanie replied. "You never cry."

"I know. Weird," Lexa said. "I really hope Conner's okay."

CHAPTER 4

WHAT PILAF SAW

CONNER WATCHED AS THE WOLF FLEW AT him. He wished he had a chance to say good-bye to his family. And Melanie. Especially Melanie.

Thwack!

A small, green blur buzzed over Conner's shoulder, hitting the wolf between the eyes. The wolf kicked and flailed in the air like a drowning giraffe before fading into wisps of smoke that blew away.

Conner looked behind him. A woman in a gray leather suit stood about ten yards away, cradling a glowing crossbow. A silver emblem sparkled on her chest: a crescent moon surrounding an eight-pointed star. The sign of the Magi. She smiled as the breeze caught her long red hair. Lieutenant Miranda Grimaldi of the Twilight Phalanx, an elite warrior force—the Navy SEALs of the Magi world.

Conner would have cheered, except he was still coughing.

Miranda walked over and knelt down next to him. "You okay, Dell?"

After spitting out roughly ten pounds of rotten seaweed-flavored sand, Conner managed a smile. "Yeah, fine." He pretended that every bone in his body was not arguing about which hurt the most.

"Just felt like a moonlight run on the beach tonight, Dell?"

Conner laughed. "Yeah, well, Fido there wanted to play fetch. With me."

A rattlesnake made out of tan Light appeared by Grimaldi's shoulder, and a heavy Texas drawl filled the air. "Grimaldi? Status?"

Conner smiled. The rattlesnake was the sigil of Colonel Lee Murrell, the commander of the Twilight Phalanx.

Grimaldi saluted the sigil. "Yes, sir. Dell's with me. I neutralized the phantumbra, and the situation appears to be normal."

The rattlesnake sigil grinned. "Nice job, Grimaldi. You always could shoot a tick off a jackrabbit's ear. Get Dell back to his bunk. We'll debrief him tomorrow."

"Yes, sir." She saluted again, and the sigil faded. "Come on, Dell. You heard the colonel. Let's get you back to your dorm. So what happened?"

"I'm not sure. I was making hand shadows with a flashlight. I made a wolf, and it jumped off the wall and started chasing me. What was that thing anyway?"

"Called a phantumbra. At least I think that's what it was. Phantumbras are like our sigils."

"If they're like sigils, does that means someone sent it to me? I mean, like me specifically?"

"Probably. No way of knowing for sure now. Good thing you outran it—nasty things. I didn't know Morgan had taught you guys how to stream yet."

"Taught us what?"

"Streaming. You know, when Magi turn into comets. You weren't quite there, maybe halfway, but you came pretty close."

"He hasn't taught us yet."

"You seriously just streamed with no training?"

"Yeah." Conner shrugged. "Just happened."

"Impressive."

"Thanks. And thanks for shooting that—whatever that was."

"No worries," Grimaldi said. "You know, I've gotta give Morgan Timberi credit. He asked Colonel Murrell to detail some of the Phalanx on this trip to watch out for you three. I thought he was being a little paranoid—no way Umbra was gonna try anything so soon after we kicked their butts so bad two months ago. But it's a good thing Colonel listened to him."

"Have you seen Dr. Timberi?" Conner asked. "Is he okay?" Dr. Timberi had been recuperating since their last battle, and none of the students had seen him.

"Colonel Murrell saw him. Said he wasn't doing very well. He's lucky to be alive at all. The Stalker almost killed him. Nice job with those pizzas, by the way. Tactical Telemanipulation's usually a pretty advanced skill."

Conner, Lexa, and Melanie had managed to stop the Stalker by bombarding him with frozen pizzas they had filled with Light.

As Conner and Grimaldi walked back onto the

grounds of the research station, Conner heard Mr. Keller calling his name. He also saw flashing lights from over where the bus had been. Not good.

"I was hoping to get you back before they noticed you were missing," Grimaldi whispered. "Have you ever seen someone sleepwalk?"

"Yeah, on TV," Conner answered.

"That's your best chance. Start sleepwalking."

Conner closed his eyes and walked out into the light from the building.

"Conner!" Mr. Keller grabbed his arm. "Where have you been?" Conner stared at him and blinked, trying to look confused. Forcing a yawn, Conner said, "I guess I was sleepwalking. I do that at home sometimes when I get really tired. Sorry, Mr. Keller. Good thing you were here. I could have walked into the ocean. You saved me!"

Mr. Keller didn't seem all that pleased or proud of himself.

Right then Mrs. Sharpe bustled up, and Conner relaxed a little. As one of the Magi, she'd be on Conner's side.

"Conner, where have you been?" While she pretended to frown at him, her worried thoughts flowed into his head.

Are you all right, Conner? She sounded concerned. *Lexa and Melanie are worried sick about you.*

"Sleepwalking," Conner said aloud. In his thoughts, he said, *Yes, ma'am. I got chased by something called a phantumbra. Miranda—Lieutenant Grimaldi—shot it. I'm trying to convince Mr. Keller I was sleepwalking. Sorry about the school bus.*

He looked ahead to the smoldering remains, now surrounded by firefighters and police. Really not good.

Don't worry about that right now. They can't possibly guess what happened. I'll handle Ned. Mrs. Sharpe turned to Mr. Keller. "His mother warned me about this. When he gets overly tired, he's prone to sleepwalking."

Mr. Keller frowned at Conner. "Conner, did you do something to the bus?"

Mrs. Sharpe stepped in front of Conner, blocking him from Mr. Keller's skeptical stare. "Yes, Ned, of course. Conner blew up a school bus while he was sleepwalking." She rolled her eyes and sighed.

Mr. Keller rubbed his mustache. He seemed to be thinking of possible methods of school-bus combustion. After a few tense seconds, he shrugged. "I guess you're right, Norma. It's sure strange timing, though. Let's get Conner back to his room. We've got a full day tomorrow, plus the lunar eclipse tomorrow night . . ."

Mr. Keller froze as he stared at the back doors of the dorm, one of which featured a large, teenage boy–sized hole. The metal around the edges of the hole looked melted, as if it had been cut with a welding torch.

Oh my, Mrs. Sharpe thought. *We used the other set of doors when we came to look for you. My goodness, Conner! You must have been almost streaming to do that. Well done!*

"Conner," Mr. Keller said, "did you do that?"

"Now honestly, Ned." Mrs. Sharpe sighed and shot Mr. Keller a piercing stare. "How in the world could Conner have done that? Just run through them like a cartoon character? It would take a welder an hour or more to cut through a door like that. And your room is right inside.

How could Conner cut through a door like that without you hearing? And with what equipment?"

"I guess you're right," Mr. Keller muttered, still staring at the door. "Hey, is that water all over the floor? Who left the showers on?" He ran toward the bathroom, shouting about a plumbing emergency.

He'll never guess what really happened, Conner, Mrs. Sharpe thought. *Simply say nothing at all. That's an old Magi trick. Since unexplainable things tend to happen when Magi are around, we don't even try to explain. Much better than lying. Now, go back to your dorm and go to sleep.*

Yes, ma'am. Conner followed Mrs. Sharpe inside.

Conner! Are you okay? Conner smiled at Lexa's familiar squeal, which happened whenever she got excited.

Yeah, I'm fine, Lex. Sorry to worry you.

Oh. My. Gosh. We seriously need to talk. I had a really strange dream tonight. It's either crazy Benadryl or a vision, and I'm pretty sure it's a vision. Anyways, Mrs. Sharpe won't let us leave our room, so we'll have to talk tomorrow, but just remember everything that happened so you can tell us—

That will be enough, now, Mrs. Sharpe cut in. *Back to bed, Lexa.*

Conner tiptoed to his bed and slipped into the shredded remains of his sleeping bag. How did a shadow do that? He gulped, thinking about what it might have done to him. Now he had to figure out what to tell Pilaf. Since he wasn't one of the Magi, Pilaf couldn't have seen the wolf, but how would Conner explain diving on the ground, then running out of the room like a possessed chimpanzee?

"Conner," Pilaf whispered. "What was that?"

"I, uh, just had kind of a sleep terror," Conner stammered. "I got a little freaked out."

"Yeah," Pilaf nodded. "I'd be freaked out if a big shadow-wolf jumped off the wall and attacked me!"

Conner froze. What had Pilaf seen? He shouldn't have—couldn't have—seen the phantumbra. And yet . . . Conner finally managed to ask, "What?"

"That shadow-wolf—hey, does this have anything to do with the way you and Lexa and Melanie have been glowing lately?"

Conner tried to gather his spinning thoughts. Two months ago, he, Melanie, and Lexa had Kindled, which meant that their sleeping Magi powers had woken up and exploded to life. Kindling gave them the ability to use the Light, turning them into Adepts—sort of junior Magi. Dr. Timberi had mentioned that using the Light would leave a sort of glow around them but only Magi should be able to see it, and Conner thought it would be the same with stuff like the wolf.

What should he say? Hadn't Dr. Timberi talked about pretty strict rules that directed how you told people about Light and Dark?

The air above him shimmered silver, like it does on a hot summer day. A unicorn made out of pink Light appeared in the shimmer, and his heart ricocheted around inside his chest. Melanie's sigil.

Melanie had sent a sigil. Since all the Magi could hear head-talking, that meant she wanted the message to be private. So did that mean that she liked him?

"Conner, are you okay?" Her voice sounded like

peaches and cinnamon, the way her hair smelled. "I was really worried about you."

"Wow!" Pilaf's voice interrupted their private chat. "Conner, look at the unicorn! Do you hear Melanie's voice? That's so cool!"

"Is that Pilaf?" Melanie asked. "Can he see my sigil?" The pink unicorn seemed to blush.

"Hi, Melanie," Pilaf said.

Sorry, Melanie, can you give me just a second here? Conner reached out in his thoughts to Mrs. Sharpe. *Mrs. Sharpe?*

Yes, Conner? Her thoughts popped into his mind. *Didn't we agree that it was bedtime?*

Sorry. But Pilaf just asked me why a shadow-wolf was chasing me. Then he asked why Lexa and Melanie and me have been glowing lately. No need to mention Melanie sending him a sigil.

Pilaf said all this?

Yes, ma'am. Has he Kindled too?

No, I'm quite sure that no one else has Kindled lately.

"Conner?" Pilaf whispered. "Is it just me or do you hear Mrs. Sharpe's voice?"

Pilaf? Mrs. Sharpe thought. *Can you hear me right now?*

"Yes, ma'am," Pilaf replied.

He said yes, Conner added. *I don't know if you can hear him.*

Yes, I can hear him through your thoughts, Mrs. Sharpe thought. *This is very strange. Conner, you might as well explain the basics. I don't suppose there's any chance either of you will sleep now. Pilaf, we'll talk more tomorrow.*

"Awesome!" Pilaf cheered.

Conner thought for a minute. *How* DO *you explain all this stuff?*

"Just tell him about Light and Dark," Melanie spoke through her sigil. Then in a quiet thought-whisper, she said, *You'll be amazing. I'm going to tell Lexa.*

What's going on? Lexa jumped into the conversation.

Pilaf can hear head-talking and see Lightcraft, Melanie said.

Pilaf? Lexa squealed in her thoughts. *No way! Is he a Magi too?*

Magus, Melanie said. *Magi is plural.*

Um, I need to explain this to Pilaf now, Conner said. *So can you two keep it down?*

We'll help you! Lexa said.

Conner decided to talk out loud to keep things more organized. "Okay, well to start, you have to understand that there are two basic powers in the universe: Light and Dark. I don't mean just having a light on or off. These are like active, living powers."

"Wow!" Pilaf shouted.

"Shhh!" Conner hissed. "Um, Pilaf, can you please not interrupt me until I'm done? This is harder than it looks."

Pilaf clamped his mouth shut and sat on his hands.

"Did you hear me, Pilaf?"

Pilaf didn't respond.

"Pilaf, did you hear me?"

"Yes, but you said not to interrupt you."

"Okay. Thanks. Anyway. So Light is everywhere—all around, like oxygen. Some people are sort of magnetic and they attract the Light. Here's the thing. If you can control the Light, you can do all kinds of things—shoot the light, make stuff move, even turn into a comet."

Pilaf's eyes stretched so wide that Conner worried he might sprain something. He shook with excitement, but he didn't say anything.

"People who use the Light are called Magi. They—we—belong to a secret group called the Sodality of the Midnight Star. A couple months ago me and Melanie and Lexa all Kindled, which is when your Magi powers explode out—"

Lexa jumped in. Conner was a little surprised she'd been quiet this long. *Pilaf, remember how Melanie shoved Zach and sent him flying? Or when Geoffrey's gym shorts caught on fire? That happened because Conner was mad at Geoffrey for bullying you. When you Kindle, stuff like that just happens—the Light follows your thoughts and strong feelings.*

There's also bad guys, Lexa continued. *They use the Darkness like we use the Light. Their group is called Umbra, but we call them Darkhands.*

Pilaf raised his hand, so Conner called on him.

"Yes, Pilaf?"

"Is this why I can see dark or light around people? Sometimes it looks like they're covered with a thin piece of dark, sparkly fabric. You guys are different. Light sort of swirls around you. Kind of like when the moon on a cold night has a glow around it."

Yes, Pilaf, Melanie said. *That glow's called a nimbus, and it surrounds anyone who performs Lightcraft. The dark layer is called a miasma, and it covers people who use Darkness. For some reason, it's especially obvious on their hands, which is why they're called Darkhands.*

Conner cleared his throat and continued his lecture. Covering all the basics was harder than he'd thought—especially with interruptions. "Magi can talk to each other in our thoughts, which you can hear. And we can send messages with these things called sigils, which are part of our souls mixed with Light. Melanie's is a unicorn, Lexa's is a dolphin, and mine's a German shepherd."

Pilaf looked like he might explode. His hand shot up, bouncing up and down.

"Go ahead, Pilaf."

"This. Is. So. Cool!" Pilaf sounded like a text in all caps. "Hey, Conner?"

"Yeah?"

"Do you know the guy outside?"

"What guy?" Conner paused but didn't hear any Magi head-talking.

"There's a guy outside the window looking for you. I can hear his thoughts too."

It's probably just Colonel Murrell, Melanie said. *But I don't hear anything either.*

Me either, Lexa added. *Why can Pilaf hear him but not us?*

Conner walked over to the window and lifted the corner of the blinds.

For a moment, all Conner saw was his reflection in the window. But then the reflection scowled, and Conner realized that the reflection staring at him had black eyes, dark, greasy hair, and pale-gray skin.

A paralyzing chill froze Conner.

The Stalker was back, staring at him with a haunted, desperate look. Shocked, Conner froze, unable to move. Luckily, his thoughts were still connected to Lexa's and

Melanie's. Sensing what happened, Melanie called Mrs. Sharpe, who called Lee and the other soldiers in the Phalanx.

The Stalker looked over his shoulder, scowled, and vanished. No smoke, no cyclones—he simply vanished as three comets blasted into the courtyard between the dining hall and the dorm.

"Cool!" Pilaf had joined Conner at the window, staring with Christmas-eyed excitement at the skirmish outside. "Can you do that too, Conner?"

"Not exactly." The comets faded, resolving into human shapes: Grimaldi, Colonel Lee Murrell, and some really ripped guy Conner didn't recognize. They each wore the same gray leather ninja-suit, with the shimmering, silver crescent moon surrounding a star.

"Hey, that star and moon pattern is carved into the courtyard at school! Cool!" Pilaf didn't miss much.

Lee grinned at Conner. His leathery skin crinkled, amplifying his smile as he ran his fingers through his messy, steel-gray hair.

Did you get the Stalker? Conner asked

The Stalker? Lee looked at the other two soldiers. *Grimaldi? Brighton? Either of you see anyone?* Grimaldi shook her head, and so did the tall, ripped guy they called Brighton. Lee looked back at Conner. *He wasn't here. No one is. Just us. Now get some shut-eye, son. We'll be patrolling all night.*

They blasted away in their comets, circling all the buildings.

"You know those guys, Conner? Wow, that is so cool! Can I meet them?"

"Hey, Pilaf, we should probably go to sleep, okay? Mrs. Sharpe can explain it all tomorrow."

Pilaf asked a few more questions, but Conner didn't answer them, so after a long time, Pilaf fell asleep.

Conner couldn't sleep. They hadn't found the Stalker, which meant he still lurked out there, hiding in the shadows, waiting to pop up again. That thought kept him wide awake, his heart pounding like he'd chugged a six-pack of Red Bull.

Remembering the Stalker's brutal cruelty to Dr. Timberi and the painful death he had planned for Conner, Lexa, and Melanie, Conner shifted and rolled in his bed.

On top of that, what had happened earlier, with the shooting black fire? That scared him more than the Stalker, because he knew what it meant.

With sleep shunning him, Conner got up and looked out the window. He scanned the area, eyes drawn to the places where light from the building spilled into the shadows, creating undefined shadowy-light areas that were neither completely light nor dark.

A flicker of movement caught his eye. The shadows by the dining hall stirred and seemed to boil, jumping to life and twisting into various shapes. The courtyard looked like a petting zoo of horror movie animals: snakes, rats, bats, giant spiders, all made out of shadows. They spoke to him, chanting in that hissing growl.

Conner, Conner, come and join us. Free the shadows in your heart.

These words hit Conner like a gut-punch, taking him back to the Shadowbox, where shadows had chanted those words. Images of the terrible things he had done stampeded through his head again, followed by guilt crashing over him in a hot tidal wave.

And now he could hear shadows. They spoke to him. It confirmed what he'd guessed, and despair rushed into his mind and heart, filling any gaps that guilt and shame had left open.

The voices got louder, and the shadows moved closer to his window.

"No!" Conner yelled, shutting his eyes and cupping his hands against his ears. "Leave me alone!"

The voices stopped, and the animal forms melted back into the shadows pooling on the ground.

"Conner?" Pilaf sat up in his bed.

"Sorry. I had a bad dream," Conner muttered as he walked back to his bed.

A bad dream that might never end.

· CHAPTER 5 ·

Gathering Clouds

MELANIE LOOKED AROUND THE CAFETERIA. Conner *never* came late to meals. Was he all right? Mrs. Sharpe would have told them if there'd been another attack, right? She bit the inside of her lip with her teeth.

Next to her, Lexa chattered about the auditions for next year's fall musical. Normally, Dr. Timberi held try-outs at the end of the school year. But since he'd been recuperating, no one knew when auditions would happen, or even if the play would go on. That possibility caused Lexa extreme anxiety since she collected leading roles the way some kids collected soccer trophies or baseball cards. She dealt with that anxiety by talking. And talking.

Wanting to be a good friend, Melanie corralled her straying thoughts and tried to listen to Lexa instead of worrying about Conner.

". . . so Lily Martin said that auditions for the *The Sound of Music* would get pushed back, but why would Dr. Timberi tell her and not us? He's in the Sanctuary resting, right? So, hello! How would she even talk to him? Anyways, I was thinking. What if I got to be Maria and you got to be one of the main kids? That would be so much fun!" Lexa charged ahead with her hypothetical casting, exploring every possible combination of student actors and potential roles—although every new version of the cast list featured her as Maria.

Conner walked in, looking haggard and worn. Something seemed wrong with him, more than just being tired.

Are you okay? Melanie asked as he sat down.

Kind of a wild night, he replied.

Lexa slammed on her conversational brakes, made a U-turn, and pelted Conner with questions about what had happened the night before.

Conner answered Lexa's questions without ever quite making eye contact.

As she listened, Melanie felt something powerful inside that she couldn't quite define. The thought of Conner being alone and being chased by monsters disturbed her more than she could say. It made her want to keep him close, to not let him leave her sight ever again.

"What about the Stalker?" Melanie asked when he finished. "Did they find him?"

Conner shook his head. "They said he wasn't there."

"Ohmygosh!" Lexa squealed. "That reminds me! In that dream I had last night, the creepiest part was when the Stalker morphed into Dr. Timberi and then back into the Stalker. Like, seriously, weird." She paused. "I really wish Dr. Timberi was here to help us figure all this stuff out."

Melanie stared at Lexa. Something about that dream nibbled at Melanie's consciousness. It seemed important, but she couldn't understand why, or what it might mean. With great care, she made a note on the whiteboard in her mind, filing that piece of information away. She knew from past experience that the information would come back when she most needed it. The whiteboard would come alive, the symbols moving and humming, and answers would snap into place. For now, she needed to be patient and keep gathering data.

Melanie looked over at Conner. "Did anything else happen last night?

Conner kept his eyes on the ground. "No."

Melanie waited for several seconds, but Conner never looked back up. He stared at his eggs as Lexa talked through a detailed analysis of her odds of getting the lead in *The Sound of Music.*

Through a window, Melanie watched a cloud pass in front of the sun, painting the room gray. It seemed appropriate. Weird things were happening: dreams, attacks, and the Stalker coming back. Worse, something had happened to Conner. Something he wouldn't talk about.

Melanie felt like she was in the beginning of a horror movie, the part where the soon-to-be victims wander around without a clue that the killer is about to jump out.

After breakfast, everyone walked fifty yards from the Sea Lab complex to the beach. Melanie's ominous feeling continued as Mr. Keller, Mrs. Sharpe, and the Sea Lab staff members bustled around, putting everyone in pairs and distributing large two-person nets, about six feet long and four feet high.

"Now, the procedure is simple," Mr. Keller said. "Working in pairs, each person will hold one side of the net. Carry it above your heads and walk out until the water is chest-high. Slide the net into the water, stretching it tight. Count to thirty before you move so you don't scare all the sea life. Take small, slow steps back to the shore, skimming the sea floor with the bottom of the net. When you get to the shore, place anything you caught in the buckets"—he pointed to a long row of five-gallon buckets filled with seawater—"then carry the bucket and transfer your organism to the aquaria in the lab. Don't go too deep. There shouldn't be any strange currents, but remember this is the Gulf of Mexico, not a swimming pool."

Melanie and Lexa had been paired, as had Conner and Pilaf. Each partner grabbed one end of the net and waded out until the water was chest deep. Melanie liked the fact that Conner ended up about three or four feet from her.

Everyone slid their nets down, and Conner started to walk to the shore, but Pilaf looked at him with worried eyes. "Mr. Keller said we were supposed to wait for thirty seconds before we moved. One, one-thousand. Two, one-thousand . . ."

As Pilaf counted, Melanie bit back a smile. Pilaf was the only seventh grader more worried about following rules than she was.

Through the corner of her eye, she saw Conner shiver and twitch.

Melanie looked over at him. "Are you okay?"

"Yeah. Something brushed against my leg. There aren't any dangerous animals out here, right? Like, nothing that could grab me and drag me under the water? Or that craves human-flavored sushi?"

"It might just be seaweed," Pilaf said. "But we should probably talk quieter or we'll scare the wildlife."

Conner jerked and thrashed under the water. "Yeah, well something just touched me again, so maybe scaring the wildlife is a good idea. Something's down there."

Conner shouted, uttering a cry of surprise and pain as he disappeared under the waves.

Conner! Conner! Melanie shouted. But he didn't answer. And he didn't reappear. Melanie dove under the water, braving the bacteria, pollution, and parasites. She searched for Conner, but the water was too murky.

When she surfaced, the teachers and the entire seventh grade had fanned out, splashing through water, calling for Conner. But he didn't come back.

Sharp needles of freezing fear stabbed Melanie's heart. She studied the choppy, gray waves, choking on the same desperation she'd felt seven weeks earlier when Conner had been captured by the Darkhands after rescuing her little sister, Madi.

As time passed, a cold, emotional haze crept over her, followed by a raw, throbbing ache. He'd been gone for too long. No one could survive being underwater that long.

CHAPTER 6

SHADOW IN THE SEA

ONNER SHOOK HIS LEG, TRYING TO KICK off whatever had him. It burned, sinking through his skin, down into his soul.

He gagged from the ocean water that had rushed down his throat before he'd shut his mouth. With his eyes stinging from the salt, Conner couldn't see much—except the sun above the water, rushing farther and farther away as the water around him grew darker and colder.

Beneath him, a blurry, shadowy shape with tentacles swam deeper, towing Conner along. Pushing through his surging panic, he managed to shoot a hot blast of red Light at the tentacle around his ankle, but the Light faded away before hitting the tentacle. He tried again, but the Light didn't stay together in the cold, dark water.

Shadowy figures flickered into shape, floating in the darkness all around him.

Conner, Conner, come and join us—

Conner thrashed against the pull of the monster,

anxious to get away from the shadows coming at him. Desperate, he tried to send a sigil for help.

A red German shepherd made out of Light doggy-paddled away but faded after a few yards.

Conner's lungs burned like he'd inhaled Flaming Hot Cheetos, and black spots appeared in his eyes, expanding to fill more and more of his vision.

Fwooooshhh!

Something massive and bright flew past him. A giant shark—glowing like it had guzzled nuclear waste.

The shining shark plowed into the black shape below him, and the grip on Conner's ankle relaxed. He kicked away, swimming for the surface, but he'd been dragged too far down. His oxygen would run out before he could get back to the surface.

The sound of singing startled him. Voices that didn't sound human. Angels? He must be getting close to heaven. The voices grew louder, singing complex harmonies unlike anything he'd ever heard. He wished Dr. Timberi could hear them.

The shark rushed up toward him and then seemed to explode, dissolving into thousands of tiny colored lights. The lights circled, surrounding him in a glowing tornado of sparkling neon colors. They swirled faster, creating a current that pushed him up toward the surface.

Conner's body wanted to black out and die, but his mind refused. Not now! Not this close! He kicked and paddled, and the lights seemed to give him extra strength. He kept fighting until, between the effort of him and the lights, his head finally broke the surface.

He choked and gasped but couldn't get any air. For a

minute, he thought it might be too late, but then his lungs expanded and he inhaled, gulping air down the way his Uncle Buddy went through a buffet line.

Somehow he managed to float and doggy-paddle back to the shore. By the time he dragged himself onto the beach near an old fort at the end of the island, total exhaustion washed over him, like the tide coming over the sand. So tired. And cold. Chills followed the waves of exhaustion. He knew he couldn't walk or even crawl an inch farther. Focusing on the last, shredded bits of his strength, he held his hands up long enough to organize a sigil. His arms felt like old rubber.

Tell Mrs. Sharpe I'm down by the fort. His arms collapsed back into the sand as his red German shepherd disappeared with a flash.

About thirty seconds later, a cream-colored comet shot over the beach, turning into Mrs. Sharpe.

"Conner! Conner! Are you hurt?"

"No, ma'am," he mumbled. "Shadows . . . light . . . shark . . . singing . . ."

He didn't remember anything else.

CHAPTER 7

MELANIE'S VOW

MELANIE FOLLOWED MRS. SHARPE'S comet, tripping and splashing through the waves all around her.

Conner was alive!

His loss had sent bleakness beyond words creeping through her, creating winter in her soul. She'd cried through all her tears as she mourned over Conner.

Now, with new hope, fresh tears flowed. Melanie followed the comet, running fast enough to put her cross-country championships to shame. By the time she found Conner, sea spray had mingled with her tears, soaking her face and shirt in bitter salt water.

"I'm going to get some help," Mrs. Sharpe said. "Watch Conner. I'll be right back." She streamed away, leaving Melanie alone with Conner on the silent beach.

She felt a tiny pinch of guilt for not going to get Lexa before coming to Conner. They'd been separated in the chaos, and Lexa had gone farther down the beach. But

Melanie hadn't wanted to wait. She soothed her conscience by sending a sigil to Lexa.

Conner lay on the sand, eyes closed, his normally tan face pale. But his chest moved up and down, regular and steady. Conner shivered. An army of tiny goose bumps dotted his arms and torso. He shivered again.

Remembering Dr. Timberi's lesson in Translocation, Melanie closed her eyes and ran through pre-algebra equations—her method of opening the gateway that connected her to the Light. Translocation, the ability to move objects from one location to another, had been one of the first Magi skills they'd learned.

Visualizing the blanket folded on the edge of her cot, Melanie focused on the white board in her brain. Mentally adjusting some of the symbols on the board, she thought about time and space, and—

Silver light flashed in the air and Melanie's blanket fell to the sand. Shaking it out, she draped it over Conner. His shivers slowed and eased, before disappearing.

In the privacy of her thoughts, Melanie allowed herself to acknowledge how she felt about him. How she'd always felt about him.

Stray strands of hair covered Conner's eyes, and Melanie reached down to brush them aside. As her fingers touched his forehead, something like electricity crackled and flowed between them.

Conner disappearing hurt more than she could describe. Her life didn't end or anything melodramatic, but it hurt more than she wanted to endure. Just as it had when the Darkhands had taken Madi. On both of those occasions, it felt like someone had reached inside of her soul and torn part of her out.

She never wanted to repeat that. But in this dangerous world, filled with forces fighting against human life and happiness, losses seemed inevitable.

Unless you were more powerful than the Darkness and destruction.

When they'd Kindled, Melanie had been reluctant. She'd hesitated, not sure she wanted to join a secret battle between Light and Dark. Her father fed that hesitation, opposing her involvement with the Magi in general and Dr. Timberi in particular.

Now, all lingering hesitation evaporated, and Melanie vowed that she would become the most powerful Magus she could possibly be. She would learn every trick and explore every secret. She'd develop as much power as she could and would never again stand by, helpless and panicked, while someone she loved was in danger. If she lived in a dangerous, predatory world, she would learn to fight back. No person, no power, no creature, no force would hurt anyone she loved.

She repeated her vow. No one would hurt someone she loved ever again.

Especially Conner.

CHAPTER 8

A SKUNK THAT DON'T SMELL

L EXA TUGGED HER PONYTAIL AS PARAMED-
ics arrived, followed by staff members from the Sea
Lab. They checked Conner for broken bones, strapped
him onto a stretcher, and carried him back to the com-
pound. As she and Melanie followed the procession, Lexa
noticed the air shimmer around them—like heat waves
reflecting off the pavement on a hot day—and she guessed
the members of Phalanx were there.

*About time! Where had they been earlier? The Twilight
Phalanx might be legendary in the Magi world, but, hello!
Letting someone almost drown when you were supposed to be
protecting them seemed pretty sloppy.*

She frowned harder at the shimmering air, grateful that
being annoyed at the Phalanx helped push away the abso-
lute, gut-twisting panic she'd felt when Conner had disappeared beneath the waves. She'd been terrified. Good thing
Melanie had been there to hug and comfort her. Such a good
friend—she seemed almost as worried and upset as Lexa felt.

Speaking of Melanie—*Hey, Mel? Is that your blanket on Conner?*

Melanie nodded and looked away. *When I got there, he was shivering really bad, so I Translocated it over. I didn't want him to get hypothermia.*

Nice job, Mel! How cool that we can do stuff like that! It is going to be A-Maz-Ing when we get trained and learn even more stuff! I can NOT wait for us to start! I hope Dr. Timberi gets better soon. Lexa didn't mention that she also wanted him to get better so they could have auditions for *The Sound of Music.* Something told her that might seem a little tacky.

They followed the stretcher into a small, wood-paneled office that doubled as a sick room. Charts of first-aid directions alternated with pictures of dangerous wildlife and cheesy, old motivational posters.

The men lowered the stretcher onto an old army cot in the corner and then left Lexa, Melanie, Mrs. Sharpe, and Mr. Keller alone with the unconscious Conner.

Mrs. Sharpe looked at Mr. Keller. "Ned, we can handle it from here. The rest of the kids are unsupervised."

He nodded. "You're right, Norma. You think he's okay?"

"I'm sure he'll be just fine. I'll contact his parents."

Mr. Keller walked out of the room, muttering, "Sure has been a strange trip so far."

As soon as Mrs. Sharpe closed the door, Lee and Grimaldi flickered into visibility, like images on a super-old TV that took a few seconds to warm up.

Lee looked down at Conner and shook his head. "Poor kid. Tell you what, you three attract trouble like stink draws flies. The Trouble Trio's what you are."

"Did you see what happened, Lee?" Mrs. Sharpe asked.

"Not really, Norma. Just saw him go under. How 'bout you? Did you notice anything?" Lee asked.

"As Conner went under, I felt a great deal of dissonance. I'm sure there were massive adumbrations."

"Dissonance and adumbrations?" Lexa asked.

"Adumbrations are the shadows created when Darkness is used," Mrs. Sharpe said. "Dissonance is the jarring sensation Magi feel or hear when it happens. At any rate, a few minutes after Conner disappeared, I felt a tremendous burst of Light."

"Me too," Lee said. "I'm glad you felt it too, Norma. Thought I was crazy at first. Boy, that's stranger than a skunk that don't smell."

"What do you mean?" Lexa asked.

Lee frowned. "Well, water's kind of funny. It ain't real responsive to the Light, so it's just about impossible to do Lightcraft underwater."

"Most Magi could do Lightcraft in a bathtub, or possibly a swimming pool," Mrs. Sharpe said. "It's not deep or dark, and it doesn't have wild currents. But the ocean is different. Light doesn't exist naturally in deep water. Additionally, water distorts light waves, and the currents provide opposition as well. So the amount of energy needed to perform Lightcraft underwater in the ocean is far beyond the ability of any human."

"Most Magi just stay away from water," Lee added.

"Lee, that makes two attacks in less than twelve hours." Mrs. Sharpe always managed to seem slightly impatient. "Can you get some extra people down here? I'm feeling a little outnumbered."

"Yeah, that's easy. Grimaldi?"

Miranda saluted, blurred into a comet, and shot out of the room.

Lee looked at Lexa and Melanie. "Did you two see anything?"

Lexa lowered her voice, pitching it for maximum dramatic effect. "We had just grabbed our nets and were walking out into the ocean. Suddenly, the water grew dark. The sun went behind a cloud. We heard a splash, and Pilaf started to shout—"

"Pilaf!" Mrs. Sharpe slapped her forehead. "I forgot all about him. Lee, Pilaf is Conner's friend. He hasn't Kindled, but hears Magi head-talk and sees Lightcraft. I needed to talk with him today, but this distracted me. Melanie, can you please go ask him to come here? He was Conner's partner, so perhaps he saw something and can tell us more about what happened."

Lexa felt just a little deflated.

"Yes, ma'am," Melanie said.

"Thank you," Mrs. Sharpe said as Melanie walked out.

A knock on the door interrupted them. Lee vanished, flickering out of view as an old man walked in, carrying a battered black bag.

"Excuse me, is this the young man that got pulled out by the current?"

"Yes." Mrs. Sharpe stood up. "I'm Norma Sharpe, one of Conner's teachers. Thank you for coming."

"Happy to help. I'm Joseph Walker—everyone just calls me Doc. Let's see what we've got here. Son, can you hear me? I need you to wake up." He tapped Conner's hand with his fingers until Conner stirred and opened his eyes.

44

Relief stampeded through Lexa. Hearing Conner would be okay was one thing—seeing him awake made her feel much better.

"I know you're probably worn out," Doc said. "But I need to make sure you're okay. Can you tell me what month it is?"

"May," Conner croaked. "Almost June."

Doc Walker poked, prodded, and pulled. When he established that Conner didn't have a concussion, broken bones, or water in his lungs, he put his stethoscope away. "Just needs some rest. If there are any problems, the staff will know how to reach me."

"Thank you, Doctor Walker." Mrs. Sharpe sounded as if she was dismissing class.

The doctor left and Lee reappeared. "Dell, can you tell us what happened out there?"

Conner told them about a shadow-monster and a Light shark. When he finished, Mrs. Sharpe and Lee looked more and more surprised.

Lee let out a low whistle. "Well, I'm stumped. What you just described is about as strange as a pig singing opera. If I didn't know better, I'd say you were crazy or a liar. Or both." He ran leathery fingers through his shock of white hair. "But I believe you. I'm gonna head over to HQ and talk to Hortense and some of the Adumbrators. See if they picked anything up." He exploded out of the room in a dust-colored comet.

"Some of the what?" Lexa asked.

"Adumbrators. They study shadows. Adumbrators are like the CSI investigators, FBI, and CIA of the Magi world," Mrs. Sharpe replied. "Which reminds me. Conner, did you . . . ?"

No answer. Lexa looked over at him. He'd fallen asleep.

"Never mind. We'll let him sleep." Mrs. Sharpe straightened Melanie's blanket just as Melanie walked back in with Pilaf behind her.

RHOMBI

MELANIE LOOKED AT CONNER, UNCON-scious again, and felt cold, suffocating fear return.

"Now, Pilaf, we need to talk," Mrs. Sharpe said. "Please take a seat."

"Yes, ma'am. Is Conner okay?" Blotches of sunscreen still covered Pilaf's face.

"Yes, he'll be fine. He's just sleeping. Pilaf, did you see anything when Conner went under the water?"

"No, ma'am. But a while after he disappeared, I felt something that seemed like an explosion a long way away."

"Thank you, Pilaf. I know you have some questions, and I'll try to answer them. First, I need to do some simple tests."

Pilaf, can you hear me? Mrs. Sharpe asked in her mind. *If so, please blink twice.*

Behind his giant glasses, he blinked once. Then once more.

Pilaf, please think a message to us. What day is it? Talk to us in your mind.

Silence.

Did you try to head-talk with us? Blink your eyes twice again if you did.

Blink. Blink.

"Very interesting," Mrs. Sharpe said out loud. "Apparently, you can hear head-talk, but not join it."

Mrs. Sharpe held her hand up and a ball of cream-colored Light appeared. "Do you see anything, Pilaf?"

"A sphere made out of cream-colored light! Wow! This is so cool! Can you do a rhombus? I love rhombi!"

Mrs. Sharpe smiled, and the sphere stretched itself in a rhombus as Pilaf cheered.

She dropped her hand and the Light faded. "How long have you seen things like this, Pilaf?"

"Only for a little while. Remember that big storm before Spring Break? It started just a few days after that."

"Remarkable." Mrs. Sharpe shook her head. "That was when these three Kindled."

"Has Pilaf Kindled too?" Lexa asked.

Mrs. Sharpe shook her head. "No. I'm quite sure he hasn't—when someone around you Kindles, it's obvious. You can't miss it. And yet, he shouldn't be able to hear head-talk or see Lightcraft, or the phantumbra last night. I don't understand what is happening here. I'm going to contact the Magisterium—that's the Sodality's governing body, Pilaf. They can send some experts to do further testing. In the meantime, Pilaf, it's very important that you not say anything about this to anyone beyond myself, Conner, Lexa, and Melanie."

"What about Dr. Timberi, Madame Cumberland, and Mrs. Grant? They all glow. Are they Magi too? And Mrs.

Davis, Mr. Duffy, Coach Jackson, and Mr. Miller?"

Mrs. Sharpe continued to look surprised. "Yes, they are all Magi. And you may discuss this with them, but no one else. Not even your parents. That could cause serious problems. Once we understand what's going on, we'll meet with your parents and explain everything. Until then, we need to be careful."

Pilaf looked at Mrs. Sharpe, blinking faster and faster. He raised his hand.

"Yes, Pilaf?"

"So are all Magi teachers? And is our school a secret base?"

"No, Pilaf. Not all Magi are teachers. You'll find Magi in nearly every field—scientists, police, performers, businessmen and -women, on and on. However, most Magi are not paid for their work in the Sodality. A few work directly for the Magisterium, but most of us provide for our own needs, so we have jobs.

"The reason so many of us are at Marion Academy is because it is a wonderful place to work. Madame Cumberland was hired at Marion years ago, and over time she helped other Magi find jobs there. Quite logical, really.

"The real question is how the four of you all ended up there at the same time. And honestly, I have no idea. One of life's little mysteries."

Mrs. Sharpe nodded and dusted her hands, clearly finishing the subject. "Conner needs to rest, and there's nothing more we can do here. I'll come back and check on him periodically. You three should really get back to class. They're on to plankton, I believe."

Melanie bit back a laugh at Lexa's dramatic, almost persecuted sigh. *I was hoping we could get out of the plankton class,* Lexa said. *Leah Owens came last year and told me it was sooooo boring.*

Lexa, Mrs. Sharpe's voice popped into her head. *You'll really have to remember that any Magi nearby can hear you when you head-talk.*

"Wait, can you hear everything we think?"

Mrs. Sharpe smiled. "No, Lexa. Not your private thoughts. Although, if a Magus is particularly excited about something—very happy, for example, their thoughts might be quite loud and easily heard."

Pilaf raised his hand. "But when two Magi are head-talking, any Magus can hear?"

Mrs. Sharpe nodded. "Head-talking is similar to normal conversations, and all the same variables apply. If someone is head-talking, I may not hear depending on how loud their thoughts are, how close I am, whether I'm distracted, and how closely I am paying attention. Some Magi are particularly gifted at hearing thoughts. Mrs. Grant, for example can hear thoughts very easily." Melanie now understood why Mrs. Grant often seemed annoyed when they head-chatted during English.

Mrs. Sharpe continued. "Other Magi only hear head-talking when thoughts are directed specifically at them with some force—just as some people can hear acutely well and others can't."

Pilaf raised his hand again. "What about the range?"

"It varies. Usually it is limited to sight, or roughly the same range as hearing. However, if you know someone well and have a close bond, it is not uncommon to be able to head-talk at much greater distances—a few miles, perhaps."

"How come we don't usually hear the teachers head-talking," Melanie asked, "unless you're trying to talk to us?" Mrs. Sharpe smiled. "Good observation, Melanie. If you want to talk privately when other Magi are around, you'll need to send your thoughts to one person and block everyone else out. We call that shielding, and it's a useful skill."

"How do we do it?" Melanie wanted to know more.

"If you'll just wait to be trained—"

Another enormous sigh belly-flopped out of Lexa's mouth.

Mrs. Sharpe raised an eyebrow and frowned at Lexa. Then her face softened into a smile. "I suppose you have heard that a lot lately, haven't you? With Morgan being out of commission, your training's had to wait longer than usual. Very well. I'll take a few minutes now and teach you the basics of private conversations. Pilaf, you're welcome to listen, but it might not make sense. Like most Lightcraft, it's quite simple in theory.

"If I want to shield a conversation with Melanie, then I visualize a stream of Light flowing from my mind to hers, connecting us like a network cable." A thin cream-colored cord of Light appeared between Mrs. Sharpe and Melanie's heads. "Now, if I head-talk, only Melanie will hear it. Once you get the basic idea, it is simple to manage. You can even have multiple connections. That's the theory—you can practice on your own.

"Now, head to class—and do please try to listen at least a little. Don't spend *all* your time practicing this. Ned is so excited for you to learn about plankton. I think I'll stream back to Nashville and tell your mother about Conner."

CHAPTER 10

FRIES AND FIGHTS

WHEN EVERYONE LEFT THE ROOM, Conner opened his eyes. He'd pretended to be asleep because he didn't want to talk anymore. He especially didn't want anyone to find out that shadows talked to him or that he shot black fire, and if he kept answering questions, he worried he might slip.

Deep down, a cold, growing fear wrenched his stomach. When Lady Nightwing had locked him in the Shadowbox, he'd watched himself do terrible things. After it ended, Lady Nightwing's creepy little helper, Mr. Stanley, told him that he'd become a Darkhand. That thought terrified Conner more than all the nightmares he'd ever had, pumping him full of panic and chilling his blood into a snow cone of terror.

Being a Darkhand meant hurting and killing people. It meant tearing up families and ruining people's lives. He couldn't stand that thought, but Mr. Stanley told him he had no choice. At first Conner hadn't believed him.

He'd brushed it away, but now he wondered. He'd done some really bad things in the Shadowbox. Last night, he shot black fire, and now, shadows spoke to him. Had his actions in the Shadowbox warped his soul? Planted some kind of slow-growing, spiritual virus that would turn him into a Darkhand?

These questions wrapped him in a thick, black depression. He wanted to talk to someone, to ask questions and find out what it all meant, and to try to understand what was happening.

But he couldn't.

No one could know about hearing shadows and shooting black fire and becoming a Darkhand. No one could know about the Shadowbox and what he'd done there.

"Conner?"

Conner jumped as a deep voice interrupted his brooding. A swan made out of pale golden Light flickered in the air. Dr. Timberi's sigil spoke again. "Conner, are you there?"

"Hi, Dr. Timberi!" Conner forced a cheerful tone into his voice. "How are you?"

The sigil flickered in and out. It didn't seem as bright or strong as usual. "I am certainly better than I was last time we were together."

"Um, last time we were together the Stalker had almost killed you and Darkness was eating your spirit," Conner said. "So being better than that isn't saying too much."

Dr. Timberi's sigil chuckled. "A fair point. The question is, how are you? Mrs. Sharpe told me about the attack."

Conner thought about telling Dr. Timberi everything. Maybe Dr. Timberi could help him somehow. Or would he call some kind of Magisterium police? Would they kick him out of the Sodality or cart him off to a secret Magi prison? Could they take away his powers somehow? Even worse, what would they think of him? Madame Cumberland. Dr. Timberi. Melanie.

"I'm fine," Conner lied.

"I'm glad to hear that. But please tell me what happened—last night and today. I'm worried about you. We need to figure out what is going on."

Conner shifted. The direction of the conversation made him uncomfortable. "Well, last night a shadow-wolf jumped out at me and chased me down the beach."

"You outran a phantumbra?"

"Well, I sort of streamed—not quite, I guess, but pretty close from what they say. I accidentally blew up the school bus."

The swan sigil flashed bright and vivid for a moment. Could swans look proud? "Well done, Conner! That is truly remarkable—the streaming, I mean."

Yeah, Conner thought in a private message to himself. *The bad news is that I'm becoming a Darkhand, but on the bright side, I can run slower than your average comet.* "Thanks."

Conner re-explained all that had happened—as much as he could without mentioning the shadows talking to him.

"Amazing," Dr. Timberi said. "That kind of Lightcraft underwater is unheard of. Something unusual is happening, Conner."

Conner decided to change the subject. "So, Dr. Timberi, how are you doing? I mean for real. You don't sound like yourself."

The sigil exhaled, long and slow. "To be honest, Conner, I am struggling. When the Stalker sent those shadow-knives at me, he chose some specific forms of Darkness that he thought would be most painful and destructive to me, and he accurately anticipated my greatest vulnerabilities."

When they'd first Kindled, Dr. Timberi had seemed unstoppable, almost all-powerful. Now he sounded weak and frail. The gloom and fear Conner already felt flared up and intensified. What if Darkness was too powerful for anyone to overcome?

An emerald-green comet shot in the room, and Miranda Grimaldi appeared. "Dell, I need to get some more information—" She paused and looked at the swan. "Morgan? You don't look good."

"Why, thank you, Miranda. Nice to see you too." Dr. Timberi's sigil conveyed sarcasm as well as he did in person.

"Morgan, you need to be resting. I know you're worried about Dell, but we'll look after him. Get some rest."

The swan sigil grumbled. "Very well. But keep me posted with any developments at all!"

"I promise, Morgan. Now go get some rest."

"Conner, I am glad you are safe. I will be thinking of you." Dr. Timberi's sigil disappeared.

"That man." Miranda shook his head. "Colonel Murrell says he can barely walk, but he wanted to come on this trip to look after you three. He seriously would have come except that Lee and Mona Cumberland ganged up on him and made him promise not to." Madame Cumberland taught French at Marion Academy. She was also one of Dr. Timberi's closest, most trusted friends.

"That's why we're here—the only way he agreed to stay back and rest was if the Phalanx came to stand guard. So Lee deployed us."

"Does the Phalanx go around helping whoever needs it?"

Miranda shook her head. "No. Not at all. But Morgan has a lot of connections from his days back in the Adumbrators. He was almost Head Adumbrator at one point."

"What?"

"Oh yeah. It happened right before the whole thing with his—" Miranda closed her mouth. "Never mind."

"But—"

"Drop it, Dell. That's an order. Listen, Colonel Murrell needs some more information. Last night, you said the Stalker was there?"

"Yeah, right outside my window."

She furrowed her brow. "You're sure?"

"Positive."

"Hmm. Interesting." She shook her head. "And you're sure that you didn't do any Lightcraft under the water?"

"I tried a sigil, but it dissolved. I couldn't keep it together."

She asked more questions, taking notes as he repeated his story.

"Conner?" Melanie walked in the door carrying a tray from the cafeteria. Light from the windows made her red hair glow—she looked like an angel with a halo. An amazingly beautiful angel in a T-shirt, shorts, and flip-flops.

"I brought you some lunch. Mrs. Sharpe thought—" Melanie looked at Grimaldi and froze. Her lips tightened for a few seconds before she continued. "I didn't know anyone was here."

Grimaldi looked at Melanie, then back at Conner with the hint of a laugh on her face. What was that all about?

"That's all the questions for now, Dell," Miranda said. "Thanks—and good luck. Bye, Stephens."

She blurred into a comet and left the room.

"Thanks for bringing me lunch." Conner hoped Melanie couldn't hear his heart pounding in his ears.

He wanted to say something. Wanted to tell her how he felt, what she meant to him, wanted to let his swirling feelings pour out in witty, romantic words—like the guys in the movies his mom watched.

He opened his mouth and heard himself say, "Fries for lunch again?" No! That's not what he meant to say!

Melanie nodded, handing him the plate. "With mustard. Just the way you like them." She seemed a little . . . tense.

"No way! You remembered the mustard. Thanks so much." Okay, he needed to regroup. Try again.

Melanie sat down on the foot of his cot and looked at him. Those dark eyes always made his stomach slosh and slide around. In a good way. "Are you okay? I mean, after almost drowning and everything."

"Yeah, I'm fine." He bit into a chicken finger, hoping she wouldn't ask a lot of questions. He didn't want to talk about it anymore.

"So . . ." She paused and looked at him with those brown eyes. "What happened? I'm worried."

He chewed the chicken a little more slowly. "Um, well,

I don't mean to be rude, but I don't really want to talk about it. I just had to give the whole story to Miran— Lieutenant Grimaldi."

"Oh." Melanie pinched her lips together. "So you told *her* all about it?"

"Well, yeah, but—"

"Fine." Melanie stood up. The warmth in her eyes had frozen. They looked like root beer popsicles now. With frostbite and freezer burn.

"What's wrong?"

"You'd better get your rest." She clipped her words. "We have to watch the eclipse tonight." Melanie turned and left the room.

Conner watched her leave, trying to understand what had just happened. What had started out with chicken fingers, French fries, and undying love had ended in a skirmish that he'd lost, even though he didn't even know what the fight had been about. He shrugged and bit into a soggy fry.

CHAPTER 11

CRIES IN THE NIGHT

LEXA LOOKED UP FROM HER CHICKEN FIN-
gers, wondering where Melanie was. She'd never
come back from taking lunch to Conner.

Hmmm. Suspicious. Especially considering other
things Lexa had noticed recently—a look here, a blush
there. An accidental brushing of hands that lasted longer
than needed . . .

No. No way. Not Conner and Melanie. They were
almost like brother and sister. They'd been friends for way
too long. Right?

"Lexa?"

Leaving behind the creepily disgusting image of
Conner and Melanie, Lexa looked up to see Pilaf standing there, blinking behind his lunch tray like an owl with
amnesia.

"Is Conner still resting?" he asked.

Since Pilaf relied on Conner for protection from
bullies and someone to sit by at lunch, he looked a little

59

lost—like a not-super-cute puppy that no one wanted. Lexa fought back a tiny wave of irritation. Couldn't he ever take care of himself? She had important things to think about. "Yeah, he is."

Pilaf's face fell a little. "Oh, okay." He turned away and squinted at the cafeteria, paralyzed by indecision.

Oh, honestly. Now she felt like a jerk. "Hey, Pilaf, do you want to sit by me? Melanie had to go do something."

"Thanks." Pilaf's smile sparkled as he turned back and sat down. He leaned across the table, dropping his voice to a loud whisper. "This Magi stuff is really cool." His unhidden, childlike excitement pushed away most of Lexa's irritation.

"I hope they let me join," he continued. "It sounds fun. I've never been in a group before."

Those few words opened Lexa's eyes. She'd never been mean to Pilaf, but she'd never understood why Conner went to so much trouble to protect and help him. But, with those few words, Lexa found herself wanting to take care of him as well.

"You'll be an awesome Magi, Pilaf!"

"So how does it work? I mean, are all Magi the same or do you have special personal powers like superheroes?"

"Well, we're still pretty new at this, but I think everyone has some of the same powers, plus you have a special talent that's your own—they call those gifts. Like, all the Magi can turn into comets and shoot Light out and stuff like that. But Conner has super strength—"

"You mean like how he tore Geoffrey's locker door off a few weeks ago?"

"Uh-huh. And Melanie is this thing called an

Augmentor, which is really rare, and it means she can make other people's powers stronger. And also, you know how smart she is in regular life? The Light makes her even smarter, and she can figure things out superfast, which I guess means she actually has two gifts." Lexa paused. She'd never thought about that before. It seemed a little unfair, actually. She tugged on her ponytail. "Anyways, I sometimes get dreams or visions, or just thoughts. I call them theelings cause they're actually thoughts and feelings put together—and they tell me things that other people don't know. I get theelings a lot. The dreams don't come as much. But theelings—"

"Listen up!" Mr. Keller marched into the middle of the cafeteria. "The bus leaves in five minutes for the salt marsh. Be aboard in four minutes with your lab partner. Make sure to bring a pair of old sneakers—no flip-flops or sandals. Salt marshes are fascinating places, so I think you have a real treat in store."

Lexa noticed anxiety spread across Pilaf's face as he heard the announcement.

"Hey, Pilaf, since Conner's not going, do you want to be with me and Melanie?"

The light shining in Pilaf's eyes gave Lexa all the answer she needed.

"Where did you go, Mel?" Lexa asked as they lined up to get off the replacement bus. Since Pilaf could hear head-talking, she figured whispering would be the safest. "Did you see Conner?"

"Yes." The word came out tight and tense.

"Are you okay?"

"I'm fine." Which obviously meant "no." Melanie sometimes bottled her emotions up too much.

Lexa gagged as they stepped off and a wave of foul-smelling, rotten air hit her just as she inhaled. "Gross!" She yanked her T-shirt up over her mouth and nose.

Mr. Keller distributed clipboards and diagrams. "Now as you explore the marsh, one partner will observe. The other partner will use the diagrams on the clipboard to identify the wildlife and keep an accurate record of the species you encounter. Find as much biodiversity as possible."

Everyone shuffled off, and before long, Lexa felt thick muck slurping her shoes down into the ground.

"This is so disgusting," she grumbled. "So, what's that?" She pointed to a weed that looked like a lot of other weeds.

Melanie frowned at the diagram on her clipboard. "That's black needlerush, and those things on it are periwinkle snails, I think."

"They crawl up the grass when the tide comes in because the salt in the water will kill them," Pilaf said. "I hope we see a fiddler crab!" He splashed off, peering down into the murky water.

"Sorry if Conner upset you." Lexa tossed a bit of conversational bait to Melanie.

"That must be cord grass." Melanie didn't even look at Lexa.

"Seriously, Mel. Don't be mad at him. Whatever he did—I don't think it's his fault."

Melanie shot a glare at Lexa so fierce that Lexa almost expected flames to shoot out of Melanie's eyes and barbecue the periwinkle snails. "Oh. So it's my fault?"

"No, Mel! That's not what I meant." She hadn't seen Melanie so mad in a long time. Something must have hit a nerve. "I mean, I don't know what he did, but never mind about that for now. Conner hasn't really been himself lately. I think something's wrong."

Melanie paused. She didn't look at Lexa, but her voice got softer. "What do you mean?"

Lexa paused. How much should she say? Conner would not like what she was about to do. "I started to notice it after he got back from being Lady Nightwing's prisoner. It's a lot of little things. He's übermoody. He shuts his thoughts off from me a lot, and he cries out in the night. I think whatever happened was more than just scary or dangerous. I'm worried something really bad happened to him."

Growing concern pushed the anger from Melanie's eyes. "Lexa, you're not telling me everything."

Lexa tugged at her ponytail. How much should she tell? "We-ell . . ." She decided not to worry about what Conner might say. The burden of this secret had been too heavy the last few weeks. "You have to promise, like, pinky swear, not to tell. Conner would kill me if he found out I was telling you about this."

She dropped her voice. "The other night he kept yelling out in his sleep, so I finally went into his room to wake him up. He was crying—like, sobbing. Most of what he said didn't make sense. But I heard one thing really clearly. He kept shouting, 'Melanie! I'm sorry!' over and over. Then my parents ran in and woke him up."

"What do you think he meant?" Melanie asked.

Lexa couldn't quite decipher the emotion on her face. "I don't know. I was hoping you could tell me." Lexa hated feeling so helpless, hated knowing something was wrong, and hated not knowing what it was. And Conner, like Melanie, could not be forced into confiding. If Melanie sometimes seemed like a clam with superglue, Conner was like a clam with superglue and a padlock.

"Have you told anyone—any of the Magi, I mean?"

"No." Lexa tugged her ponytail again. "I thought about it—but I don't know. It kind of feels like I'm violating a secret. Plus Dr. Timberi's the one I would tell anyways, and he's been gone. I sort of thought that I'd see if Conner got better, and if he didn't, then I'd talk to Dr. Timberi whenever he gets back. The reason I'm telling you is so you'll understand why Conner might be tense lately. If he did something rude, he probably didn't mean to. He's just not himself."

"Poor Conner," Melanie whispered.

"Fiddler crabs!" Pilaf splashed up to them, sending droplets of mucky, murky water everywhere. Lexa cringed and ducked, turning her face away. "I found fiddler crabs! Lots of them." He beamed, panting like a proud, cartoon puppy. "You've got to see this. So cool!"

"All right," Melanie said in a bright voice. "Here we come. Show us where they are, Pilaf."

ᴀPOLOGIES

CONNER JERKED UP, PANIC RACING through his veins like runaway semis. Adrenaline threw open his gateway to the Light, and he sent bolts of red Light scything through the darkness around him. As the Light flashed, the room lit up, illuminating charts on a wood-paneled wall. How to treat a jellyfish sting. Diagrams of marine plants.

No Darkhands. No Lady Nightwing. It had been a dream.

He took a deep breath and tried to push away the adrenaline-fueled anxiety. Just another dream. He must have fallen asleep.

"Conner!" Mrs. Sharpe appeared in a brilliant bloom of cream-colored Light, brandishing her yardstick in a battle stance. She scanned the room. "Are you all right? I sensed some explosive Lightcraft."

Conner nodded as embarrassment replaced his last

bits of fear. "I had a dream that I was being attacked, and I woke up fighting."

Mrs. Sharpe flicked on the light switch, revealing the mess that Conner's outburst had created: broken glass from a medicine cabinet, blasted papers, and a hole in the door.

"This has not been an easy trip for you, has it?" Mrs. Sharpe gave him a sympathetic pat on the shoulder. She clapped her hands together and shards of broken glass jumped back into the cabinet, welding themselves back together with a flash. Scraps of paper flew up and re-organized themselves into a chart of different shark species. Splinters of wood rebuilt the hole in the door. In just a few minutes, she had the room cleaned up and put back together.

Mrs. Sharpe looked back at Conner. "I streamed back to Nashville and saw your mother this afternoon. She sends her love. She was quite worried, but I assured her you would be fine." She paused and tilted her head. "Conner, I need to ask you a question, and I want you to answer honestly."

Great. They must have found out about the shadows and the black fire.

"Last night when you blew up the bus—what happened?"

Relief washed over him. She only wanted to hear about his major act of property destruction. Not the really bad stuff.

"Well, I, when I was sort-of-streaming, I tried to jump over the bus, but I didn't make it, so my feet hit the roof and sliced through it. I ducked to miss the phantumbra and lost control. I fell down and ended up going down through the gas tank. I guess the heat made the gas explode. Sorry about that."

She shook her head. "Don't worry about it. That's not your fault. I only ask because last night several fires were started in Nashville. No one was hurt—they were all remote, uninhabited locations. But the timing seems strange. Fires there, and a fire here. I just wondered if there was any connection, but I don't see how there could be."

"Mrs. Sharpe, is it okay if I get up now?" He didn't want to keep sitting alone in a dark room.

"I don't see why not. The doctor said you needed rest, but if you feel ready, I think you'll be fine."

"What time is it, anyway?"

"Half-past nine. I assumed you would sleep through the night. It's almost time for the eclipse—Mr. Keller's got everyone down on the beach to roast marshmallows while they wait. Are you hungry?"

"Yes, ma'am."

"The cafeteria's closed, but I'll stream over to the convenience store and find something for you. Why don't you go on down to the beach and join the others? Some fresh air would probably do you some good after being in here all day." Her cream-colored comet shot out of the room.

Conner climbed off the cot, but his feet got tangled in a blanket on the floor. He tripped, then picked the blanket up, noticing the pink and white hearts and the monogrammed letters: MNS. Melanie Nicole Stephens.

Melanie's blanket? Ticklish sort of chills ran up and down his arms, and his stomach felt pleasantly fluttery.

He didn't know how the blanket had come to be there, but he liked being so close to something that had been close to her. Wrapping the blanket around him, he caught a whiff of the sweet, sort of peachy smell she always had.

But thinking about Melanie's awesomeness triggered other thoughts. Memories rushed back, overwhelming him before he could do anything about it. Memories of the Shadowbox and Melanie's anguished, frightened face and cries flared back to life. Guilt and shame slammed into him, shouting about what a terrible person he was. The blanket made him feel unclean now. He was becoming a Darkhand. He didn't deserve kindness. Especially from her. He let the soft, sweet warmth slide off his shoulders.

He knew what he'd done in the Shadowbox must have technically been illusions or hallucinations. But the Shadowbox couldn't create something out of nothing, right? Those images must have come from some swampy place deep inside of him. A new thought jumped out and twisted his spirit. What if it was the future? Like some kind of prophecy?

Thoughts and fears pelted him as he made his way down to the beach, each new thought worse than the others.

How long before the change to being a Darkhand was complete? Should he just run away and hide to protect everyone he knew and loved?

Conner trudged past the fence and over the dunes of warm sand. A fire flickered ahead in the darkness. The sound of laughter made him feel lonely. He walked alone under the stars, boiling in a miserable stew of guilt, haunted by the memories of shooting fire and by what he'd done to Melanie in the Shadowbox, and became increasingly terrified of what he might do in the future.

I'm sorry, Melanie.

How many times had he apologized in his head? Repeating the words like they were some kind of magic spell.

Sorry, Melanie, he thought. *I'm so sorry—*

For what?

He looked up, frozen.

She stood about fifty yards in front of him, her skin painted silver by the full moon as her red hair blew in the soft, salty breeze.

What are you sorry for, Conner? Melanie asked.

His thoughts scattered in a million directions, like sand crabs scuttling away. He couldn't tell her the truth. Couldn't let her find out. But he had to say something.

Thinking fast, he stammered, *For earlier.*

Me too, she said. *It was immature of me to get mad.*

Conner gulped. He took a hesitant step toward her.

She took a tentative step too.

He took another—and so did she.

A few more steps brought them within arm's length of each other.

Conner reached out and felt her fingers closing around his. How could anything be so soft and smooth? Taking her other hand, Conner basked in the chills running a relay race down his back.

Melanie's eyes sparkled as stars and moons and oceans danced in them. Conner's heart skipped two or three beats, before pounding like a conga drum convention.

He should say something. But—what? In movies the guy always knew what to say. *Melanie—*

I know. Her smile lit up the night and warmed him, covering his soul like her blanket had covered his body. *Me too.*

Shaking a little, Melanie leaned in closer.

Shaking a lot, Conner did too. Before he closed his eyes, he saw her lips quiver.

Conner! Conner, come and join us! The hissing voices returned. Tension knotted every muscle. The shadows lurking on the beach began to swim and swirl, taking shape as they called to him.

"NO!". Conner pulled away from Melanie. He raised his hand and shot his sigil into the rolling, boiling shadows. The big red dog tore into some of them, but as they faded, others took form, chanting louder and louder: *Conner, Conner! Come and join us—*

He stood in front of Melanie, trying to insert himself between the shadows and her. He started to tell her to run, but before he found his voice, pink Light flared, encircling Conner in a bubble of bright, glowing warmth. The bubble exploded, sending shock waves through the shadows. When Conner opened his eyes, both the Light and the shadows had vanished.

Six comets exploded into the area, fading into Lee, Grimaldi, Brighton, and three other members of the Phalanx all in combat stances. Lee looked around. "Stand down," he said. "At ease." They relaxed but kept scanning the area. "What happened, you two? We felt adumbrations and a whole bunch of Light."

Conner paused before speaking. How much should

he tell? This would be tricky. How much had Melanie seen? Had she heard the shadows call him?

Conner wished he had Lexa's ability to think fast and talk faster. She could spin lies so convincing that the truth looked false by comparison.

"I think some shadows were getting ready to attack. They started to form, but before anything happened, Melanie's Light pushed them away." Changing the subject might be a good tactic. He turned to Melanie. "How did you do that?"

She shook her head. "I don't know exactly. The Light just jumped out of me, almost on its own. I didn't do it on purpose."

"Stephens, are you saying that you used Light without meaning to? And it shielded Conner?" Lee asked.

"Yes, sir."

Lee whistled. "Boy, the three of you are really something."

"Are you an Augmentor, Stephens?" Grimaldi jumped in.

"Yes, ma'am."

Grimaldi nodded.

"Well, we'll have to investigate some more," Lee said. "Anything else happen? Anything else you noticed?"

Melanie stared at Conner.

He looked away, not wanting to make eye contact right then. The air between them still crackled with intensity, and he knew he couldn't hide anything from her while looking into those eyes. And he didn't want to mention the shadows talking to him. Had she heard that? Probably not. Because she wasn't turning into a Darkhand.

71

"Nope. Nothing else. Everything's good."

Above them the moon began to turn dark. Conner looked up. "Oh, hey, the eclipse! We probably better get over to the group or Keller will kill us."

CHAPTER 13

ℙENUMBRAS

LEXA KICKED AT THE STUPID SAND, WATCH-
ing to see if more stupid flashes of Light came.
Melanie had gone to get a jacket. A few minutes later,
a flash of red light had caught Lexa's eye, followed by a
ginormous explosion of pink Light. Red and pink. Conner
and Melanie's colors.

Hurt and a sudden sense of loneliness echoed in her
mind, with the reverb turned up high. What were they
doing without her?

Did you two forget anything? Like maybe me?

How could they go off and leave her out like that? Her
best friend and her twin brother! Of all people that she
should be able to trust. How long had they been practicing
Lightcraft without her now? Did this happen a lot? Hurt
tied a knotty lump in her throat.

"The kind of eclipse we'll be seeing tonight is a penumbral lunar eclipse," Mr. Keller paused for everyone to
take notes.

Yeah, right. I'm on the beach at night and I'm going to take notes, Lexa murmured in her head. Next to her, Pilaf giggled.

"This part is important," Mr. Keller continued. "Listen carefully. When the light from the sun hits the earth, the earth casts a shadow. That shadow has two parts. The darkest part of the shadow, the area where the earth completely blocks the light, is called the umbra. The umbra is totally dark—no light at all."

Lexa's skin prickled. No wonder the Darkhands chose Umbra for the name of their organization.

"However, because the sun is so large, the earth cannot block all of its rays. Some of the light spills past the earth, creating a portion at the edges where it is not completely dark. This area is a border between sunlight and shadow, a place that is not fully light or dark. We call this area the penumbra—a vague, shadowy area. Everyone repeat after me—pen-UM-bra." He paused as they repeated the word. "When the moon passes through the earth's penumbra, we get a penumbral lunar eclipse. Let me demonstrate. I'll need a few helpers. Miss Dell, why don't you come join us? And perhaps Miss Martin? Come up here."

Lexa groaned. Insult to injury. Conner and Melanie went off to do Magi stuff together while she got stuck demonstrating penumbras with Lily Martin! Stuck-up, irritating, drama queen Lily Martin.

Mr. Keller handed Lexa a ping-pong ball and gave Lily a tennis ball. "Lexa is the moon, and Lily is the earth . . ."

Lexa looked into the distance as more Light flashed—not red and pink this time. Other colors. She could feel the air shaking. What was going on?

Mr. Keller's voice interrupted her. "Get with your partners now. It's almost time for the eclipse! Look for the specific phenomena noted on these diagrams." He waved a stack of papers in the air.

As everyone partnered off, Lexa felt more alone than ever. Melanie should have been her partner.

Beneath the immediate loneliness, a freezing cold fear scratched at the doggy-door of Lexa's mind. She recalled all the recent blushes and lingering looks between Melanie and Conner lately. Was she losing her best friend? To her twin brother?

Lexa gulped and pushed down on the lump rising in her throat, forcing herself to focus on the penumbral lunar eclipse.

"Hey, Lexa?" Pilaf stared up at her with nervous eyes. "Do you have a lab partner?"

"No, and I'd love to be your partner, Pilaf!" She felt a giant smile run across her face. The fact that someone wanted to be with her right now soothed some of the sting.

As upset as she was about being excluded, Lexa found herself captivated by the ominous beauty of the penumbral eclipse. The areas that were neither light nor dark fascinated her, the way they could be both illuminated and shadowed at the same time.

A few minutes into the eclipse, Conner and Melanie walked into the group. *What did we miss?* Conner asked Lexa.

Lexa glared icicles at him, not minding that some shards spilled over and hit Melanie also. *Well, an amazing Light show for one thing. You'll never believe it, but there was a ginormous burst of Light down on the beach. Pink and red. Weird. Those are your colors. It's almost like two Magi were out practicing or something. Just two, though. Not three. No yellow.*

Lexa— Melanie started to say.

You'd better get your study sheets from Mr. Keller. You missed a lot of the eclipse already. Chin held high, Lexa turned her back to them and pretended to stare at the darkened moon. Gnawing, hungry hurt burned inside her. How could they be so mean?

Stop it, Lex, Conner's voice came into her mind, and she noticed a thin strand of Light linking their heads. Oh, a private conversation. He must have only been pretending to be asleep when Mrs. Sharpe taught them how to do that.

Stop what? She needed to stop something?

You always do this!

Do what?

You know what. When someone makes you mad, you don't just tell them. You have to drop all these hints to make sure they know you're upset. But we don't even know what we did to make you mad. What's the problem?

My problem? Let's see. Ummm, maybe that my twin brother and best friend are out practicing Lightcraft and leaving me out. Yeah, that might be it. I thought we were a team—like all three of us. The Three Musketeers or whatever.

"Four," Pilaf said.

Conner and Lexa both snapped their heads to look at him.

Pilaf, can you hear what we're saying? Conner asked.

Pilaf nodded. "Yes. Is that bad?"

Well, it's weird since it was supposed to be a private, shielded conversation. No one should have been able to hear it.

"Sorry," Pilaf said. "I didn't mean to listen. It was like you were yelling. I couldn't really help it. Anyway, sorry to interrupt. I just meant that since I am somehow involved in all of this, technically you aren't the Three Musketeers anymore."

"Good point," Conner said. *Um, Pilaf, this is kind of personal. Do you think you can maybe tune us out? Sort of plug your mental ears?*

Pilaf nodded. "I'll try. Maybe if I sing a song in my head."

This thing with Pilaf is really weird, Conner thought to Lexa. *Anyway, me and Melanie weren't doing Lightcraft. I mean, not on purpose. Uh . . .* He looked down at the ground and pawed at the sand with his foot. *Well, me and Melanie accidentally ran into each other and, well, it turns out we kind of like each other, and then some shadows started to attack me, and her Light just kind of exploded out. It just happened. I don't know how.*

Lexa stared at Conner. He liked Melanie, and she liked him back? She cringed and then shuddered. Gross. Seriously gross. She'd suspected a crush, but this sounded far worse. Lexa had seen this with other girls when they got boyfriends. Everything and everyone else suddenly became non-existent. She now risked being much further outside the Trio than she'd realized.

Lexa looked at Conner and forced a smile. *That's great!* She gave Melanie a hug and the sincerest fake smile she could manage. What did you say when someone started liking your brother? "Welcome to the family?" Or, "Are you crazy?"

Lexa finally managed to squeeze out the words, "I'm really happy for you." She spoke aloud because she didn't trust her thoughts. As she focused on the diagram of a penumbral eclipse, the knot in her throat grew bigger and tighter.

CHAPTER 14

THE ADUMBRATORS

MELANIE WOKE UP WITH A SMILE ON HER face. Conner Dell liked her! He liked her back, and he liked her as much as she liked him!

A laugh bubbled out of her mouth, filling the tiny dorm room before she could stop it. Conner Dell liked her back! How long had she been crushing on him? Since kindergarten? Or earlier?

Melanie paused as a dark cloud floated across the sunny skies of her happiness.

She could have sworn the shadows had talked to Conner last night. Called him by name. That seemed strange to her. In all the battles they'd fought, all the times they'd been attacked, she'd never noticed that. But the thing that worried her and gave the storm cloud some extra darkness was his reaction. He'd changed the subject and kept it from Lee and Miranda. Almost like he felt guilty and wanted to hide it.

She didn't know exactly what that meant, only that

it seemed off somehow. On the other hand, Conner had been through a lot lately. Maybe there was an explanation.

And the fact was that he liked her. He really liked her!

A hum buzzed through the room, interrupting her thoughts. The air seemed to shiver, and she felt quivers inside her soul—like vibrations from a speaker you can feel even when you can't hear the music.

Melanie ran through an equation in her head, opening her gateway to the Light. With the gateway open, she could tell that the vibrations were echoes from Light being used nearby. But who would be doing Lightcraft this early in the morning?

Crawling out of her sleeping bag, she tried to move without making the ancient bed springs squeak. Lexa hadn't woken up yet, and Melanie didn't want to be the one to do it. Lexa never did well with lack of sleep, and she'd been a little pouty the night before. Waking her early would not be a good way to start the day—for anyone involved.

Melanie looked out of the window. Below her, three gardeners stood chatting outside of Conner's window. One gardener, a young, skinny guy, threw a net of neon green Light against the walls while a young woman used a long metal wand connected to a laptop to scan the Light net. A third gardener stood guard, brandishing his Weed eater as if it were some kind of lethal weapon.

Melanie smiled, recognizing Colonel Lee Murrell, disguised in a straw hat and old work clothes. The other two were Donovan and Veronique, two of the Adumbrators. She'd met them when Conner had been kidnapped.

Donovan and Veronique finished whatever they were

doing and started packing their equipment as Mrs. Sharpe walked around the corner. Curious about their task, Melanie opened her mind. They didn't try to shield their conversation, so she could hear them with little effort.

Morning, Norma, Lee thought, touching the brim of his straw hat.

Good morning, Lee. I'm glad you're back. And I feel better knowing you have some extra Phalanx members now. I got a sigil from Morgan last night. With everything that's happened to Conner, he's terribly worried about the Trio.

A twinge of guilt tiptoed through Melanie. Should she be eavesdropping like this? On the other hand, they'd do private conversations if it were secret, right?

Lee chuckled. *I've never seen Morgan quite like this. He's like a mother hen fussing over those three. The man that used to make Darkhands everywhere tremble has turned into Mary Poppins. Sure loves those kids, don't he?*

He certainly does, Mrs. Sharpe replied. *I doubt they have any idea quite how much they mean to him. He's been happier these past two months than any time I can remember since everything happened.*

What did Mrs. Sharpe mean by "since everything happened"? This wasn't the first time Melanie had heard fragments of conversations alluding to a big secret in Dr. Timberi's past.

I told him you'd send regular updates, Lee, Mrs. Sharpe continued. *It was the only way I could stop him from trying to stream down here, which he almost did. Between us, I think that might have killed him. His sigil was so weak—I don't think he's doing well.*

Apprehension spread through Melanie. That didn't

sound good at all. How badly had he been injured?

'Fraid you're right, Norma. He looked at the Adumbrators, who had finished packing all their equipment. *Well, what did your scan find?*

Donovan shook his head. *Not much, Colonel. No signs of Darkhands. Only a Magi Light signature we can't identify.*

That's odd, Mrs. Sharpe said. *A Magus was here that you can't identify?*

Veronique shrugged. *It's not uncommon. Light signatures degrade quickly. It might be from you or Lee or anyone else—the quality has degraded over twenty-four hours, so it's inconclusive. But there are no signs of any Darkhands being here.*

Are you sure? Mrs. Sharpe asked. *Conner said he saw the Stalker.*

Who? Veronique asked.

Excuse me. I mean Timothy. The students call him the Stalker, so we've all taken to using that term.

Timothy? They knew the Stalker's name?

Veronique shook her head. *Whatever you choose to call him, he was not here. We did not see any adumbrations. No signs of Darkhands whatever.*

This is getting stranger than a tap dancing coyote, Lee muttered.

Conner has been under a great deal of strain lately. Veronique's patronizing tone annoyed Melanie. *After the trauma of his imprisonment, he needs to be thoroughly examined for stress-induced disorders. It would not be at all unheard of for someone who had been through what he has to hallucinate.*

Anger pulsed inside of Melanie, and she found herself

feeling both indignant and protective. They were going to ignore this and say Conner was crazy? That this was a figment of his imagination?

Lee paused, then looked up at Melanie's window and smiled. *That you, Stephens? Your thoughts are louder than a freight train on rickety tracks at midnight. Why don't you come on down here instead of just snooping up there?*

Mortified at being overheard, or over-thought, but still angry at the way Veronique talked about Conner, Melanie pulled on a T-shirt and shorts, slipped into flip-flops, and went to join them.

By the time Melanie got down, the Adumbrators had left, leaving Lee and Mrs. Sharpe chatting.

"So what was that all about?" Melanie asked.

"When Magi use Light, it leaves vibrations," Mrs. Sharpe said. "Each Magus has distinct vibrations, like a fingerprint. The Darkhands leave shadows, or adumbrations. These are also distinct and can be read. The Adumbrators were scanning the area for evidence of the Stalker, but there are no adumbrations. Just a Light signature that's not clear enough to read."

"So, because they can't figure it out, they'll conveniently accuse Conner of being crazy?" Melanie felt herself flush.

"Keep your feet in the stirrups, Stephens," Lee said. "We're on your side. I didn't see the Stalker, but if Conner says he did, I believe him. But you never wanna argue with a bureaucrat. It's worse than pointless—it's like trying to poke a porcupine. We all just need to keep our eyes open and figure out what's going on."

He stretched and yawned. "I've been streaming back and forth from HQ all night, and I'm bushed. I'm gonna get me some shut-eye. Grimaldi has command."

"Thank you, Lee," Mrs. Sharpe said. "Melanie, I'll be waking everyone up soon, so why don't you go back upstairs now.

"Yes, ma'am."

Back in her room, Melanie checked the travel alarm clock on her dresser. 6:51. She ran over and sat on the foot of Lexa's bed. "Lexa, we have to talk. I was just outside, and they were Adumbrating. Donovan and Veronique and—"

"What?" Lexa seemed to have a chorus of frogs in her throat.

"Remember those two Adumbrators who came and helped you when you were sending your sigil to find Notzange and Conner?" Notzange was another Magus who worked for the Magisterium. She'd been imprisoned but had been saved when her sigil found Lexa.

"Oh yeah, they were cool." Lexa woke up just a bit more.

"They were doing some kind of scanning thing—looking at Light signatures and adumbrations."

"What?"

"They're like fingerprints for Magi and Darkhands. But here's the thing. They said the Stalker wasn't ever here. And they apparently know the Stalker's name."

Lexa started to look more interested than sleepy. "Are you serious?"

"Yes. It's Timothy." Melanie paused. "I guess it's not necessarily weird that they know his name. But I get the idea they know a lot more. Like the name's just the tip of the iceberg."

"I think you're right," Lexa agreed. "I really wish Dr.

Timberi was here. At least he usually tried to answer our questions. Everyone else just brushes us off." Lexa looked at Melanie, and her eyes lit up. She leaned forward and dropped her voice. "So what happened last night with you and Conner? I mean, he said you both like each other and that shadows started to attack, but your Light jumped out and made everything go away."

Embarrassment slithered around Melanie, strangling her train of thought and leaving her speechless for a few seconds. "Uh, well, I—I don't know how that happened. I mean—" She couldn't believe how self-conscious she felt. "Lexa, can we talk about this later? I need some time to think everything through."

The light in Lexa's eyes cooled. When she spoke a few seconds later, her tone had grown brittle. "Oh. Sure." Lexa wrapped her words in a chilly, distant voice that hurt Melanie more than yelling or any number of mean names. "Well, I'd better go shower." Lexa grabbed some wadded-up clothes from the floor by her bed, rummaged through a pile for her towel, and swept out of the room.

Melanie cringed and wrinkled her nose. Lexa had left a wet towel crumpled up under her dirty clothes? She shivered as her skin crawled, an involuntary response to the resort for mold and mildew Lexa had created.

And now, even worse, Lexa was in full-blown martyr mode. Every time her feelings got hurt even a little, she turned it into a major drama where she played Joan of Arc or some persecuted saint. Melanie loved Lexa. But the drama was starting to get a little old.

· CHAPTER 15 ·

THE AQUARIUM

CONNER WOKE UP A LITTLE LATE AFTER A refreshing, undisturbed sleep. Pilaf waited for him to get ready, and as they walked to the cafeteria together they ran into Lexa, who seemed tense.

"Hi, Lex," Conner said. "Where's Melanie?"

Lexa glared at him. "I'm fine, Conner. Thanks for asking. Glad my brother cares so much about me."

Conner never failed to be amazed by how much sarcasm Lexa could generate. It was like her words were a tiny hamburger surrounded by a giant bun of sarcasm.

"Am I in charge of Melanie now?" Lexa snapped. She turned to Pilaf. *Hey, Pilaf,* she thought. *Want to be my partner today at the aquarium?*

Pilaf blinked and looked a little surprised. "Uh, sure."

Good! Lexa thrust her chin up, spun on her heel, and swept back to the dorms like an angry Greek goddess.

"What's wrong with Lexa?" Pilaf said as they went through the breakfast line.

"Who knows?" Conner said. "It doesn't take much to trigger an Oscar-worthy performance from Lexa. She's such a drama queen."

"Yeah, she is an amazing actress," Pilaf said, apparently missing Conner's ironic tone. They found a table and sat down.

"Can I sit here?"

Conner looked up and almost choked on his rubber eggs. Melanie stood there—impossibly beautiful behind her tray of plain cold cereal and orange juice.

"Sure." He felt self-conscious. What should he do? What should he say? He risked a smile—and almost jumped out of his seat when she smiled back.

"Have you seen Lexa?" Melanie asked.

"Yeah. She just stormed off. She seems kind of touchy this morning. Maybe you should talk to her."

Melanie frowned. "She's your sister."

Conner frowned back. "She's your best friend. Plus you're a girl."

Melanie laughed, making Conner want to do flips or something. "Let's just try to be patient with her. I think she needs to adjust to"—Melanie looked at Pilaf, who slurped his cold cereal with great relish—"to things."

Conner nodded. "Lexa asked Pilaf to be her lab partner today. Do you, uh, maybe, uh, want to be lab partners at the aquarium today?" He stammered and stumbled around, tripping on awkwardness. Why was that so hard to say?

"Sure! I'd love to."

She looked so beautiful when she blushed.

Conner stared through the glass at the sharks. He couldn't believe how evil they looked, and, when one of the sharks darted toward them, Conner *might* have screamed a bit as he and Melanie jumped back. Thank goodness for thick glass.

Trying to recatch his breath, and more importantly, his coolness, Conner looked around. Why did they keep it so dark in here? Shadows puddled, thick and heavy, in so many places.

"Oh, wow, sharks! Cool!" Pilaf walked into the room.

"Did Lexa finally dismiss you?" Conner asked.

"She's getting a drink." Pilaf stared at the sharks. "She told me to meet her here."

She's getting ready to make sure we know she's ignoring us, Conner thought to Melanie.

"Hey, Pilaf." As Lexa walked into the shark observation room, Conner thought it got several degrees colder. She looked around, ignoring Melanie and Conner in the most obvious way possible. "Let's go see the stingrays now." Lexa swept out of the room, full of queen-like contempt for the dirty peasants.

Melanie followed her. "Hey, Lexa. Wait." She disappeared out the door and down the hall.

"Sorry." Pilaf looked at Conner when they were alone.

"You don't need to apologize, Pilaf," Conner said. "Lexa's mad at me and Melanie, so she's trying to make sure we know it by ignoring us. We're supposed to ask what's wrong, and then she'll go into this big persecuted heroine monologue. She does this all the time. You're basically a prop in Lexa's little drama. You're really nice to hang out with her."

Pilaf shrugged. "I like being with Lexa. She's funny."
He blushed a bright flaming red that made Conner think
of a fire truck. "And pretty."

Conner stared at Pilaf. *Lexa pretty? Pilaf had always
been a little strange but—oh well.* Whatever. "Go for it. If
Lexa latches on to you, that just forces me and Melanie to
spend time together."

Pilaf giggled. "So, do you—you know, like Melanie?"

That giggle always made Conner smile. "Yeah. A lot."

"She likes you too. I can hear her thoughts sometimes.
When you're around, they're sort of like loud heartbeats."

Conner grinned. "I'm really glad to hear that. Can
you hear my thoughts too?"

Pilaf nodded. "Uh-huh. When she's around, yours are
like screams at a football game."

Conner laughed. "That doesn't really surprise me.
She's amazing. I mean, she's beautiful. And super-smart.
And she thinks I'm funny and cute. And, well—she's just
incredible. We're going to go see a movie when we get
back. Hey—can you hear all of our thoughts?"

"No, not very often, actually. Just really, really strong
ones. Don't worry, I don't hear much. Well, I better go
find Lexa."

"See you, Pilaf."

Alone, Conner studied the sharks, trying to identify
the different body parts on the worksheet Mr. Keller had
given them.

Conner! Conner, come and join us!

The shadows pooling in the room began to swim and
swirl, taking shape as they called to him.

Pink Light flashed, and the shadows vanished.

"Conner!" Melanie's voice pierced the darkness, and she ran in and grabbed his hand. "I felt something again—vibrations—and then Light jumped out of me again. Are you okay?"

"I'm fine. Just shadows. Before they could do anything, your Light pushed them away."

She scrunched her nose. "Maybe it's because I'm an Augmentor and your, uh, you're my friend, so my Light automatically comes to help you?" She looked at him more closely. "Are you sure you're okay?"

For half a second, he felt tempted to tell her everything—to pour his heart out about the Shadowbox and—no. No. What was he thinking? He couldn't risk how she would feel about him if she knew what he'd done. Time to change the subject. He tightened his grasp on her hand. "It's all good. No big deal. Seriously. I'll be fine. So, did Lexa talk to you? Or do you have to grovel a while longer?"

She looked at him with worried eyes for a few more seconds. "Conner, I really think—"

"Trust me. Everything's fine. So, what's up with Lexa?"

"Well, once I got her to talk to me, she said she feels left out and hurt since you and I are, are—since we've been spending time together. Anyway, I think I convinced her that she's still part of the Trio and that we're still friends. But here's the thing. You know Lexa—she got all excited. Now we're BFFs again, and she wants to go see a movie as soon as we get back. I sort of promised her I'd go see *Endless Night* on Friday after we get back."

Conner felt like he'd been kicked in the gut. By a family of kangaroos. "I thought we were going to go see a movie on Friday night." Lexa was destroying his first time out with Melanie. *Thanks a lot, sis.*

Melanie took his other hand, and he forgot all about Lexa. "I know—and I'd rather go with you. I don't even want to see that movie." She rolled her yes. "Vampires are not my thing. But Lexa needs to feel like she's still important to me. If we can just be patient with her for a while, she'll get everything worked out. Please don't be mad."

"I'm not mad at *you*," Conner grumbled.

"Don't be mad at Lexa either. It's kind of hard for her right now." Melanie's deep brown eyes caught the light reflected from the glass around them. Her soft voice extinguished Conner's frustration like rain falling on a fire.

"Fine." He sighed. "Zach wanted to get a bunch of us to go see *Dark Marauder*. Maybe we'll go watch that while you watch *Endless Night*."

Melanie smiled. "That's a great idea. We can at least drive together—and maybe go get some ice cream after?"

That made Conner feel better. "Yeah, there's that new frozen yogurt place in the mall. We could go there."

"I'd love that! Thanks for understanding." Melanie gave him a hug, then blushed and pulled away.

Conner realized that his memories of the Shadowbox and fears about the future had faded.

CHAPTER 16

FROZEN YOGURT

NOTHING HAPPENED FOR THE REST OF THE trip. Well, nothing much. A few times, Conner thought he saw shadows stir. But whenever shadows started to appear, a pink glow flashed, and they evaporated.

Additionally, the fear and guilt Conner had been feeling disappeared. He knew they still lurked somewhere in his unconscious mind, but they seemed unable to get to him, like sharks behind a glass wall. They'd tear you apart if they could get to you, but as long as the glass held, you were safe. Melanie and her Light seemed to be the glass wall, and Conner began to feel safe from shadows, both inside and out. He even grabbed onto a tiny sliver of hope that he wouldn't become a Darkhand after all.

They got home safely and, on Friday night, went to the movies. Melanie and Lexa saw *Endless Night* while Conner, Pilaf, and a bunch of other guys watched *Dark Marauder*. After the movies, the other guys left, and the Trio plus Pilaf went to get frozen yogurt. As they walked out of the theater toward the shop, Conner rolled his eyes and cringed as Lexa squealed. Again. Lexa's squeals made the food court of the mall feel a little crowded.

"No way, Mel! Jackson is *waayyy* cuter than Charles! I can't believe you don't like him!"

How did Lexa produce so much volume with two small vocal cords?

"Lex, you don't have to yell," Conner said. "We're only a few feet away from you. And can you stop squealing? You sound like a possessed chew toy."

"Be nice," Melanie whispered from his immediate left. He liked having her lips that close to his face.

From Melanie's other side, Lexa glared at him, although she did lower her volume by a decibel or two. "Seriously, Mel. How can you like Charles?"

Conner forced himself to swallow a sarcastic remark. Would Lexa go on with her cute vampire play-by-play all night long?

Sorry, Melanie whispered in a private thought. *Thanks for being so patient. I'm trying to change the subject, but—*

Pilaf, who had been walking on Conner's right, crossed over next to Lexa. "Hey, Lexa, can you tell me about the movie? It sounds really good."

Thanks, Pilaf, Conner thought, glad for once that Pilaf could hear even private conversations. *You're a real friend, taking one for the team like that.*

"Oh. My. Gosh," Lexa squealed. "You can*not* even believe how good it was! You totally should have seen it. Anyways, there's these two vampires, Charles and Jackson, and they're both in love with Lucy . . ."

Lexa talked all the way to the frozen yogurt place

without stopping for breath. With Pilaf distracting Lexa, Conner wondered about holding Melanie's hand. Nothing like that had happened since the aquarium, and he thought it might be time again.

Taking a deep breath, he reached down for Melanie's fingers—just as she reached for a cup with one hand. With her other hand, she pulled the lever on the machine, filling the container with a small amount of chocolate frozen yogurt. Bad timing. He hadn't been thinking clearly.

Executing a strategic retreat, Conner filled his own cup and followed Melanie to the toppings bar as Lexa rattled on at full-throttle behind them.

". . . so then these swimsuit models attack Charles because they're jealous of his love for Lucy, but they're really beautiful zombies and he's outnumbered, and since he doesn't have his shirt on—"

Pilaf blinked, staring at Lexa with genuine confusion. "Why would he be walking around in winter without a shirt?"

Conner snickered. From what he could tell, vampires did seem to be especially reluctant to wear shirts.

"Anyways, so, then Charles burns down Lucy's house and kills her family because he's *sooooo* heartbroken and he just can't stand to lose her . . ."

"Wait," Pilaf interrupted. "That's romantic? Also, does he have a shirt on yet?"

Conner refocused on his objective. Melanie held her yogurt with her right hand, leaving her left hand free. He shifted his own container and reached out again. Just then, she almost dropped her cup, grabbing it with both hands. He dropped his hand, lamenting his bad luck as they walked up to the cash register.

"I've got this," he said. The cashier punched a few buttons. "That will be $13.97." Conner handed her a wadded-up twenty-dollar bill and got the change.

"Oh, sorry!" A gum-chomping employee bumped into Lexa, knocking her skyscraper of mixed yogurt flavors and toppings onto Melanie, whom she also plowed over. "I'm so sorry," the woman said. "Let me help you!" She dropped to the floor next to Melanie. A moment later, Melanie's eyes got wide and her face grew pale.

Guys, Melanie's thoughts wobbled, *she has a knife! She says not to do anything and she's got the knife really close. She'll stab me before you can do anything.*

Conner clenched his fists so tight he thought he might break his fingers. He would kill this woman if he had the chance.

"I can't believe I did that!" the gum-chomping woman said in a loud voice. "Come in back to the break room and we'll get you cleaned up. Your friends can come too." She "helped" Melanie up, pulling her close, and Conner saw the flash of a silver blade. "Don't try anything," she hissed, spewing spearmint-scented bad breath. "Go past the machines, then into the back room. We're right behind you."

Conner fumed as they walked past oblivious customers, through a doorway, and into the back area of the store. Memories of Kyle Black marching him through Disney World with a knife in his back rushed back. He clenched his fists tighter, imagining them connecting with the gum-chomping Darkhand.

Gum-chomper nodded her head toward a storage closet. "Inside." Conner opened the door and walked in, followed by Lexa and Pilaf.

As they trudged inside, the fun-sized cashier walked by, standing guard outside the door.

"Lock us in, Avery," Chomper said as she pushed Melanie into the closet in front of her. "Then let Lady Nightwing know we have them. Call her—no Noctigavation. Don't make any adumbrations for the Magi to pick up." The cashier nodded and slammed the thick metal door shut. The slam echoed in the small room followed by the sharp click of a lock.

Conner tried to calm his burning rage. He needed to focus. Think clearly. This woman would kill or maim Melanie without a second thought. He couldn't risk any incomplete passes here. He looked around, hoping for inspiration—a plan of some kind. Large cans and boxes rested on dust-covered shelves. A few aprons hung on a hook. Not very promising.

The woman sniffed a few times. "Spread out." She looked at Conner. "You get in front of the aprons." She nodded at Pilaf and Lexa. "You two get by the shelves. Everyone put your hands together in front of you and don't try any Lightcraft. My knife is against her spinal column, and you can't move fast enough to stop me from paralyzing her for life." She sniffed again and swiped her nose with the back of one hand. "Lady Nightwing will be here soon."

Conner, Lexa said. *She's allergic to dust. We need to get lots of dust in the air. I have an idea. Make sure you stand right in front of the aprons and block them so she can't see.*

Are you sure, Lex? She's got a knife in Melanie's back. We can't mess this up.

Trust me. I have a theeling. Just be ready to grab the knife. Lexa didn't move, but Conner saw faint yellow Light glow around the aprons. He wished he had as much confidence in Lexa's theelings as she did.

Animated by Lexa's Light, the aprons moved back and forth, fanning small clouds of dust from the shelves into the air.

The woman sneezed, then sneezed again. Each time she sneezed, Conner's heart lurched, terrified she'd accidentally hurt Melanie.

Hurt Melanie.

The thought filled him with rage, and he choked back seething anger as Melanie winced. Without thinking, and in less than the blink of an eye, Conner saw a tunnel of red Light open up in front of him. He felt himself stretch out, shooting across the tiny room as if he were a rubber band.

Before Conner could blink, he'd shoved Melanie away, clamped his fingers around Chomper's wrist, and yanked her other arm behind her back. Chomper cried out and dropped her knife, which clattered to the ground.

"Make one sound and he snaps your wrist like a fortune cookie," Lexa growled.

"Two sounds and it's your neck," Conner added.

"Let's just tie her up and get out of here," Melanie said.

Lexa removed her shoe and tugged a sock off. "Open wide." Chomper turned her head away and clamped her jaws shut, but Conner squeezed her wrist—hard. The woman groaned and opened her mouth, allowing Lexa to stuff a dirty pink sock inside. Conner noticed Melanie cringe a bit, but the woman deserved it.

"Pilaf, hand me those aprons," Lexa ordered. Pilaf grabbed three aprons, and Lexa and Melanie wrapped one of them around Chomper's mouth to hold the sock-gag in, while Pilaf tied her hands and feet with every knot he'd learned in Boy Scouts.

"How do we get out of here?" Lexa asked. "Conner, can you break the—"

Outside, a key moved in the lock and the doorknob turned. The cashier said, "Hey, Lady Nightwing says— "

Melanie raised her hands, and her pink unicorn sigil charged through the crack in the door, dropping the cashier to the floor in an unconscious heap. Conner dragged her inside, and Lexa locked the door behind them as they walked out.

Creeping through the back of the store, they stopped at the doorway that led to the public area of the store. Conner peeked out and stopped—his blood as cold as frozen yogurt. Only a few hundred yards away, a group of six people walked through the food court toward the yogurt place. Six people with shiny, black miasmas.

We're about to have company, Conner warned. *We need a distraction or something—*

A high-pitched shriek pierced the air, and small strobe lights blinked.

"How's that?" Pilaf yelled. Conner looked over his shoulder and saw Pilaf's fingers on the handle of the fire alarm, sporting a giant grin.

"You're a genius!" Lexa wrapped her arms around

Pilaf—whose face grew redder and redder until it matched the fire alarm.

Conner peeked through the doorway again. Spurred by the fire alarms, a flash flood of people from all over the mall rushed into the food court, heading for the nearest exit. *Okay, I think we should be able to get lost in the crowd,* he thought. *Keep down and stay together.* Inspiration struck him. *Everyone hold hands!* He grabbed Melanie's hand. Victory! Of course, the downside was that Pilaf grabbed his other hand. Oh well . . .

Running in a half-crouch, they dove into the chaotic crowd of people. But the crowd pushed back against them, making it difficult to maneuver. Staying low made it even more difficult, and soon they couldn't move at all.

Conner thought he saw some Darkhands coming toward them. As they tried to decide what to do, Lexa yelled, *OUCH!*

What's wrong? Melanie asked.

Someone smashed my foot—the one without a shoe. Let's go hide in there before we get crushed! Lexa nodded toward a large department store. *We can leave when the crowd is gone.* Together, they managed to push through the mass of bodies and duck inside the men's section.

Battle of the Men's Department

MELANIE FOLLOWED LEXA INTO THE MEN'S section of the department store. Lexa stopped and pointed to the narrow gap between two long rows of racks filled with men's suits. *In there!* She darted into the opening, and Melanie went in behind her, wondering why Lexa always had to be in charge.

Behind Lexa and ahead of Conner, Melanie felt a little safer. They crawled to the center of the racks, and Melanie had to admit Lexa had picked a good hiding place. Sandwiched between the backs of two solid, wooden racks, no one could see them.

We should probably let the teachers know what's going on. Lexa raised her hands to send a sigil—

Don't! Melanie shouted. *That might give our location away—*

Too late. Before Melanie had finished, Lexa's sigil, a yellow dolphin, leapt into the air and vanished in a silver shimmer.

BOOM! A mannequin on top of the rack exploded, showering them with plastic splinters.

"I'm guessing that's not the teachers?" Pilaf squeaked.

A familiar tearing sound ripped through the air.

"What's that noise?" Pilaf looked around at everyone. "I hate not knowing this stuff!"

They're tearing holes in space, Conner said. *They're coming through another dimension called the Otherwhere.*

Pilaf's already-large eyes grew bigger as he whispered, "Cool!"

His eyes got even bigger as part of the rack blew apart behind them, blasted into toothpicks by smoldering Darkness.

Come on! Lexa crawled toward the opening at the other side—then froze. Everyone bumped into her from the behind.

What are you doing, Lex? Conner said.

Guys, look up there, Lexa said.

Looking past Lexa, Melanie saw two black-clad legs appear at the other end of the racks, apparently waiting for them.

Another section exploded in back of them as Lexa looked back, a question on her face. *Which way, guys?* Behind them, more sections blew apart like china plates being hit with a baseball bat. *Explosions or waiting Darkhand?*

Just then, a multi-colored comet whistled through the air right above them. It crashed into the waiting legs, and a man in black clothes fell down, unconscious.

Guys! Quick! A sharp Wisconsin accent filled their heads. *Get out of these racks and hide somewhere else!*

"That's Mrs. Davis!" Pilaf yelled.

We can help fight, Conner said.

No! She replied. *I can't fight and watch out for you at the same time. I sent a sigil to the others, but until they get here, it's just me. Hide—and stay hidden.*

Everyone followed Lexa as she dashed out from the gap between the racks, jumped over the unconscious Darkhand, and dove inside a circular rack of sweaters.

The colored comet landed on top of a shelf stacked with socks, fading into Mrs. Davis, their art teacher.

She dropped two shopping bags, whipped out a paint-brush, and sent hundreds of multi-colored Light spatters across the store. Her jeans and sweatshirt shimmered, transforming into long robes covered with bright, shifting geometric shapes.

Melanie followed the Light with her eyes and had to fight to prevent her breath from running away. Lady Nightwing, the evil mad-scientist Darkhand who'd almost killed them a few months ago, stood across the store. She waved her arms, and thick pillars of black fire flared up, suffocating Mrs. Davis's Light flecks. The stench of sulfur filled the store as the last bits of Light disappeared.

"Okay, scratch pointillism," Mrs. Davis muttered.

Pilaf distracted Melanie from the battle with a loud sneeze. "Sorry," he said, pointing to the sweaters. "I'm allergic to wool."

As Melanie looked back through the sweaters, Lady Nightwing sent a big cloud of Darkness at Mrs. Davis, who then painted a glowing rectangle in the air. The rect-angle intercepted Lady Nightwing's Darkness, and as they collided, additional lines shot out from each side of the rectangle, creating a 3-D cube that trapped the Darkness. Mrs. Davis continued to retaliate, waving her paintbrush in broad strokes. Across the room, a rack of suit coats started to glow, each a different color of Light. Flying off their hangers, they circled around Lady Nightwing like a spinning color wheel.

"Terrifying." Lady Nightwing smirked.

The jackets sped up, whipping Lady Nightwing's face with glowing sleeves. She held her arms out to block them, but as she did, one of the floating jackets slid backwards onto her outstretched arms. It flashed, and the sleeves crisscrossed, wrapping around her torso and trapping her in a straitjacket. She struggled, but the jacket held her tight.

Melanie stifled a scream as two more Darkhands appeared right outside the rack—a man and a woman.

Mrs. Davis shot squiggly neon lines at them, but they both ducked. The man countered, firing black fire at Mrs. Davis, while the woman ran over to help Lady Nightwing, freeing her from the glowing straitjacket with a cloud of Darkness that smothered the Light.

Free now, Lady Nightwing shot more sulfuric black fire at Mrs. Davis. The man near Lexa raised his hands, pointing at Mrs. Davis too. Dark energy crackled around his fingers, but Mrs. Davis was too busy ducking Lady Nightwing's flames and returning fire to notice him.

He pulled his hands back, ready to hurl a ball of sizzling Darkness at Mrs. Davis's back. Melanie raised her hands to stop him, but before she could do anything, a pale, sneezing figure jumped out of the sweater rack and tackled the back of the man's knees.

As Pilaf hit the man's legs, the Dark energy in his hands disappeared. The man gasped, turned pale, and collapsed in a heap on top of Pilaf.

As Mrs. Davis battled Lady Nightwing and her remaining sidekick, Conner dashed out of the rack and used his Light-enhanced strength to pull the unconscious Darkhand off Pilaf.

"Thanks," Pilaf said, back in the rack. "I didn't realize he'd fall on me like that." Pilaf sneezed, and Melanie noticed a bright red rash stretching across his face. He wrinkled his nose. "The fire they use stinks! It must have a high sulfur content." More Darkhands appeared in clouds of smoke, just as six colored comets blasted into the room: cream, silver, blue, purple, green, and orange—but, sadly, no gold.

Conner started out of the rack, but a sharp southern accent cut into their thoughts. *Y'all can't help us!* Their English teacher, Mrs. Grant, materialized atop a rack of men's underwear across the store. *Just keep hidden!* Wielding her red pen, she sent neat, blue bolts of Light everywhere. Madame Cumberland, Mr. Duffy, Mrs. Sharpe, Coach Jackson, and Mr. Miller joined Mrs. Grant and Mrs. Davis in the fight. As they appeared and fought, their street clothes changed into colored Magi robes, alive and burning with Light.

Blasts of Darkness flew all over, crashing into bolts of Light. Magi comets chased Darkhand cyclones through the air, and black flames burned everywhere.

One of the Darkhand cyclones whirled over them, paused, and doubled back, landing and forming into Lady Nightwing.

"Conner, so nice to see you again." Lady Nightwing smiled with a mouthful of icy-white teeth. "Are you ready to join us yet? Has the change started?"

Melanie looked at Conner. He had frozen with a look of terrible agony etched on his face. He dropped his head and stared at the floor.

Lexa shot a snarling cheetah at Lady Nightwing, who laughed and dodged it. She smirked at Melanie. "Oh, the girl from the Shadowbox. Ask Conner about the prophecy he saw—"

Melanie sent steaming bolts of pink Light at Lady Nightwing, who laughed again and dissolved into smoke.

From her perch on the underwear rack, Mrs. Grant didn't see Lady Nightwing reappear on a shelf a few yards behind her.

Mrs. Grant! Behind you! Melanie yelled in her head, but Mrs. Grant didn't hear her. They'd learned during a battle at Disney World that head-talking didn't work well in the heat of battle.

Let's go warn her, Mel. Lexa had seen it too. *Come on!*

The two of them ran forward to warn Mrs. Grant, but black fire burst up, boxing them in and separating them from each other.

Melanie screamed as Lady Nightwing raised her arm and threw a knife at Mrs. Grant's back. Once again, the explosions around them drowned out her warning.

At that moment, the Stalker appeared, faint and blurry, behind Mrs. Grant and kitty-corner from Lady Nightwing. He shot a blast of Darkness at Mrs. Grant, who remained unaware of the Stalker's Darkness and Lady Nightwing's knife, both hurtling toward her back.

The Darkness moved faster than the knife, and they collided just before hitting Mrs. Grant. The knife exploded, and the crash seemed to suck the energy away from the Darkness, which faded away.

Alert now, Mrs. Grant jumped up into the air and, in the middle of her backflip, transformed into a comet. She loop-de-looped toward Lady Nightwing, who rushed away in a cloud of thick smoke. The Stalker vanished as well.

As Melanie retreated back to the sweater rack, a strangled squeal got her attention. She looked back and saw a massive, muscle-bound Darkhand emerge from the flames and grab Lexa in a choke hold, pulling her into the air. Lexa struggled, but the thick arm round her neck didn't move. As Lexa dangled, the Darkhand from the frozen yogurt shop stepped in front of her. In one hand, she brandished a knife. In the other, she waved a dirty, pink sock.

CHAPTER 18

A Face in the Crowd

As Lexa struggled to breathe and black spots squished everything else out of her vision, a gold comet roared between her and the yogurt Darkhand with a crackling sizzle. Gold sparks shot all over as the comet exploded, throwing Lexa several feet away and blinding her with blazingly bright gold Light.

When she opened her eyes, she took some deep breaths and then squealed for joy.

A middle-aged man in striped pajamas and a paisley bathrobe stood in front of her, leaning on a cane and pointing a conductor's baton at the frozen-yogurt Darkhand. "Leave her alone!" Dr. Timberi's voice burned with menace, and he launched into an angry song from *Les Misérables* as his pajamas faded into glowing gold robes.

The Darkhand lunged at him with her knife, but Dr. Timberi swung his cane upward, hitting the underside of her wrist. As the knife flew through the air, he sliced downward with his baton, and gold Light shot out and wrapped around the woman, pinning her arms to her sides.

The woman struggled, but before she could escape, Dr. Timberi opened his mouth and sang a loud, high note, finishing the song. He pounded the floor with his cane, and a thick geyser of gold Light burst up from the floor, engulfing the Darkhand, who collapsed and hit the floor.

Everything became quiet, and Lexa realized the battle had ended.

"Dr. Timberi!" Lexa ran over and threw her arms around him. He tensed beneath her hug, keeping his arms at his side, and his back stiff and straight. He seemed surprised and awkwardly uncomfortable—but Lexa didn't care. He'd saved her life a few weeks ago, sacrificing himself to protect her and Melanie. And now he'd just saved her again. She didn't know what to say, so she poured all of her overflowing affection and gratitude into the tightest, longest hug she could give.

Thank you, thank you, thank you for saving me! she thought. *I'll never ever, ever, ever forget.*

Dr. Timberi struggled to pull one arm out of her hug and gave her an awkward pat on the head. *You are most kind, Lexa.* His thoughts had the same milk-chocolate warmth that his voice did.

"Dr. Timberi!" Melanie joined the hug, and he tensed up again. "Are you okay?" Melanie asked. "Should you be out of bed?"

Since Melanie mentioned it, Lexa noticed he did look pale and *waayyyy* older. His chest rose and fell quickly, and he seemed to struggle to catch his breath. Lexa hugged him once more, a little tighter. When she did let go, Lexa kept hold of one arm to make sure he didn't fall.

Hey, Doc! Conner didn't hug Dr. Timberi. He gave him a manly pat on the shoulder instead. *Good to see you! Likewise, Conner.* Dr. Timberi seemed a little relieved not to get another hug. He turned and scanned the ruins of the store. His eyes gleamed with a sarcastic glint, and for the first time, Lexa thought he seemed like himself. "My goodness, possums! You've outdone yourselves. I thought destroying the Small World ride at Disney World was an accomplishment. But this . . ." Dr. Timberi gestured at the heaps of smoking rubble.

Madame Cumberland walked toward them, still brandishing her pointer stick, flanked on the left by Mrs. Grant, who was gripping her red pen. Mrs. Sharpe stood to their right, clutching her yardstick. Coach Jackson came next with his lacrosse stick. Mr. Miller followed, clutching his mop, and Mr. Duffy brought up the rear, his large wooden compass still glowing. Mrs. Davis marched over from a different part of the store. The teachers all appeared grim. And grimy. Their shining robes had disappeared, replaced now by their regular clothes all decorated with rips and scorch marks. Scrapes, cuts, and black smudges covered their faces.

Mrs. Grant frowned at Dr. Timberi and clicked her tongue. "Morgan, you shouldn't be up. The doctor said—"

"Thank you, Carol. I've been confined quite long enough." He smiled at Pilaf. "Well, Mr. Larson, I see you've joined our merry band as well."

"Let's clean up a bit, and then we'd better be going," Mrs. Sharpe said. "Firemen and police will be here any moment."

All of the teachers, except Dr. Timberi, shot Light

into different areas of the store. Chunks of wood, metal, and plastic flew back together, reforming themselves into shelves, racks, and mannequins. When they were repaired, the items of clothing jumped up, folded themselves, and got ready for display.

Dr. Timberi looked at the four students. "You can't stream yet, and we need to get out of here quickly without anyone seeing. We will phase—which means turn invisible. If you will each grab one of us around the waist, I think we can manage to cover you for a short time too. Mona, perhaps you can escort Melanie? Carol, if you take Lexa, then Joseph can cover Conner, and Mary will have Pilaf. I fear I don't have enough strength to cloak someone else."

Melanie stood behind Madame Cumberland and wrapped her arms around her waist. With discomfort so obvious it made Lexa laugh, Conner put his arms around Mr. Duffy, which left Pilaf with Mrs. Davis. Lexa did the same with Mrs. Grant.

All right, Lexa this might feel a bit odd, Mrs. Grant thought. *Stay as close to me as you can, or I won't be able to keep you hidden.*

A strange, tingly-tickly feeling covered Lexa—like swimming through hundreds of tiny feathers. She watched as Madame Cumberland and Melanie vanished, followed by Conner and Mr. Duffy, Mrs. Sharpe, and Dr. Timberi. Mrs. Davis and Pilaf flickered—but didn't vanish. They just stood there, with Mrs. Davis frowning more and more.

What's wrong, Mary? Madame Cumberland's invisible voice asked.

I-I don't know. I can't phase. I can't use the Light at all.

Just then, Pilaf sneezed twice. The second time, he sneezed hard enough that he let go of Mrs. Davis. She disappeared, leaving Pilaf there by himself.

Pilaf, touch me again, Mrs. Davis said. Pilaf poked a single finger out in front of him. When his finger connected with Mrs. Davis, she reappeared.

Let go again, Mrs. Davis said. He did, and she vanished once more. So did Pilaf's rash.

No one said anything for a few seconds, until the sound of sirens crescendoed.

We need to get out of here, Mrs. Sharpe thought. *Pilaf will have to walk out of the store on his own. I'll stay close to him in case of trouble. Let's go!*

They escaped through the nearest exits before anyone arrived, and, one by one, the teachers returned to visibility again, walking out into the parking lot where they blended in with the crowd. Except Dr. Timberi, who stood out in his pajamas and paisley bathrobe. When two elderly women stopped to stare, he shot such a withering glare at them that Lexa thought one of them might have a heart attack.

Madame Cumberland looked at Mrs. Davis. "Great Caesar's ghost, what a fight! Mary, how did you get here so fast?"

"I was here doing some birthday shopping," Mrs. Davis replied. "When I felt adumbrations, I streamed to the source and found the kids being chased around the men's department by Darkhands."

"My goodness!" Madame Cumberland exclaimed. "It's lucky you were here tonight. By the time we got Lexa's sigil, it might have been too late."

Right then all the kids's phones began vibrating, ringing, chirping, and beeping.

Lexa looked at a text from her mom while Melanie answered a call. "Hello?" A loud man's voice carried well beyond her phone.

Ah, the dulcet tones of Frank Stephens, Dr. Timberi thought-muttered.

"Yes, dad. Yes. We're fine. I promise. Okay. We'll be waiting. The teachers are with us, so we'll be safe."

She hung up. "My parents just watched the news and they were talking about gas leaks and explosions at the mall. They kind of freaked out." She winced. "Especially my dad. He's a little, um, upset."

"I can't imagine that," Dr. Timberi said.

"My mom's a little freaked too," Lexa said as she typed a reply message on her phone.

"Mine, three." Pilaf giggled as he texted his mom.

Another message pinged on Lexa's phone. "My mom's on her way," Lexa said. "She'll be here in a few minutes."

"Very well," Dr. Timberi said. "Go on home now and we'll talk tomorrow. We need to start your training. We've waited far too long as it is. I shall arrange it with your parents. I will wait here until—"

"We'll wait with them, Morgan." Madame Cumberland put her hand on his arm. "You go on home. Mary, did you drive here tonight? Could you give Morgan a ride home?"

Dr. Timberi opened his mouth and Lexa thought he might argue, but Madame Cumberland smiled bigger and stared him down. After a minute or so, he nodded and sighed. "Yes, that would probably be best. I am a bit worn. I'll see you tomorrow, little goslings."

Lexa watched Dr. Timberi limp away with Mrs. Davis. Before long, they disappeared into the large crowd of people evacuated from the mall. As they walked away, Lexa caught a glimpse of a face that looked familiar.

"You guys, isn't that the girl that got kidnapped by the Darkhands? What was her name—um, Taylor?"

"Where, Lexa?" Melanie asked.

"Right there." Lexa pointed at a blonde girl wearing an employee uniform of one of the mall restaurants. A theeling told her that was important somehow. She started to say something but stopped. Conner looked pretty bad— like throw-up-at-any-minute bad. "Con, are you okay?"

Lexa realized he hadn't said anything since the fight.

"Yeah, I'm fine," he said after a few seconds. "Just don't feel well."

Lexa's dream returned again that night. She saw Taylor and the other kids who had been kidnapped as part of Lady Nightwing's experiment. They ran through dark, misty pathways, chased by shadows in the shape of wolves until black flames exploded everywhere, blocking Lexa's view.

The flames faded, replaced by Conner's face, twisted with rage and hatred, yelling and screaming at someone until he too disappeared in flaring black flames.

Melanie's face appeared next, sobbing and sobbing, heartbroken in a way Lexa had never seen before. Lexa wanted to comfort her, and in her mind, she tried to call out. But as she did that, the dream shifted one last time.

Dr. Timberi writhed and screamed on the floor. The

Stalker stood above him, scowling and grimacing. Their faces flashed back and forth so quickly, Lexa grew dizzy in her sleep, and soon they seemed to become one person.

When Lexa woke up the next morning, she had a vague memory that she'd dreamed, and that the dreams were important somehow. But she couldn't remember much beyond seeing shadows, faces, and black flames everywhere.

CHAPTER 19

FAMILY PORTRAIT

IT'S TOO BAD CONNER COULDN'T COME, Melanie thought as they drove to Dr. Timberi's house the next day. The backseat of her mom's minivan felt empty without him.

Lexa sighed. *He says he's sick, but I don't think so. I'm really worried about him, Mel. He won't talk to me. I tried for like two hours last night to get him to tell me what Lady Nightwing meant, but he wouldn't say anything, and then he got mad and just closed his mind off completely. I have a theeling that what Lady Nightwing said is really important. But what could it have to do with you?*

Melanie didn't know, but she thought about the shadows talking to Conner. Were they connected? She hadn't told anyone about the shadows yet—mostly because she was waiting for Dr. Timberi to be better. Maybe today was the day. *I have no idea. But I think we need to tell Dr. Timberi about all of this stuff.*

Lexa shook her head. *I don't know, Mel. Conner really,*

really, really hates it when people tell his secrets. It makes him furiously mad, like not-speak-to-us-ever-again mad. When we were five I told my mom a secret Conner told me, and he still gets mad when he remembers.

I don't know what to do then, Melanie replied. *It's not like we're going to figure this out on our own.*

But, Mel, we totally figured out the Darkhands's plan a few months ago! With my theelings and visions and your freakishly-smart, Light-enhanced super brain—

It's one thing to put clues together, Lexa. It's another thing to figure out what's in someone's mind.

Let's try it! Last time, we started with a list of all the weird things we noticed. We can do that now.

Melanie sighed. Arguing with Lexa was the dictionary definition of "futile." Maybe it wouldn't hurt to wait a little longer before telling anyone about the shadows. Conner might be waiting to tell Dr. Timberi himself. She really should give him a chance. Melanie pulled out her phone and started tapping notes onto the screen.

"Okay," Lexa said. "First thing—what happened to Conner at the Darkhand base?"

"Secondary questions"—Melanie tapped her phone, —"what about the shadow attacks on Conner? Where did the Light-shark come from, and why didn't the Stalker show up on the scanning the Adumbrators did?"

Lexa jumped back in. "And what's up with Pilaf seeing all this stuff and the way he made Light and Dark stop or disappear? And why was Taylor at the mall last night? I have a theeling that's important."

Melanie's irritation faded, soothed by the balm of list making, which she loved. She saved the notes on her phone as Mrs. Stephens pulled up in front of a row of neat town houses.

"That's it," Melanie's mom said. "The one at the end. Now don't stay too long—he's still recovering from your battle over spring break. I'll be back after I run a few errands."

It sounded bizarre to the tenth power to hear her mom refer to a battle in such a casual way, as if Dr. Timberi had the flu or something. It reminded Melanie again of the dramatic way their lives had changed since they had Kindled.

Lexa jumped out of the car, and Melanie followed her to the door. Grabbing the lion-head doorknocker, Lexa swung the brass handle against the door.

A swan made of gold Light appeared, hovering in front of them. Speaking through the sigil, Dr. Timberi said, "Won't you please come in?"

Gold Light flashed and the door opened.

Inside, the scent of cinnamon and other spices filled the entryway, wafting up from a big brass bowl of pot-pourri on a table by the door. The swan led them through a long hallway. Melanie noticed dozens of reproductions of famous paintings—but something felt off. She realized after a minute that she saw no photographs. Nothing personal.

They walked into a cozy living room where maroon paisley wallpaper punctuated the small portions of wall that weren't covered by wooden bookshelves stuffed with leather-bound books.

"Welcome, dear ones!" Dr. Timberi smiled from a big armchair by the fire. He looked comfortable in navy-blue pajamas, a dark green smoking jacket, and corduroy slippers. "Forgive me for not getting up. Please sit down and make yourselves comfortable." He slipped a bookmark into the book he was reading, which Melanie noticed was *The Adventures of Sherlock Holmes*.

That would be like trying to make yourself comfortable in a museum, Lexa private-messaged Melanie as they sat down on the slippery leather sofa.

"I'm so glad to see you both, but where is Conner?" Dr. Timberi asked, looking past them into the hall.

"He didn't feel well." Lexa spoke in a casual, matter-of-fact voice.

"I'm sorry to hear that. How have you all been? How are things at school? I feel so out of touch."

"Everyone misses you," Melanie said.

"Yeah, a lot. No one likes your substitute," Lexa added. "He's mean. He gave Zach detention because he sang like a girl."

Dr. Timberi rolled his eyes. "Oh dear. One of those uptight music teachers who believes fervently that the proper observance of sixteenth rests and perfect quiet in class are far more important than the soul of the song and the experience of the singer. He teaches but hasn't the first idea how to understand adolescents."

"Wow," Lexa said. "That's totally him. Do you know him?"

"Not personally. But I've encountered his sort for my entire professional life: pinched souls who use music as a ruler to smack people's knuckles instead of lifting hearts and inspiring minds. So, Zach sang like a girl?" Dr. Timberi chuckled, but his smile didn't light up his face the way it used to. He looked tired and worn, and the lines in his face seemed to be carved much deeper than normal.

"Is it so bad, Melanie?"

"Sir?"

At least his eyes twinkled a little. "Do I really look so bad? That is what you were thinking, correct?"

"Well, I—"

Dr. Timberi held his hand up. "You are quite right. I do look awful."

A whistle from the kitchen interrupted him. "My tea," he explained. "I don't suppose either of you would like some herbal tea?"

"No!" Lexa pulled a terrible face.

"No, thank you," Melanie said.

Dr. Timberi almost smiled again. "Good, because I do not really want to share. I was merely being polite." He raised a hand and stared at the kitchen, concentrating with visible effort.

As a cup, tea bag, and a steaming kettle floated out from the kitchen, strain jumped up all over Dr. Timberi's face. Melanie had never seen him work so hard at Lightcraft. He grew pale and started shaking. Following his lead, the tea things shook as well, threatening to drop.

As she worried about him, something inside of Melanie jumped, like a rabbit leaping in her chest. Without conscious thought, a stream of pink Light rushed out of her, shot across the room, and wrapped around Dr. Timberi. As soon as her Light enfolded him, both he and the tea service stopped shaking. He relaxed, and everything landed on a table in front of him.

"Thank you, Melanie. Quick thinking. It is a useful thing to have an Augmentor around. Augmentation is a rare and useful marvel." Dr. Timberi smiled as he opened the tea bag and poured the hot water into the cup, filling the room with the scent of black cherry. "I didn't realize you had learned to do it remotely."

"You're welcome." She felt confused. "But I didn't do anything. At least not on purpose."

He looked at her with new interest. "Really?"

She nodded. "Really. I was getting worried about you—and then it just happened."

"Remarkable. Truly remarkable. What you did is called a Remote Autonomic Response. It is a form of very advanced Lightcraft generally done only by Magi of great power and experience. Essentially, the Light did what you wanted it to do, even though you didn't consciously guide it. It's similar to the way your heart beats without being consciously told to do so—your autonomic nervous system keeps it going even without conscious thought." Dr. Timberi took a sip of tea and sighed. "Your Light essentially Augmented my own power without any conscious effort, but it also happened remotely—meaning that you had no physical contact with me. Usually, Augmentation requires contact. Very interesting. Very interesting, indeed."

"Should you even be doing Lightcraft?" Lexa asked.

Dr. Timberi laughed. "Actually, the Magi doctor told me I should do more Lightcraft each day to try to get my strength up again. However, after the rigors of last night's battle, I am weaker than usual. It was unwise to try Translocation, but I felt too weak to get up, and it seemed rude to ask my guests to wait on me."

"Are you okay?" Lexa asked. "I mean, really? Cause you don't look like it."

"As I told Conner the other day, the Stalker wounded me severely. I have improved a great deal, but the wounds inside my soul may take some time to heal."

What if he never got better, Melanie wondered. *What if he stayed sick and weak forever because of us?* Tears bloomed in Melanie's eyes, rolling down her cheeks, faster and faster. She swiped at them, hating that she always cried in response to any emotional situation.

Lexa seemed to be thinking the same thing. She ran over and gave Dr. Timberi a big hug. "Thank you for saving us. I'm so sorry that it hurt you so bad!"

Melanie joined Lexa, hugging Dr. Timberi. As she did, she felt him tense, just as he had the night before.

"You are both kind. But, please, no more of that." Dr. Timberi patted both of them on the head with stiff, embarrassed fingertips.

"But you saved our lives!" Lexa said. "And now you're so sick."

Melanie cried harder and felt Lexa tighten her hug.

"Now, now." Dr. Timberi sounded uncomfortable and tried to pull away. Being seated in the chair made that difficult, though. "I will be just fine. Lexa, if I know you, I am sure you are full of questions."

Lexa's eyes lit up. "Oh yeah! Lots!"

"Very well. Why don't you sit down and we'll discuss them."

As Lexa and Melanie let go and returned to the couch, Dr. Timberi seemed to relax.

"Okay." Lexa wriggled into the couch. "First of all, I

don't mean to be pushy or anything and maybe this isn't the right time, but what's going to happen with the fall play?"

"The play will go on as planned. However, instead of having auditions now, as we usually do, they will be delayed until the end of the summer, the day before school starts, to be exact. Now, the next question goes to Melanie."

Melanie opened the list of questions on her phone. One of them seemed like a good subject for Dr. Timberi.

"Conner said he saw the Stalker, but the Adumbrators did some scans and couldn't see any traces of him. What does that mean? Could they be wrong?" It irritated her that they didn't seem to take Conner seriously.

Dr. Timberi paused, and Melanie recognized the thoughtful frown he wore when explaining something complicated.

"When either Light or Dark is used, it sends ripples through the universe. Some of these ripples are large, some are small. If I throw a large boulder into a pond, the ripples created will be significant. A small pebble will, of course, create only minor waves." Dr. Timberi sipped his tea.

"Adumbrators try to understand what is happening by reading these ripples. It is similar to looking at the ripples in a pond and trying to figure out what caused them. Adumbrating is a very complex art, and there is little that even gifted Adumbrators can say with total certainty. So, keep that in mind.

"Now, consider what they found. Anytime a Magus uses Light, that interaction leaves unique waves behind, like a fingerprint. However, over several hours, they begin to fade. The Adumbrators saw a Light signature that had degraded to the point it couldn't be read clearly. It might have belonged to any Magus there. At the same time, they saw no traces of a Darkhand.

"But lack of evidence does not prove something didn't happen. Especially when dealing with Darkness. So all they proved was that a Magus had been at Dauphin Island. Something we already knew.

"Remember, the fundamental nature of Darkness is to hide, obscure, and deceive. That is what it has done since the beginning of time. Those who serve it are expert deceivers," Dr. Timberi finished, taking another sip of tea.

That reminded Melanie of something. "So is that why we couldn't see miasmas on the Blacks?" she asked. The Blacks had been a young couple that befriended their two families at Disney World. It turned out that they were working for Umbra. They'd kidnapped Melanie's little sister, Madi, and when Conner freed her, they took him instead. It still annoyed Melanie that she hadn't realized they were Darkhands.

"Yes, Melanie. Possibly. But strictly speaking, a Darkhand is someone who uses Darkness as the Magi use the Light. Darkhands have supernatural powers and will generally have visible miasmas. However, Darkhands employ many other people, running the spectrum from everyday thugs and petty criminals to highly trained professionals. Only true Darkhands will have visible miasmas.

"I would guess that the Blacks were well-paid mercenaries working for Umbra, who did not have visible miasmas. They were most likely physically attractive, skilled con artists, with a sympathetic story. Evil, dear ones, is not always obvious. Seeing through the Darkness is a difficult task, and even those with years of experience and special gifts do not always discern with perfect clarity."

"Okay, next question. What's going on with Pilaf?" Lexa asked.

"Curiouser and curiouser, is it not? I honestly do not know. Pilaf has been a rather startling development. No one in the Sodality has ever heard of anything quite like this before. The Magisterium is supposed to send someone to test him, but heaven only knows when they will get around to coming. When one adds Pilaf's unusual abilities to your triple Kindling—well, it gets very interesting."

Lexa jumped in, sneaking in an extra question. "How did all three of us, I mean four of us, end up at the same school with a bunch of Magi teachers?"

Dr. Timberi smiled. "I do not know. That seems too significant to be a coincidence. And yet, you will frequently find such 'coincidences' in your work with the Magi. There are powers beyond this world we don't understand. Somehow, the Light organizes events in remarkable ways, and in the stories of individuals and civilizations, we often see the quiet evidence of an unseen hand, guiding and ordering. That seems to be what happened to bring you to us. I do not understand how it all works—but somehow it does. And I find that a comforting thought.

"Now, on a less comforting note, I'm concerned about the attacks on Conner at Dauphin Island. At some point, we need to talk more about that. Clearly, something is going on. However, without Conner here, I don't know that a discussion would be productive."

Melanie considered ignoring Lexa and telling

Dr. Timberi about the shadows talking. Or what Lady Nightwing had said in the mall. It wasn't much, but those were the only clues they had. She opened her mouth.

Don't say anything, Mel, Lexa warned in a private message.

Irritation jabbed Melanie. Why did Lexa's opinion always have to be the deciding factor? If she and Lexa disagreed, somehow Lexa always ended up breaking the tie. Melanie took a deep breath and tried to focus on Dr. Timberi—who hadn't seemed to notice her hesitation.

"Now, last night was the second time I almost lost you three, and that is unacceptable. We really must start your training. Monday is the first day of summer vacation, correct?"

"Yes," Melanie said.

"Good. I shall speak with your parents about starting your training." He sank back into the chair, looking much, much older. "Now, little ducklings, I fear I am exhausted. Would it offend you if I asked you to leave?"

"It wouldn't offend us at all. I'll text my mom," Melanie said. "Get some rest."

"Yeah," Lexa said. "Definitely get some rest."

"Thank you. Forgive my rudeness, but I really must lie down. You are welcome to wait inside until Elise comes. I shall see you on Monday."

He stood up and took a step but staggered and started to fall. Melanie and Lexa jumped up, each grabbing an arm before he hit the ground. Using their arms, he steadied himself and struggled to his feet.

"Awk-ward," Dr. Timberi said in a perfect imitation

of Conner. "Thank you. I apologize. The battle last night left me weaker than I realized. Melanie, could you please hand me that cane?" He pointed to the polished wooden cane leaning against a bookshelf. As Melanie retrieved the cane, a framed photo on a shelf caught her eye, but she forced herself not to stare at it.

Melanie gave him the cane and a quick hug. He seemed surprised but was a degree or two less stiff and uncomfortable this time.

"Thank you, Melanie," he said in a soft voice. Then, leaning on the cane, he limped to a closed door. "Have a good day, possums." He opened the door, slipped inside, and closed it behind him.

"I think getting hugs kind of makes him nervous," Melanie said when the door had closed.

Lexa looked at the door. "Yeah, which means he really needs them. We should probably give him at least one a day."

"I think you're right. Sometimes I feel like there's so much hurt inside of him." Melanie dropped her voice to a whisper. "Lexa, look at this." She pointed to the small photograph on the bookshelf. The only photo in the house as far as she could see. Framed in a delicate gold frame was a picture of a much younger Dr. Timberi, a beautiful young woman with long red hair, and a smiling, chubby baby boy.

Lexa's eyes got big as she turned to face Melanie. "Dr. Timberi was married? And had a baby?"

Melanie met Lexa's surprised gaze. "As Dr. Timberi would say: curiouser and curiouser."

What happened to his wife and baby? Lexa private-messaged as they got into the minivan. *It must be really sad since no one talks about it.*

Melanie didn't say anything. She didn't know what to say—but Lexa went on.

Anyways, I'm so excited that we're still going to do the play! And that I have extra time to get ready for auditions now. I've been practicing, and I really think I'm going to do amazing. I'm not trying to brag, but the songs are right in my range, and I can totally act it too. I'm going to be Maria, Mel. I know it! I have a theeling, and I'm so excited! It's going to be so much fun. Maybe you can be the oldest daughter, and we'll be at rehearsals together. Oh wait! What if Conner was that guy on the bike and you two got to be in love in the play? That would be so cute!

The thought of having her feelings displayed in such a public way made Melanie cringe. But even worse was the growing concern she felt for Conner. And the pressure of knowing that she was part of a secret that she didn't understand.

CHAPTER 20.

EAVESDROPPING

WHEN LEXA GOT HOME, HER MOM MET her at the door. "Lexa, I need to talk to you."

Urgh. That was not usually a good thing. Lexa's mind hurtled back over the past few weeks. Had she done anything punishable? No demerits or anything recently, right? The worry clouding her mother's eyes told her it was more serious than just being in trouble.

"It's Conner. Ever since he got back from being kidnapped, he's been moody and withdrawn. At first, your father and I tried not to worry too much. The Magi doctors said he was okay physically, so we thought we'd just give him time. We didn't want to overreact, but it's been almost two months now, and he's not getting better. Today, he seems much worse. You've heard him screaming out at night. We're starting to get worried about emotional or psychological damage, but taking him to a regular therapist won't work. 'Hi, my son belongs to a secret group of

Magi and he got kidnapped by some dark wizards and now we're worried he has PTSD.'"

"What do you want me to do?"

"I don't know, exactly. But I wondered if Conner had said anything to you. He won't talk to us, but I know you two talk a lot. I realize he doesn't like you to tell his secrets, but this is important, Lexa. If you know anything, anything at all, I really need to know so I can figure out how to help my son."

Lexa paused. Should she mention Lady Nightwing's comment? It did seem like an important clue. On the other hand, it wasn't anything concrete or specific. And Conner really, really hated it when people talked about him or told his secrets. This felt like a secret. On the other hand, her mom had good reason to be worried. She decided that deflecting the question might be her best bet.

"Um, you know, they have Magi doctors, so maybe there are Magi counselors too? I'll bet Dr. Timberi could help you get in touch with someone—I can send him a sigil and let him know you want to talk to him."

Her mother nodded. "Yes, I'd appreciate that. I probably should have called Dr. Timberi to begin with, but he's been so sick, and since he was at the Sanctuary, I didn't know how to reach him. And with your father being out of town, everything's piling up and—" She took a deep breath. "I'm just rambling now. Go ahead, please."

Lexa connected to the Light and waved her arms, using extra flourishes and gestures. With her mom watching, she wanted it to look good.

Lexa's yellow dolphin sigil appeared in the air in front of her.

"You are doing something, right, Lex? I mean, waving your arms will make something happen?"

"Yes, ma'am." It still seemed strange that her mom couldn't see any Lightcraft when it had become such a huge part of Lexa's life. Lexa thought a message to Dr. Timberi, and the dolphin sigil dove into the air and disappeared.

A few minutes later, her mom's cell phone rang. "Hello? Morgan—thank you so much for calling. I probably should have just called you sooner, but I've been so worried that I haven't been thinking clearly. Brent's in China on business, so I'm all alone . . ."

Lexa's mom walked into a different room, and Lexa went upstairs. She couldn't keep this quiet forever. Conner needed to open up at some point. She knocked on Conner's door. *Con? Are you okay?*

Yeah, just tired.

Silence.

Dr. Timberi said to say he missed you.

Thanks. I'm pretty tired now, so I'm going to go to sleep.

Conner shut his thoughts off completely, leaving Lexa grappling with growing frustration. They'd always been close—hello, twins! Now, on top of being twins, they were Magi together. Now, more than ever, he should be talking to her. But she knew pushing him wouldn't accomplish anything.

Trying to ignore her frustration, Lexa went to her room and dug out the script for *The Sound of Music*. She'd ordered it from Amazon so she'd have plenty of time to prepare for auditions.

Losing herself in the script, Lexa poured her heart

out to Reverend Mother, confessing her feelings for the Captain, when a knock at her door interrupted her.

"Lexa?" Her mom poked her head in. "Thanks for your suggestion to call Dr. Timberi. I feel a little stupid—it seems so obvious now. Anyway, Dr. Timberi thinks that getting Conner to the Sanctuary place we went before would be a good start. I guess that's what Dr. Timberi had to do to recover after his attack. He says you need to start your training anyway, so that will work out well. And he promised that if Conner didn't improve, he'd send for some people who could help. So, you guys are going to leave Monday."

"For how long?"

"Well, most of the summer. That's the plan."

"Finally!" Time to start training! Lexa's heart jumped up and down like her chest was a trampoline. "Wait, but how will we get Conner to go? He won't even leave his room."

"Dr. Timberi said he has an idea he thinks will work. My job is to convince Mr. and Mrs. Stephens to let Melanie go."

Lexa snickered. "You mean convince Mr. Stephens. Mel's mom will be fine with it. But Mr. Stephens is so—"

"Lexa, be respectful." Her mom sighed. "But you're right. He will be hard to convince. He's never liked Dr. Timberi, and the whole Magi thing set him over the edge."

"Why did he freak out so much? What's his thing about Dr. Timberi?"

"I don't know. Elise doesn't say anything. But it seems pretty deep-seated. Frank settled down after the Disney

World incident, but having Melanie leave home to go train for the whole summer might be tricky."

"It's just like summer camp," Lexa said. "Melanie's done that before. And this is free. He'll like that."

"Hmmm. Good point." Her mom smiled. "Your persuasive skills amaze me even after all this time, Lexa. Thank you."

She left, and Lexa danced around her room unable to contain herself. Training! They were going to learn to be real Magi! Lexa opened her thoughts to tell Melanie—and found Melanie already head-talking in another, unshielded conversation.

. . . it will be so much fun! Melanie said. *We'll get to be at the Sanctuary together and everything.*

Yeah, that does sound cool. Conner didn't sound convinced.

Oh, a conversation between Melanie and Conner. Dr. Timberi's secret plan to get Conner to go was to have Melanie talk to him? Why did that feel like a slap in the face?

Conner, you have to come! It won't be the same without you—no fun at all. You always make everything way more fun.

Oh. Nice. Conner made everything fun. It wouldn't be the same without him. As opposed to his sister, who apparently did not make anything fun and whose presence didn't matter much at all.

So promise me you'll come? Please? Melanie asked.

Okay, Conner replied. *But only if we can hang out when we're not getting trained. Since you had to go to the movie with Lexa, it's my turn now.*

Melanie *had* to go to the movie with her? *Had* to? Melanie must be so relieved to have that terrible chore out of the way. After all, who would ever want to go to a movie with Lexa Dell?

Once more, Lexa found herself outside looking in, excluded by her best friend and by her twin brother.

She picked up her script and jumped back in, seeking refuge from the aching lump of loneliness in her throat. She tried to push it away. Monday, they would all be together for training. Just the three of them. It would get better—like it used to be.

Lexa hid in her script for the rest of the weekend, feeling more in sync with the role every time she finished another read-through. She could do this! She felt it with everything she had. She rehearsed, packed, rehearsed some more, and anticipated the training, feeling better and better each hour. Things would be like they used to be. The Trio would be back.

Monday morning, Melanie's mom drove them to Dr. Timberi's house. Conner and Melanie sat together in the back of the minivan. The third seat was conveniently filled with Conner's stuff. So, Lexa sat in the middle row, next to Madi, Melanie's seven-year-old sister.

"Are you excited to go get trained?" Madi asked.

Madi's question reminded Lexa that at the end of their last adventure, Madi had seen Conner shoot a sigil. Something she shouldn't have been able to do since she hadn't Kindled yet.

"Yeah, I'm excited, Madi," Lexa said. But not excited

to spend the summer being excluded by Conner and Melanie.

"Melanie's excited too," Madi said. "My daddy didn't want her to go. He yelled so loud I could hear him. He said Dr. Timberi's a—"

"That's enough, Madi," Mrs. Stephens jumped in. "Daddy was just a little caught off guard." Lexa noticed, though, that the lines around Mrs. Stephens's mouth got tighter.

Madi stopped talking, but she looked at Lexa with a conspiratorial smile. After a few minutes, she whispered, "My daddy doesn't like Dr. Timberi very much. He punched my dad in the nose."

Lexa nodded, remembering how she had to try not to cheer as Dr. Timberi swung his fist into Mr. Stephens's face.

Madi dropped her voice even more. "I heard him talking to my mom, and he said he could never forgive Dr. Timberi. But my mom won . . ."

Never forgive him for what? A punch in the nose? Or something much bigger? She turned back to Conner and Melanie, but they didn't look at her. Strands of Light ran back and forth between their heads as they indulged in a private conversation.

"Here we are," Mrs. Stephens said as she pulled up in front of the house.

They all got out of the car, carrying their luggage— well, Conner carried Melanie's, but Lexa carried her own.

Melanie said good-bye to her mom. Madi cried and threw her arms around Melanie. "Bye, Melanie! I'll miss you!"

Melanie started to cry as well. "I'll miss you too, Madi," she said.

Mrs. Stephens ushered Madi back into the car, and the Trio walked to Dr. Timberi's house.

Dr. Timberi greeted them with a big smile. "Welcome, platypi! Conner, I'm so glad you are feeling better. We have a wonderful summer ahead of us."

He still leaned on his cane but seemed a little less worn today. The creases in his khakis had been pressed within an inch of their lives, and his button-up shirt seemed to crackle with starch.

"Now, we'll be going to Mockingbird Cottage for your training. Since you have not yet learned to stream, the only way is through the Otherwhere. Once you have learned to stream, you can travel there directly. Until then, we will travel through the Shroud."

He reached inside of his shirt and pulled out a chain from around his neck. Several keys hung from the chain, and Dr. Timberi chose a small, old-fashioned key, which he then pushed into the air in front of him. He whispered something and turned it. The key disappeared, and the air in front of them shimmered silver, then pulled open, like two curtains.

He smiled and gestured to the opening. "After you." Dr. Timberi paused, staring at Conner. "Conner? Are you ill? You look quite green."

CHAPTER 21

Through the Shroud

"Conner?" Dr. Timberi repeated.

Conner was frozen, stuck in panic like a prehistoric bug in petrified tree sap. He hadn't thought about this. Hadn't remembered that going to the Sanctuary meant getting past the cherubim.

Fear warmed up inside of him, getting ready for a major workout. How could he face the cherubim? They were powerful, fiery beings that would see inside him, see what he was becoming.

He remembered when they'd dragged the Blacks away, carrying them off kicking and screaming to some terrible fate. They hated Darkhands in their realm. Images of the screaming, wild-eyed Blacks flashed through his mind.

On the other hand, he'd gone through the Shroud right after being in the Shadowbox and the cherubim hadn't done anything. They even told him not to worry, that it hadn't been real. Of course, that was two months ago. Before he shot black fire. Maybe the virus growing in his spirit hadn't been strong enough yet.

On the other hand, what was he supposed to say? "Sorry, Dr. Timberi. I can't go because shadows talk to me, I shot black fire, and I'm becoming a Darkhand."

He *might* get past the cherubim again, but saying something guaranteed that everybody would find out. Okay. Curtains and cherubim, then. Hopefully they were in a good mood.

"Conner? Can you hear me?" Dr. Timberi stepped closer and looked him in the eye. Conner squared his shoulders and took a deep breath. "Sorry. Just thinking."

They stepped through the curtains, and fear went from warm-up stretches to a full-blown scrimmage. Conner tried to stop his muscles from shaking.

The entrance to the Otherwhere looked the same as Conner remembered—a space about ten feet square, bordered on each side by soaring arches carved from gold, silver, pearl, and polished wood. Thin curtains shimmered in the space under each arch. The fabric looked silver until it rustled, and then colors of every kind flashed across the surface.

The corridor had no walls or ceilings. The only thing between and above the arches was a dark purple sky glowing with lightning-bright stars, moons, and planets. Swirling mist covered the floor, rising to their knees.

The gold arch in front of them glowed until it burned almost too bright for Conner to look at.

"Who is there?" The voice pierced Conner as the air crackled with power—a kazillion watts of electricity with a voice. What had he been thinking? Trying to fool the cherubim? They would fry him. Hopefully it would be quick . . .

Dr. Timberi stood taller. "I am Morgan Timberi. I follow the Light. I seek passage through your domains with these young Adepts. I must take them to the Sanctuary for training."

Blinding, blazing Light shot out of the curtains and hovered around Dr. Timberi for a moment. Conner winced, remembering what the cherubim did next.

Three comets shot out, surrounding him, Melanie, and Lexa.

The air around him heated up as the Light ran through his spirit from head to toe, prying his soul open, examining everything he'd ever thought or done. It didn't exactly hurt, but the feeling was intense and uncomfortable as the Light played his life like a YouTube video at super high speed.

A voice came into his head, powerful and piercing, but not as overwhelming as the first voice.

We know you, Conner Dell.

What did you say to cherubim? *Uh, nice to see you again too.*

You are troubled in your heart.

Nah, I'm fine. Really. But thanks for asking.

Focus on your choices and the future, Conner Dell. Not the past. And do not fear. You may pass. Go in the Light.

Thanks, Conner thought. *Bye. I mean, farewell. Live long and prosper?*

What did they mean, telling him he could pass and not to fear. Did they not sense the Darkness? Not care?

The voice returned, but didn't seem quite so

intimidating. "You may pass through, but they are not to enter either the Between or Beyond."

"I understand. Thank you."

"Go in the Light, Morgan Timberi."

"Shine brightly in the Darkness," Dr. Timberi replied with a bow.

As the gold arch stopped glowing, the pearl-colored arch on their right lit up.

The glow spread from the arch to the curtains below, which flashed and flew open.

Dr. Timberi led, followed by Melanie and Lexa. Conner came last, and when he had passed through, the curtains closed behind him. As the curtains closed, the entire arch disappeared, leaving the four of them in a long hallway made of curtains on both sides. About five feet wide, the hallway seemed to stretch on forever in a slow curve, both in back and in front of them.

"The way the cherubim look into your spirit—will that happen every time we come through?" Melanie asked.

"As I mentioned several weeks ago, the Otherwhere is essentially a hallway between dimensions. The cherubim who guard it cannot bear Darkness in any form."

That thought grabbed Conner's attention. Seriously? So did that mean—

"Anyone who comes through the Otherwhere must be free of Darkness. The process we just endured resembles a needle being put in a flame. The fire burns away impurities without harming the needle. That is what happened to our spirits. It is not pleasant for anyone, but if you had more Darkness than Light inside your heart, you would be consumed.

"So, only people with Light can come here?" Conner asked. "Darkhands couldn't come through?"

"Correct. Darkhands could not endure the cleansing. Now, as we saw a few months ago, they sometimes tear through the Shroud. However, the cherubim vigorously fight such incursions into their home, so that is dangerous and relatively rare. No, Conner, Darkhands cannot come here."

The fist of terror in Conner's heart unclenched, allowing a few flutters of hope. What if Lady Nightwing had been lying? What if everything was going to be just fine?

On the other hand, it almost seemed frightening to consider that possibility. What if he was wrong? His dad always said if something seemed too good to be true it probably was.

Yet the cherubim didn't seem like they'd be easy to fool.

Conner looked around. "So what's on the other side of the curtains?"

Dr. Timberi pointed to their left. "That is where the cherubim live. We know very little about it." He pointed to the curtains on their right. "This side borders our own world. I will teach you later about the mysteries of the Otherwhere. It's really quite a remarkable place. Here we are." Dr. Timberi grabbed the old-school key from inside his shirt again and pushed it into a panel of curtains. The key flashed, and as the Light spread across the curtains, they parted.

"After you," Dr. Timberi said.

As Conner and Melanie walked out, he took her hand. Success!

She smiled at him and leaned closer.

Guilt and fear had gang-tackled him after Lady Nightwing taunted him the other night. For a day or two, he'd been lost as darkness tore into him. But when Melanie head-talked him into coming for training, her voice and presence had pushed the guilt and fear away. Now, they circled him, like the sharks at the aquarium, but Melanie's wall kept them away.

And with that separation, Conner realized things were going to be okay. It was all just a bad dream. It seemed so obvious now, here in the quiet of the Light-filled Otherwhere, next to Melanie. Yeah. Things were totally going to be okay.

As they stepped through the curtains, Conner was surprised to see that, from the other side, it looked as if they had walked out through an opening in a high wall of thick clouds.

"Welcome to Mockingbird Cottage," Melanie said. She squeezed Conner's hand as she led him past a big, old-fashioned house, surrounded by flower beds stuffed with colorful flowers. Leaving Dr. Timberi and Lexa behind, they walked around the side of the house, past some gardens, and into the backyard, where a long, gentle hill rolled down toward thick woods. The only noises that interrupted the silence were some birds singing and bees buzzing. A heron splashed down in a pond through some trees.

Melanie pointed at the wall of thick clouds spinning in a giant orbit around the entire property. "This is a

Sanctuary. Somehow, the Magi made it so it's not really a part of our world anymore. Dr. Timberi said it's kind of like an island in space and time." They walked around, ending up under a pergola covered in flowers and vines. Melanie smiled. "We came here after you got captured. It's a lot better having you here." She looked away from him, blushing so deeply that Conner could almost feel the heat rise from her face.

He squeezed her hand and smiled. "Yeah, I like this a lot better than where I was too."

She looked back at him, eyes sparkling with concern. "You were really brave to give yourself up to save Madi."

Her admiration made him feel bigger, taller, and stronger, and Conner wanted to deserve that admiration. He would have killed dragons or fought armies or faced a pre-algebra exam right then and there. All at the same time, if it would have made her happy.

He leaned in closer. Not only did she not pull away, her eyes sparkled with more suns and stars and lights than the whole universe had ever contained.

Oh, gosh, she was beautiful.

Now Melanie leaned in closer, and it hit Conner like a whole defensive line that she was thinking about kissing him.

Oh yeah!

As she blushed, he leaned in even closer, brushing his lips against her cheek.

Did sparks literally jump between her cheek and his lips, or did it only feel that way?

Excitement, love, and Light ran through Conner,

growing stronger until he felt he might explode in one huge burst of complete awesomeness. Which was what happened.

A wild shout jumped out of Conner's mouth, and his body followed it straight up into the air. He had the sensation of stretching out and shooting higher and higher into the air, surrounded by a tunnel of red Light.

Conner blasted through the sky, a full-fledged Magi comet. Executing a flip, he zoomed back down, grabbing Melanie with arms that felt invincible. She wrapped her arms around him, gripping him tightly as he shot back into the sky, carrying her with him.

You know what you're doing, right? she asked.

No—but it's really cool, he replied.

They flew together, shooting through the air like a roller coaster gone wild. Soaring out over the trees, they painted the forest below them bright red.

Do you think we should be doing this? We're going pretty fast, she said.

Yeah, he replied. *Yeah. I definitely think we should be doing this.*

Conner forgot everything else that had happened before that moment. Right then, nothing else seemed to matter.

ᗷLINKING

LEXA BLINKED AS RED LIGHT EXPLODED AND kicked her farther out of the Trio.

Buckets of cold, bitter water splashed over the excitement she'd felt about training, the hope she'd had that they'd all hang out together again, like they used to.

She tried to swallow, but the knot in her throat had grown larger, almost squeezing it completely shut. Conner had kissed Melanie. The Trio had just become a Duet. Maybe she could be a back-up singer.

Dr. Timberi walked around the side of the house. He looked up at the red Light in the sky with a shocked expression, then turned to Lexa. Understanding, kindness, and sincere sadness all flashed in his eyes.

Oh, Lexa. His thoughts sounded warm and comforting, like milk and chocolate chip cookies. *I am so sorry. I did not realize things had advanced to this point. They do not mean to be unkind. But that doesn't make it less painful.*

Understanding rolled off him in great waves, and Lexa threw herself into a hug, hiding her face in his shoulder. Dr. Timberi seemed surprised. He tensed and pulled back, and she thought he might pull away altogether, but a moment later, she felt a few light pats on her back with the tips of his fingers. His awkwardness almost made her laugh in spite of feeling left out.

Lexa wondered again about Dr. Timberi's discomfort with hugs and any kind of normal affection, as well as the hurt she sometimes heard in his voice or saw in his eyes. For all his jokes and sarcasm, Lexa suspected that he carried around a lot of pain, and she assumed it had to do with the family portrait they'd seen. No wife or child seemed to be in his life.

Well, since Melanie and Conner were obviously going to leave her out, she decided to have her own project. She'd adopt Dr. Timberi and see if she could help ease some of that pain. Nothing major—a hug here, a few kind words there. He'd nearly given his life for her. It was the least she could do.

Right then, the red comet plummeted to the ground.

"Well, they're back," Dr. Timberi said. "I'm glad they made it. Carrying someone while streaming is difficult and is considered dangerous to the point of reckless." He smiled. "Not exactly a word we generally associate with Melanie, at least." The idea of Melanie being even a little reckless made Lexa laugh.

Conner's comet landed and faded, revealing Conner holding Melanie in his arms. Melanie's blush glowed so bright that it outshone the comet, and Conner's eyes shined like a demented cat.

Until he dropped Melanie. She fell to the ground with a heavy "Ooph." Then he just looked embarrassed.

"Sorry," he muttered, as he tried to help her up. "That's a lot harder than it looks."

☾ ✦

CHAPTER 23

STREAMING

CONNER HID HIS EMBARRASSMENT AT DROP-ping Melanie by focusing on helping her up and making sure she was okay. Kinda awkward to kiss a girl, fly with her, and then drop her. Really awkward. Like even more awkward than an old person trying to act young and cool.

Well, now he knew. Streaming with a non-streaming person was much more difficult than he would have guessed. Melanie didn't weigh very much, but the faster he streamed, the heavier she seemed. Not at all like just giving a piggyback ride or something.

"Very well, little froglings." The dry sarcasm in Dr. Timberi's voice reminded Conner of the old Dr. Timberi. "Since Conner has apparently started to stream instinctively, I think we should start there. Streaming is, of course, the ability to turn into a comet, and the proper technique is critical. It can be quite dangerous if you do not know what you are doing."

Conner noticed Melanie's eyes grow a little wider, and he swallowed, feeling increasing self-consciousness. Oops. Maybe that hadn't been such a great idea. Looking around, he noticed a giant smirk on Lexa's face, which really annoyed him.

"Incidentally, when you are streaming, you cannot carry a non-streaming person. The physics of it all are complicated, but it's like trying to float a lead balloon in a stream of water from a hose," Dr. Timberi continued. "Now, the term 'stream' refers to a Lightstream. A current in time and space, which carries you along, just as a current in the ocean carries a boat. Now listen. This is important." He pierced them with The Stare that had become famous all over Marion Academy. "Before starting, you must have a clear image of where you want the current to stop. You cannot simply jump in and go. You could lose control and end up anywhere—China, outer space, or even back in time. Streaming is just as dangerous as driving a car, perhaps more so. So, the first lesson is: Never start streaming without first deciding where you want to stop. Do you understand?"

"Yes, sir," everyone said. Melanie's coloring had faded to old gym-sock gray and Conner didn't feel so great either. *Note to self—never use the Light after kissing a girl again.*

"Now, kindly open your gateways, and let the Light fill you. Allow it to absolutely saturate you."

Conner had never found his gateway. Not officially. Lexa said lines from plays. Melanie solved pre-algebra problems. He didn't have one. Except maybe adrenaline. And Melanie.

He sneaked a glance at her out of the corner of his eye.

Amazing. She made him feel like Christmas and summer vacation and winning the conference championship all put together. Around her, he wanted to be the best, smartest, nicest, bravest, strongest guy in the world, and—

Red Light sizzled in the air around Conner, and he crackled like a human bug zapper.

Dr. Timberi pointed to some fruit trees about a hundred yards away. "Choose one of the fruit trees and direct a beam of Light at the tree—"

Yellow Light erupted out of Lexa's hand, blasting a cherry tree into popsicle sticks.

Dr. Timberi winced, but his voice stayed low and even. "Remember, the Light responds to your thoughts and feelings. If you are angry, the Light you channel will be destructive. Instead of an explosive burst that you would use in battle, think of a gentle stream."

Lexa blew up another fruit tree. Conner laughed. *Sheesh, Lex, what do you have against fruit trees?*

She glared straight ahead, not looking at him. *Don't disturb me. I'm trying to concentrate.* Sharp icicles seemed to dangle from each word.

Melanie looked over at him and mouthed the words, "Not now," with soft, pink lips.

Conner shrugged. What was up with Lexa lately?

With tremendous effort, he pulled his thoughts away from Melanie's lips and directed a steady stream of red Light at one of the remaining trees. A minute later, Lexa resolved her anger issues enough to manage a non-exploding stream of yellow Light. Melanie's pink Light joined them a second later.

"Good." Dr. Timberi flicked his fingers, and a large

five-gallon bucket appeared, full of ping-pong balls.

"Have you ever thrown a stick into a river and watched it float? That is similar to what you are going to do now. I will throw the ping-pong ball into the stream in front of you, and you will focus on having the Light carry it along."

He tossed a ball into Conner's Light stream, and Conner gasped at the sudden weight he felt on his body, mind, and spirit. It felt like trying to hold a bowling ball up with his pinky.

"Let the Light hold it up, Conner."

Conner strained spiritual and physical muscles he didn't think he had ever identified. Focusing harder, he imagined the Light supporting the ball, making it float. The strain stopped, and for just a few seconds, the ball bobbed in the Light, then shot forward and hit the tree trunk with a pop.

"Well done, Conner!"

"Whoa!" Conner yelled. "Cool!"

Lexa's ping-pong ball followed Conner's, but Melanie couldn't make it work. Her ping-pong ball kept falling.

"Conner and Lexa, please practice while I work with Melanie." Dr. Timberi reached into his pocket, pulling out a long, silver whistle, something a captain would use on a ship. He blew the whistle and violin music played.

The bucket glowed with gold Light, and two balls jumped out, one landing in front of Conner, the other in front of Lexa. Each ball hovered for a few seconds before plopping down into the Lightstreams.

Again, Conner strained and focused, and once again the ping-pong ball shot forward and hit the tree. Lexa squealed as her ball hit a tree as well.

Dr. Timberi whistled and more ping-pong balls jumped out, flying at Conner and Lexa like they were being pumped out of a pitching machine.

When Conner thought he had a good rhythm going, he risked a glance at Melanie, hoping she was okay. She looked upset, but amazingly beautiful with her nose scrunched. Dr. Timberi stood next to her, talking in a soft voice. As Conner pondered the way Melanie's hair caught the sun, one of his ping-pong balls flew past Melanie's scrunched nose and smacked Dr. Timberi in the forehead.

The glare that Dr. Timberi shot back at Conner needed no explanation. Conner refocused his attention on firing balls at the fruit trees.

CHAPTER 24

ΛUGMENTATION AND PERCIPIENCE

MELANIE HEARD A WHISTLING SORT OF shriek, and a graceful silver comet flew through the clouds, fading into Madame Cumberland, their French teacher. "Great Caesar's ghost, are they getting ready to stream already?" She beamed her saintly smile, and Melanie felt just a little less frustrated. Madame Cumberland had that effect on people.

"Hello, Mona." Dr. Timberi smiled back. "One day of summer break and you're bored already?"

Madame Cumberland laughed a silver-clinking-on-crystal laugh, and Melanie felt even less frustrated. "I have a delivery. Melanie, your mother called me because a letter came for you in the mail today. She wondered if I could bring it by. So I thought I'd come and see how you all were getting along." She held up a letter and Melanie reached for it, but Dr. Timberi said, "Thank you, Mona. Melanie, you can get it when we have a break."

"I'll leave it on the piano, Melanie."

"Thank you, Mona. Melanie, please try again. Focus on the tree."

Melanie's frustration came rushing back. Aside from the fact that she wanted to read the letter, why was she having such a difficult time doing this? She'd felt so good earlier, after Conner's kiss, and after the way he streamed and carried her. But now, nothing?

She managed to get the Lightstream, but dropped the ping-pong ball again. She kept trying but found her attention wandering to the conversation between Dr. Timberi and Madame Cumberland.

"Any news, Mona?" Dr. Timberi asked.

"Well, I heard from the Magisterium about testing Pilaf."

"And?"

"They said they 'regret very much that they are currently unable to send anyone from the Bureau of Testing and Assessment because of other pressing concerns, but will send someone at the earliest possible opportunity.'"

"Honestly," Dr. Timberi grumbled. "Useless bureaucrats. Anything else?"

Madame Cumberland frowned, which Melanie always thought looked out of place on her. "Well, another fire."

"Another one?" Dr. Timberi asked.

Madame Cumberland's frown crept down deeper. "Yes, and this one happened in a bakery near homes and businesses, so there were witnesses this time."

"Mona, I know that look. There's something more. What is it?"

"The flames were black. And they smelled of sulfur. But they seemed spontaneous. No one could be seen, and nothing showed up on the security cameras nearby."

The sunshine seemed to fade when Melanie heard that.

"Why would the Darkhands burn buildings down?" Dr. Timberi asked. "What value could that have for them?"

"No one knows. But the Adumbrators think the Stalker is behind it. They've picked up traces, and apparently he's been seen." Madame Cumberland looked at Dr. Timberi with her sad, sympathetic smile. "Morgan, Hortense is going to come and see you, I think. In addition to the fires, there have apparently been some attacks on the kids that were kidnapped and then freed last spring. It sounds like shadows have been attacking them, just like with Conner."

The anger that blazed in Dr. Timberi's voice almost scared Melanie. "If Hortense thinks she can just swoop in and—" Dr. Timberi seemed to notice everyone staring at him. "All right, back to work, possums." Conner and Lexa scurried back to shooting ping-pong balls.

Dr. Timberi turned to Melanie again. "Now, Melanie—"

Another ping-pong ball flew up and popped Dr. Timberi in the forehead. This time, Lexa looked at him with a penitent smile. "Sorry," she said as Madame Cumberland laughed. "I didn't aim very well."

Dr. Timberi started to scowl, but he shook it off, even laughing a bit. He'd never been able to stay mad at Lexa long. "That's enough with the ping-pong balls. Melanie, please give me a moment to get the Dells doing something else before they play David and Goliath again. Conner and Lexa, you will now make one modification. Instead of shooting ping-pong balls, you will shoot yourself.

"Yes!" Conner yelled. "Finally."

"Before you start, remember to set a stopping point. And I suggest it not be the fruit tree, or you might end up with a mouthful of wood bark. Pick a point about two hundred yards away and direct a stream of Light there." Lexa and Conner both nodded as Dr. Timberi grabbed his whistle.

"When I blow the whistle, jump into the Lightstream you create. Jump in all the way. Don't step in cautiously, or you will find your toes at the end of the yard and the rest of your body still up here."

Dr. Timberi blew the whistle, filling the air with show tunes. Lexa and Conner both shot streams of Light in front of them and jumped forward. For a second or two, each of them stretched out into long blurry lines— a trail of dozens of fuzzy Lexas and Conners. They reminded Melanie of a bite of pizza with cheese trailing behind. Then they vanished, blurring into red and yellow comets. Conner shot down to the very end of the yard, where he reappeared a second later, grinning and breathing heavily.

Lexa, on the other hand—

CRAAASSHHHHHH!

Shards of yellow Light filled the air, mixed with treebark shrapnel.

"Lexa!" Madame Cumberland yelled and hurried over to where Lexa lay on the ground next to a tree. Dr. Timberi limped along behind them at snail-speed.

Lexa moaned, and Melanie suspected her of embellishing things just a bit. After several dramatic groans, Lexa said, "I'm fine."

"What happened, Lexa?" Dr. Timberi asked.

Lexa winced as she sat up. "I forgot to set my stopping point." She looked at a large dent in a tree. "Sorry."

Dr. Timberi laughed through his frown. "You are awfully hard on trees today, Lexa. Now, what did I tell you at least three times? You are fortunate this tree stopped you. You could have ended up heaven-only-knows-where."

Melanie turned to Dr. Timberi. "Wait a minute. You and the other Magi go through walls and all kinds of things. Why did the tree stop Lexa? And why did Conner burn a hole in the doors at Dauphin Island?"

"And blow up the school bus," Lexa muttered.

Dr. Timberi smiled. "An excellent question, Melanie. Frederich von Weingarten studied that extensively. Simply put, it has to do with the ratio between Light and physical matter. When you first start streaming, you tend to have more dense physical matter and less Light. As you practice, you will merge with the Light more completely, becoming much finer and less dense, and therefore able to pass through objects.

Lexa got back up, looking determined.

"Race you, Lex," Conner said. "Down to the bottom of the yard—mark, get set, g—"

Lexa didn't wait for the last syllable—she dove into her Lightstream, appearing at the bottom of the yard before Melanie blinked. However, Conner got there first, welcoming Lexa with a big grin. They ran another race. And another. Backwards, forwards, side-to-side.

Lexa struggled to control her stops, but she could at least stream. Melanie, who had sworn to become a superpowerful Magus, couldn't do anything at all.

Melanie suppressed the urge to pout or something

equally childish as Dr. Timberi said, "Melanie, let's work on the ping-pong balls."

After working all morning, Melanie managed to shoot a grand total of two ping-pong balls.

Wonderful. Next time Darkhands attacked, maybe she could take out a bad guy with a ping-pong ball to the forehead.

When the sun had crept much higher into the sky, Dr. Timberi finally blew his whistle and gave them a break.

"Well done," Dr. Timberi said with a big smile. "We've made some good progress this morning. Why don't you rest for a few moments?"

Conner raised his hand. "When you all stream, you just start running. You don't shoot a beam with your hand."

"You will get to that eventually. But this is how you learn. Think of it as training wheels. The running start works better when you have more control."

"Thought you all might want something cool about now." A tall, skinny woman with wispy gray hair stood a few feet away, balancing an immense pitcher of lemonade on a tray with four glasses.

"Why thank you, Sadie," Dr. Timberi said, and everyone else thanked her as well. "Sadie, let me introduce you to Conner Dell—he was otherwise occupied last time, but I believe you know Lexa and Melanie. Conner, Sadie is the caretaker here."

Sadie gave them a nod and a shy smile. "Nice to meet you, Conner. Good to have y'all here."

Lexa guzzled her lemonade and started on another glass. Conner inhaled three cups, while Dr. Timberi swirled his glass, taking small swallows. Melanie sipped hers, trying not to be grumpy, and Madame Cumberland just smiled at everyone while seeming to savor every drop.

When they had drained both pitchers, Sadie collected their glasses. "I'll have some lunch ready in a bit." She smiled and walked back to the house.

"I think I'll join Sadie," Madame Cumberland said. "It's getting a little warm out here."

As she walked to the house, Dr. Timberi pulled out his whistle again. "You've run ladders in physical education, I believe? Lexa and Conner, when I blow the whistle you will stream halfway up to the house and back again. Touch the trees and stream three-quarters of the way up, and back again. Then, all the way to the house, and back to the tree. Repeat that procedure consistently until you hear the whistle again. Melanie, you and I will continue to practice while they run those drills. Ready, go!"

He blew the whistle, cuing more classical music. Melanie thought she recognized the Lone Ranger theme.

As Conner and Lexa streamed, Dr. Timberi turned to Melanie. "Are you all right, Melanie?" he said in a soft voice.

"I just can't make it work!" Her words seethed in a thick stew of frustration.

"It is common for individual Magi to struggle with particular skills, especially during the initial training. When I was first trained I couldn't stream either. It took me months. I've never been coordinated, and I took much longer to learn physical aspects of Lightcraft than others. Even now, I don't stream as fast as many Magi. I suspect you are similar. Consider your gifts, Melanie. You are a powerful Augmentor and also a Percipient, I think."

"Percipient?"

"Yes—one who perceives. Do you remember how you took the stray bits of data and figured out the Darkhands' plans a few months back?"

She nodded, remembering how the white board in her mind had just come alive all of a sudden. Symbols had buzzed and clicked—and then she somehow knew what the Darkhands had planned.

"A Percipient connects facts and perceives patterns. Assisted by the Light, your brain works so quickly that it may seem like a flash of insight. In reality, you are reasoning, or perceiving, at a very high speed, processing like a super-computer."

"Is this like the theelings Lexa gets?"

"No. Your brain organizes known facts and data in such a way as to perceive patterns and understand the truth of a situation. Lexa's gift is quite different, more intuitive. Her dreams, feelings, and thoughts—theelings, as she calls them—reveal things not previously known. She is a Seer, I think, one who basically pulls truth out of thin air."

"That makes sense."

"Augmentation and Percipience are both internal processes, coming from the inside out. You will probably struggle with the more physical, external aspects of Lightcraft, but you are not flawed or defective. It will simply take some time."

Conner streamed past them, flipping a loop-de-loop. "Conner's gifts are physical." Dr. Timberi chuckled. "Strength and speed. If I were to sit Conner down in a classroom and discuss something like Adumbrating, he would likely struggle. But when it comes to streaming, he's like an otter swimming."

He paused for several seconds, frowning his thoughtful frown. "You know, I have not thought about this before, but it is fascinating how complementary your abilities are."

"What do you mean?"

"Consider the gifts the three of you possess. Conner has strength and speed. He excels in the physical aspects of Lightcraft. You are an Augmentor and a Percipient, specializing in the mental aspects of Lightcraft. Lexa is highly attuned to the emotional and spiritual aspects and has great potential as a Seer. The three of you together encompass every branch of Lightcraft and represent the entire human being: body, mind, spirit. Very interesting. But I'm wandering. At any rate, don't worry about not being able to stream right away."

Melanie felt a little better. "Thank you. So what do I do?"

Dr. Timberi smiled again, fingering the whistle. "You practice, Melanie. A lot."

He blew the whistle and Melanie groaned.

CHAPTER 25

HORTENSE BENET

CONNER STREAMED EVERYWHERE AND back again. The rush that came from streaming mixed the adrenaline and endorphins of the best workout ever with the total happiness that came with Lightcraft. He'd never felt so good in his life, so exhilarated and excited, but also peaceful and content. The guilt about the past and the fear of the future all seemed like a lifetime ago.

The situation with Melanie made it all even better. Streaming and a beautiful girl. Summer was looking pretty good.

After lunch, Dr. Timberi made them practice for a while longer, before giving them the afternoon off. Lexa went off somewhere on her own, so Conner and Melanie explored the yard around Mockingbird Cottage. The property had lots of hidden nooks, and they discovered chickens, a goat, and rabbits, as well as horseshoe pits and a volleyball court. Sadie said they could swim in the large pond, but after Dauphin Island, Conner didn't have much desire for swimming, and Melanie thought the water looked full of bacteria.

So they wandered, ending up in the front yard as a fuchsia pink comet burst through the clouds with a loud, shrieking whistle. The comet faded into a tall woman with short, spiky gray hair and too-tan skin.

"Good afternoon, children." Her smile didn't quite reach her voice or her eyes. "Melanie, nice to see you again." She looked at Conner. "And you must be the famous Conner Dell." She extended her hand. "Hortense Benet. It is nice to finally meet you." A French accent flavored her words.

"Uh, thanks," Conner said.

"You don't know me, but I am the Director of the Adumbrator Office. I met Melanie and Lexa when you were taken a few months ago."

"It's nice to meet you," Conner said. Should he bow or something?

"Likewise, Conner. Is Morgan here?" Madam Benet's eyes narrowed.

"Yeah, I think I saw him around back in that pergola thing."

"Thank you for your assistance."

"Sure," Conner said.

She left, and Conner and Melanie sat on the steps of the front porch, not doing anything, just holding hands and enjoying being with each other. Until then, Conner had never realized doing nothing could make his heart race harder than doing wind sprints.

Madame Cumberland poked her head out of the front

door. "Do you two know where Morgan is?"

"Yes, ma'am," Conner said. "I think he's in back talking to that Adumbrator lady. The director. Or something."

Madame Cumberland's smile faded. "Hortense? Here? With Morgan? Oh no—" Distant shouts interrupted Madame Cumberland, who ran into the house. Conner and Melanie followed her through the kitchen and out the back door.

Outside, they watched Dr. Timberi limp toward the house with a furious scowl on his face as Madame Benet strode behind him.

As they reached the steps, Dr. Timberi turned around, huffing and wheezing. "No!" He pounded his cane on the ground. "No, Hortense!" Another pound. "No! I refuse! And it shows a complete lack of decency on your part to even ask. Not that I am surprised."

Hortense glared knives and guns and bombs at him, but did not yell. "Your personal feelings do not matter, Morgan. This situation demands your assistance."

"No!" Dr. Timberi bellowed. He took a breath, then spoke as if he were talking to a deaf person—or a small child. "I. Re. Fuse. Mona, kindly translate that into French, because Madame Benet does not seem to understand English." Dr. Timberi's eyes crackled with a fury Conner had never seen directed at anyone but Darkhands. And Melanie's dad.

Madame Benet paused and pulled herself up to her full height. "Then I must order you."

Fireworks of fury exploded all over Dr. Timberi's face and gold sparks literally crackled in the air around his eyes. "You can't do that!"

She glared back, matching his outburst with her own quiet anger. "Oh, but I can. You were merely given leave. Transferred, not released. Your oaths are still binding."

The gold sparks around Dr. Timberi flared and flashed. His face turned purple, and he shook with rage. "How dare you?" he hissed. Then his voice swelled to a roar. "How dare you!" Conner worried Dr. Timberi might have a stroke, or explode in one massive gold fireball.

"No, Morgan! How dare *you!*" The Head Adumbrator faced him down, her voice shaking with just as much emotion. Frustration. Anger. And—hurt? "How dare you let your personal pain blind you to the urgent need for your assistance! How dare you continue to be an insufferable, arrogant martyr! And how dare you make me suffer every day for your pain! You are a cruel, cruel man."

Hortense turned away and took a deep breath, forcing her voice back into some semblance of control. "I shall send a sigil with instructions later.

"Good-bye, Mona." Hortense looked at Madame Cumberland, who gave her a sad smile and whispered something in her ear. Hortense nodded, then looked at Conner—who felt super-sized awkward. "It was nice to meet you, Conner." She jumped into the air and streamed away in a sizzling, fuchsia comet, passing through the clouds with that distinct whistling sound.

A long, painful silence fell over the deck. As he tried to find some unawkward place to look, Conner noticed that Lexa had her face pressed up against the inside of a second-story window.

"She's right, Morgan," Madame Cumberland said in a gentle voice.

Conner flinched, preparing himself for more fireworks, but Dr. Timberi exhaled and seemed to deflate. "I know." He spoke in a strained whisper. "That's why it rankles me so. Excuse me, please. I need to gather myself. Then I shall apologize to Hortense and get to work."

He looked at Conner and Melanie.

Now, possums, whatever could you all be staring at? Is there a squirrel at the bird feeder? Back to your business. The Morgan Timberi Show is over for the day.

He walked into the house and slammed the door hard enough to shatter a gymful of backboards.

CHAPTER 26

FAMILY SECRETS

LEXA BACKED AWAY AS DR. TIMBERI slammed the door below, rattling the window and the whole back of the house. He'd fought major battles with less anger than she'd seen in his confrontation with the Hortense lady. Lexa hadn't meant to eavesdrop—well, not really, but they'd shouted so loud, and she couldn't help it.

Now, curiosity swarmed her, like ants on a dropped popsicle. Wondering about what she'd just heard, Lexa resnuggled into the couch.

After Conner and Melanie's little kissing and streaming incident, Lexa wanted to be alone, and she'd discovered a small circular room up at the top of the house. Lined with bookshelves, it contained a fireplace, a small sofa, and an armchair. It felt safe and snug, a place to retreat and hide.

With Dr. Timberi's performance over, Lexa went back to what she had been doing before all the yelling interrupted her—staring at one of the bookshelves.

Most of the shelves in the room groaned under big, old books. But this one was different. On the shelf in front of her, soft, colored Light pulsed inside a dozen different sealed containers—boxes, jars, bowls, cups, and vases, each containing something that seemed bright and alive.

Next to the shelf, afternoon sunlight floated through a window, mixing with the colored Light from the shelf, creating a stained-glass effect and making the room feel powerful and almost sacred, like a church. Lexa could practically hear angels singing heavenly chords.

Among the containers, three caught her eye: an elegant silver vase etched with a graceful rose bush, a blue jar with a twirling ballerina worked into the clay, and a gold box carved with an intricate flock of swans.

Heavy footsteps pounding the spiral staircase below made Lexa jump. She turned around as Dr. Timberi stomped up the stairs.

He froze, staring at her with apparent surprise.

"Sorry, I didn't know I wasn't supposed to—" she began.

Dr. Timberi waved his hand. "Don't be silly. This room isn't off-limits. I am simply not accustomed to finding anyone here." He strode over to the window and glared out at the empty yard, radiating waves of strong emotion. Anger and deep sadness filled the air around him. "You are free to stay if you like," he mumbled.

Sympathy tugged at Lexa—he looked so upset, so lonely somehow. But what could she do about that? And what did he need more of—privacy or sympathy?

As she wondered what to do next, a theeling jumped into Lexa's mind. Go to him. Touch him. Now.

Lexa hesitated. That seemed a little risky, something with seriously super-awkwardness potential, but she'd learned to follow her theelings, so, tugging her ponytail, Lexa walked over and touched his elbow as gently as she could.

As her fingertips made contact, the air seemed to crackle, and images and feelings stampeded through her, intense and almost overwhelming.

Faces flashed in her mind—the faces from the photo at Dr. Timberi's house. The beautiful woman, the chubby baby. Years of memories flooded into Lexa—bits and snippets of cherished moments.

Dr. Timberi rolling on the ground with the baby, making faces and funny noises while the chubby baby giggled, his black eyes shining.

Dr. Timberi and his wife walking through the park, pushing a stroller with one hand, clasping the fingers of their other hands together.

Time passed and the stroller vanished. Now they walked with a toddler between them, clutching their fingers in his own tiny hands.

The Timberis danced together in a small living room by candlelight while the baby slept in an adjoining room.

Dr. Timberi was young and surprisingly handsome, sparkling with life and energy. The woman took his breath away. Her long red hair flowed everywhere, and her smile lit up the world around her, but it especially lit up Dr. Timberi's eyes.

She took his face in her hands and pulled him down to look at hers. They laughed, and then they kissed—like a couple in a movie.

Smoke billowed in, covering the images. Thick black smoke and black flames. When it faded, Lexa recognized the living room. Charred and blackened. Dead. A gold comet blasted in, and Dr. Timberi looked around the ruins, his face contorted with wild, raging grief. He looked up at the sky and shouted, a terrible, heart-shredding cry that twisted Lexa's soul.

A silver comet streamed in, and a younger Madame Cumberland reached out to touch his shoulder—

The vision ended with an abrupt jerk as Dr. Timberi yanked his arm away from Lexa. He glared at her, and the furious look on his face frightened her. She jumped back, and his expression softened. Lexa realized that all of that had happened in a second or two.

"I am sorry to frighten you, Lexa. You caught me off guard." His face and voice grew even softer. "Generally, it's best not to tap into someone's memories without advance warning. It can be unsettling for the other person."

"I'm sorry," she stammered. "I didn't mean to—I didn't know—"

He waved his hand and gave her a small smile. "I understand. Driven by that generous heart of yours, you wanted to comfort me, and you reached out. Thank you. Forgive my initial reaction. You surprised me in a vulnerable moment." He looked back out the window, and the room got silent.

"Nicole," he whispered after a few minutes.

"Sir?"

"Nicole. That was my wife's name."

His voice stayed even, but Lexa sensed deep fires of emotion blazing beneath the surface.

"She was really pretty," Lexa said. What did you say in a situation like this?

"Yes, she was," he said.

"And your baby was cute."

Dr. Timberi turned around, and a genuine smiled flashed through the grief and stress. "Adorable. We used to wrestle on the living room floor. I'd let him pin me, and he'd laugh and laugh. All these years later, that laugh still makes me smile."

"So, what happened?" Lexa spoke in a hesitant voice, worried she might be trespassing.

"Nicole and I met while working in the Adumbrator Office. We fell in love and got married. Nicole had always wanted children, and our little boy came quickly. Once he joined us, she decided to stay home with him.

"With a young family to provide for, I worked as hard as I could. I was young, ambitious, full of energy, and very good at my job. I say that in all modesty, but it is true. Promotion after promotion came, and everyone knew that it was only a matter of time until I became the Head Adumbrator, one of the most coveted positions in the Sodality. Those were happy years." His voice cracked, and intense foreboding struck Lexa.

"Hortense was also an Adumbrator, one of the most gifted Seers the Sodality had known in decades. She was my senior by just a few years, and if anyone was going to get the position instead of me, it would have been Hortense. Frankly, we never liked each other much to begin with, but as time passed, we grew fiercely competitive.

"Some years earlier, a particularly vicious Darkhand had caused major problems. Nicole and I had first worked together in figuring out his plan and capturing him. About this time, he escaped, vowing vengeance." Dr. Timberi's voice stretched and grew tight. Lexa couldn't help but wonder if it was the Stalker.

"The Adumbrators worked 24/7 to track him. Word came that he was plotting something big in China. I disagreed. I felt sure it was a ruse. My own adumbrating convinced me that the real plan involved something much closer. But Hortense believed the intelligence about China. She lobbied long and hard, convincing the other Adumbrators that she was right. The department sided with her, and I was ordered to China."

Lexa gasped as she realized what happened next.

"China was a decoy." His voice stretched to the breaking point. "The real plan was close to home. To my home. While I was away, the Darkhand attacked. By the time I got word, it was too late."

He paused, and although Lexa hardly ever cried, her eyes felt a bit misty. The knot in her throat kept her from talking, so she patted his elbow.

"My dislike of Hortense hardened into bitter hatred. Over the years, that has softened to a persistent loathing, but I've never been strong enough to completely forgive her.

"I left the Adumbrator office, which is not allowed. Because of the secret work Adumbrators do, it is a lifetime commitment. But I refused to work for them any longer. I swore that I'd rot in prison before looking at another adumbration, and I meant it. In fact, I almost left the Sodality altogether, which would have meant breaking some solemn and serious oaths.

"Some of my friends went to bat for me—Lee was a rising star then, and very persuasive. And everyone knew and loved Mona. And some others you've not met. The Magisterium relented and changed my assignment. I became a Guide and ended up teaching. However, I was never actually released from the Adumbrators—I was simply reassigned. Which means my oaths still obligate me to follow orders." He took a deep breath. "And now you understand."

Yes, she did. She understood so much. Why he seemed so distant sometimes and why he kept people at arm's length. She understood the use of big words and formal manners to control the pain and anger boiling under the surface of his calm demeanor and perfectly pressed clothing. Poor Dr. Timberi.

His secret cut deep into her heart with shards of sadness. Lexa wanted to make it better, to take it away somehow. She hugged him as tight as she could. "I'm so sorry! I'm so sorry!" She repeated it over and over. He didn't hug her back, but he didn't flinch or back away this time.

"Thank you, Lexa." He gave his trademark awkward fingertip pat on her back. "You are kind, and your sweet affection is soothing. I wonder, however, if it's entirely appropriate for a middle-aged man to get so many hugs from a student."

Lexa released her embrace, and he walked a few steps away.

"It's so mean of Madame Benet to make you go back after all that," Lexa said.

Dr. Timberi shrugged. "It does appear that way. And I am tempted to indulge in that line of thinking myself. On the other hand, the Magisterium is worried. More fires happened last night, and there have been rumors about shadows attacking the children that you helped rescue from Lady Nightwing's experiments. No one understands what is going on, but it does appear quite serious. Since I am local and was reasonably skilled in my day, they feel they need my help."

He opened a cabinet under one of the bookshelves and pulled out something that looked like a whole bunch of metal hoops. "I actually came for this. Now, if you'll excuse me, I have some work to do." He walked down some of the steps on the spiral staircase, stopped, and turned to face her. "Thank you, Lexa." He smiled. "Thank you very much."

As he walked away, Lexa reminded herself again to always listen to her theelings.

CHAPTER 27

L'Horloge de la Lumière et de l'Obscurité

AFTER DR. TIMBERI STORMED INSIDE, Conner and Melanie messed around with the volleyball and then played badminton. With every minute, Conner felt happier and happier, and more deeply infatuated with Melanie.

When Sadie rang the dinner bell, they went back to the house and devoured fried green tomatoes and barbecued ribs. Dr. Timberi seemed more cheerful now and insisted that he and the Trio do the dishes. Conner and Melanie ended up getting into a battle with soap suds. Dr. Timberi laughed and helped Melanie ambush Conner at one point. Lexa ignored Conner and Melanie and disappeared upstairs as soon as the dishes were done. Madame Cumberland said she had to get home, and Sadie shooed the remaining three outside. "I'll have warm peach pie in a little bit—with homemade ice cream. I'll ring the bell when it's all finished."

Conner and Melanie went out into the yard to look

at the sunset. Technically, that was Melanie's idea, not his. But any activity involving Melanie had become his favorite thing to do.

They walked onto the deck, where Dr. Timberi sat in a chair, staring at a strange instrument of some kind.

A large metal hoop rotated on an invisible axis in front of him. Six smaller hoops of different sizes revolved inside, each at different angles, turning at different speeds. Gold Light surrounded each hoop, making them look more like spinning spheres, while tiny comets shot around each one. In the middle of everything, three clock-like hands ticked and spun around at different speeds. It reminded Conner a little bit of the internal gears of a complicated clock— except instead of flat pieces just spinning from right to left, 3-D globes spun in every direction, at different angles. He had to look away to avoid getting a migraine.

"Whoa, what is that?" Conner asked.

Dr. Timberi looked up and smiled. "The full name is *l'horloge de la lumière et de l'obscurité.*"

Conner, who took Latin, felt like an idiot, while Melanie, the A+ French student, mouthed the words a few times. "Clock of light and dark?"

"Exactly!" Nothing made Dr. Timberi smile like Melanie figuring something out. "Well done. A fourteenth-century French Magus who worked as a clockmaker wanted to create a tool to sense and display levels of Light and Dark. A clock of light and dark. For short, we call it an horloge."

"What does it do?" Melanie seemed really interested. Conner wasn't so sure that staring at spinning hoops sounded all that fun. Even with Melanie.

"Several things. Mainly, it measures levels of Light and Dark, and it can also represent them in visual form."

"Is it like a crystal ball?" Conner asked, hoping to show Melanie he could figure stuff out too.

"No." Dr. Timberi laughed. "Unfortunately not. It cannot show you anything that you do not already know. Although, it can illuminate what you thought you knew by presenting a different perspective. Sometimes the horloge can show a Seer's visions to others—there are a number of uses."

"So what are you looking for?" Conner asked.

"Shadows. Every time the Darkness is used, it causes shadows to appear—just as throwing a rock in the water causes ripples. These shadows can be studied, and through careful analysis, one can sometimes perceive the outlines of a plan or a plot."

"Is this about the fires?" Melanie asked.

"Yes."

"What's going on?" Conner looked at Melanie. The way she knew everything was really amazing. "Mrs. Sharpe said something about fires after I blew up the school bus."

"Fires have been happening all over town," Dr. Timberi said. "Growing in frequency. The Magisterium thinks the Darkhands are behind them—"

"They think it's the Stalker," Melanie said.

Dr. Timberi nodded, but continued talking. "And any time the Darkhands do things we don't understand, it's cause for concern. There have also been rumors of attacks on the children Lady Nightwing kidnapped for that ghastly experiment."

"Are they connected?" Melanie asked.

Dr. Timberi smiled. "No *apparent* connection at all. Which makes me suspicious. I think they must be. But I do not know how. Of course, after ordering me to look into this, no one at the Magisterium bothers to listen to a word I say." He muttered something under his breath, then said, "Why don't you two look? Melanie, perhaps you can help me. With your gifts, I imagine you will be a natural Adumbrator."

Conner joined Melanie, peeking in the twirling circles. Light and Darkness swirled around, constantly pushing up against each other like two cocky guys getting ready to fight. Darkness shoved forward, pushing the Light back for a few minutes. Then the Light regrouped and pushed back.

Conner looked into a different hoop, and instead of fighting, the Light and Dark took shape, whirling into the form of a small house on a tree-lined street. Everything was made of Light and Dark, and while the image was detailed and clear, it wasn't like a movie or a picture. It seemed more like something you'd see through night-vision goggles. The door of the house opened, and a girl about Conner's age walked out and sat on the steps.

"That's Taylor," Conner said. "She was one of the kids Lady Nightwing kidnapped."

"Correct," Dr. Timberi said. "And Lexa saw her at the mall the other night. I had the Magisterium place a detection net around each of the homes where those children live. If anything Dark happens in the area, I will know."

"That's pretty cool," Conner said.

Dr. Timberi looked away from the horloge and rubbed his temples. "Yes, it is. But that's enough adumbrating for now." Dr. Timberi stared at the yard below. With no one talking, all Conner heard were birds and frogs and insects, but what really got his attention were the lights. Giant fireflies bobbed and floated all over the yard.

Dr. Timberi sighed. "I love it here in the evenings. There is nowhere I'd rather be than Mockingbird Cottage as the sun sets over the trees."

"I love all the fireflies," Melanie said. "I remember them from last time we were here. I've never seen so many of them, and they seem so big."

"Look closer, Melanie," Dr. Timberi said.

Conner looked and realized that many of the lights were much larger than the others, much brighter. Some even had different colors. And, unlike the fireflies, they didn't seem to blink—their lights glowed steadily.

"What are they?" he asked. Something about them seemed familiar.

"They are called Lucents and are essentially baby cherubim—extremely rare and wonderful creatures. They are said to have great power and many old legends mention them helping particularly worthy Magi in dire trouble."

"Have they ever helped you?" Conner asked.

"No." Dr. Timberi shook his head. "Nor anyone I know. Lucents usually stay far from humans, remaining near sanctuaries. Sometimes, when they sense a particularly kind or pure heart, they might flicker around. Madame Cumberland has occasionally had one or two land on her shoulder. But they only go near truly exceptional humans, so most Magi see them from a distance."

Conner shrugged. He thought the Lucents seemed

familiar, but he'd never been to a sanctuary before. Oh well.

They sat in silence for a few more minutes, watching Lucents fly as the stars came out. Conner thought about putting his arm around Melanie, but right then Sadie walked out and rang the massive dinner bell.

Conner jumped up. "Pie!"

Dr. Timberi laughed. "Like Pavlov's dogs," he said.

"What?" Conner asked.

Melanie gasped.

"Melanie, what is it?" Dr. Timberi ignored Conner's question.

"I don't know. Something just got me thinking—the symbols on my whiteboard were flying. I almost know something—but not quite. It's like when you need to sneeze but can't. My mind almost figured something out." She smiled. "Sorry. Sometimes this happens. It usually means I need more data."

She scrunched her nose. Conner loved the way she did that. "It might have been about the fires. I'm not sure. Sorry. It's like having an equation with half the numbers in it."

Dr. Timberi nodded. "Well, please keep me posted. Until then, let's go eat."

They walked into the kitchen, and Conner sat down next to Melanie. Deep peace washed over Conner as he ate warm peach pie next to the most amazing girl in the universe. Life seemed perfect.

THE LETTER

AFTER DESSERT, WHEN EVERYONE ELSE went back outside, Melanie remembered the letter Madame Cumberland had mentioned earlier. She walked into the living room and saw it on the piano. Her pulse fluttered inside of her when she realized the letter was hand-addressed to her in an envelope from Harvard. *The Office of Undergraduate Recruitment and Early Talent Identification!* Someone had written "Extremely Urgent" across the front, and she tore it open with trembling hands.

A letter fell into her hands, which she read, with growing dismay.

> *Dear Melanie,*
> *Forgive the deception with the Harvard envelope. Unkind, but I had to make sure you would open this, and I figured the hopes of an Ivy League scholarship would do the trick. Please keep reading. I'm writing to you out of concern. Seriously.*

You're a smart girl, Melanie. Smarter than everyone else around you. I relate to that because I was the same. And while I oppose the Magi, I respect you and don't want you to be destroyed. Smart girls should be valued and nurtured.

Your friendship with Conner Dell puts you in danger. There's a lot you don't know about him. When Conner was captured, he was terrified of being killed. From the first, he begged me to let him become a Noctivagant—what the Magi rather crudely call Darkhands. He promised to give me information about the Magi and become a double agent if I'd spare him. I agreed, figuring he might be useful.

Becoming a Noctivagant involves going through something called a Shadowbox. This special device gives you the ability to hear shadows and to use the Darkness. It also shows visions of the future.

I won't go into the details here, but in Conner's vision he did terrible things to you.

And so, one more time, I'm going to warn you. Stay away from Conner Dell. One of these days, he'll hurt you.

I know you won't believe me. But let me ask two questions. First, how much has Conner ever told you about what happened when he was our guest? Second, the change to become a Darkhand is slow but steady. Have you seen anything out of the ordinary with Conner? Any unusual behavior or actions?

I won't pretend to wish the Magi well. I hate their oppressive self-righteousness, their pinched and

*limited morality. I want them wiped off the earth so
a more equitable order can arise.*

*But as one smart girl to another, I want you
to have a chance. Women need men like fish need
bicycles. But you need Conner Dell like a fish needs
a baited hook.*

Sincerely,
Emily Jacoway, aka Lady Nightwing

It took Melanie several minutes to catch her breath.
She read the letter again and again. It had to be a joke.
Or a lie. Surely she couldn't trust anything that Lady
Nightwing told her.

She crumpled the letter. Why would Lady Nightwing
send her a letter? What would the point be? Her goal?
Suspicion caused Melanie to squint her eyes.

And yet—

*The change to become a Darkhand is slow but steady.
Have you seen anything out of the ordinary with Conner?*

What about the shadows talking to him? Or Lexa's
descriptions of his cries in the night?

No. This couldn't be true. It couldn't be. She shook
the thoughts away, but they clung to her consciousness.

*How much has Conner ever told you about what hap-
pened when he was our guest?*

An idea flickered into her mind—an answer. A way to
prove this was an ugly, vicious lie.

Melanie slid the letter into the piano bench. Lexa
shared her room, and with professional-grade sneaky
skills, she would find it if Melanie kept it in the room.

Taking a deep breath, Melanie walked out to the deck.

She forced a smile. "Hey, Conner. Want to go on a walk?"

He looked a little surprised but smiled. "Again? Sure." As they walked down the steps, she saw him reach for her hand, but she slipped her fingers inside her pocket. She needed a few answers.

In the darkness of the yard, Lucents lit their way, hovering around them in a small cloud. Melanie led them to one of the secluded nooks, a bench under some vines where they had talked earlier.

"So, how are you doing?" Melanie decided to jump right in. No easy way to do this.

"Great." Conner smiled. The colored Light from the Lucents painted his hair with soft gold highlights.

"I never really thanked you for saving Madi."

He seemed a little surprised, but said, "You're welcome."

"I've been wondering if you're okay."

"I am now." He took both her hands and smiled at her. The Lucents flitted around his head, lighting his eyes with rainbows.

"No, I mean really," she persisted. "I feel like something's wrong. Like, well I don't know." She paused, wishing she had Lexa's ability to talk and weasel information out of people. "What did they do to you?"

Conner's smile faded and his hands tensed, squeezing hers in agitation. "Um, I'd rather not talk about that."

He looked at the ground, but before he did, she saw guilt flash in his eyes, and he flushed hot and bright. His hands squeezed tighter, and she winced as they began to hurt.

Conner dropped his hands. "Sorry," he said. "I didn't mean to—"

"I need to go get something." She turned and ran to the house, fighting back the tears. *How much has Conner ever told you about what happened when he was our guest?*

If Lady Nightwing was lying, what did Conner have to hide? What if the letter was true?

As she walked up the deck steps, Dr. Timberi looked up from the horloge. Should she tell him what she knew about Conner?

No. At this point, she only had suspicions. For now, she would gather data and watch for clues. And she knew which clues she needed most. She took another deep breath and swallowed her tears.

"Dr. Timberi, what's a noctivagant?"

"Noctivagation literally means, 'walking in the night.' It is the name Darkhands use for what they do."

"Thanks. What's a Shadowbox?"

Dr. Timberi's peaceful expression changed, and his voice sounded strained. "A Shadowbox is an instrument of extreme spiritual torture. We do not know many details because those that come out of the Shadowbox are usually unable or unwilling to speak to Magi anymore.

"We believe it is part of the Darkhand initiation rites. It is an evil, evil thing—an abomination. For those who do not become Darkhands, it can lead to madness or cause a profound shock that brings a welcome death." A shadow passed over his face. "It can turn even the brightest Lights into shadows and create monsters. Why do you ask?" He took a drink of lemonade.

She looked away, choking back her tears back. Not now. Not in front of Dr. Timberi. "No reason. Just something I heard the Darkhands talking about when they attacked at the mall. I kept forgetting to ask you." Not exactly a lie. Lexa must be rubbing off on her.

A high-pitched whistling noise interrupted them. Melanie looked up and saw a bright yellow comet, speeding for the deck.

"Stop, Lexa," Dr. Timberi muttered. "Lexa, stop!" he said louder. "Sto—" He and Melanie both had to dive aside as Lexa's comet plowed through the railing of the deck, exploding into the spot where they had been sitting.

The comet faded into Lexa, panting and perspiring. She smiled and shrugged. "Sorry about that. I thought I could control the landing better."

"Yes, well, perhaps, until you get the landing down, you could practice away from the elderly and infirm," Dr. Timberi said, from under his upturned chair. "Might I trouble you for some help?"

Lexa and Melanie pulled the chair off of him, and then they each reached down and took an arm. His lemonade had spilled all over his shirt, and he no longer looked very neat, pressed, or creased. As he pulled himself back up, the strain on his face made Melanie wonder just how recovered he really was.

Melanie—remember what we decided about hugs? One-two-three! Lexa threw her arms around Dr. Timberi. Giving hugs was about the last thing Melanie felt like doing at the moment, but she joined in the hug and then let him go.

Dr. Timberi looked from Lexa to Melanie. "Why do I think that I am at the center of a conspiracy of some kind?"

"You get so tense when we hug you," Lexa said. "We figure that means you need more of them."

Melanie had seen Dr. Timberi look furious, delighted, and terrified. She'd never seen him look so surprised.

He didn't speak for a minute or two. "Thank you," he said. Did his eyes get misty? "Thank you. I generally avoid physical contact with students. However, perhaps, in this case, your diagnosis is accurate." He grabbed his cane. "Now, I think I will change into something a bit less citrusy." He turned and walked into the house.

Melanie watched him, wondering again what it was that had made him so tense and afraid of emotions.

She looked at Lexa. "Lexa, are you okay?" Time to address why Lexa had been sullen and withdrawn all day. Down in the yard, Conner hit some bushes with a stick.

"I'm fine." Lexa sighed with a melodramatic twinge. Melanie dug her fingers into part of the deck railing that Lexa hadn't demolished.

Did she really want to get into this tonight? Discussing a problem honestly was one thing, but based on the normal pattern with Lexa, she would spend half an hour or more trying to coax Lexa to open up. Then, they would spend another hour or two "working through it,"which meant Melanie apologizing over and over.

Talking with Lexa often left Melanie feeling that she'd been cast as a supporting player in a dramatic scene, and suddenly, she had little interest in drama.

"Okay," Melanie said. "I'm glad you're fine." She looked down at the yard as Conner's red comet shot through a cluster of fireflies, scattering them as he practiced streaming. The Lucents re-formed and seemed to chase him.

Lexa heaved a loud sigh. "Well, I guess I was a little hurt earlier."

Melanie tried to feel sympathetic, but Lexa's drama was getting old. "And why was that?"

"On Friday, when I found out that we were going to get trained, I tried to tell you, but you were already in a conversation with Conner. I didn't mean to eavesdrop, but you weren't shielding it."

"Yes." Melanie clipped her words. "I had a conversation with Conner."

"Well," Lexa said, "you were talking about how this wouldn't be the same if Conner didn't come and how it's no fun without him and how you *had* to go to the movie with me and that was a big pain and then today—"

"Stop right there. That's not what I said."

"Huh?" Lexa seemed confused, probably because normally, Melanie would be apologizing by now.

"Actually, I didn't say that. Conner did. Not me. You can't blame me for what Conner said. And as far as that other stuff, yes, I said it! I was trying to get Conner to come. Dr. Timberi asked me to persuade him to come because Conner's health was at stake! Hello, Lexa! Your brother needed to come because he is seriously suffering and is maybe damaged!" Melanie felt the tears coming. No one knew how damaged. She forced herself to continue in spite of the tears. "This seemed like the best way to heal him, so it was kind of important to get him here." Melanie's temperature rose as pent-up feelings poured out. "And, anyway, Conner does make things fun. You used to think that too before you started being jealous of every minute I spend with him!" Melanie glared with righteous indignation at Lexa.

Feeling the tears pushing back, and not wanting to cry

in front of Lexa, Melanie turned and walked back into the house.

Melanie didn't sleep well that night. Lexa's sulky, icy silence chilled the room, creating an awkward tension.

Melanie hated conflict and normally apologized the second she perceived tension of any kind. But tonight she hadn't done anything wrong, so why should she apologize? Besides, why couldn't Lexa apologize sometimes?

So, for the first time she could remember, Melanie dug into an emotional foxhole, ready to wait. Lexa could be stubborn. Fine. Melanie would be stubborn too.

Still, conflict upset her, and she couldn't sleep. After tossing and turning in the shared bed for two or three hours, she got up, too restless to sleep and tired of trying. She tiptoed out of the room and down the hall. Maybe she could get a drink or some fresh air on the deck. As she passed Conner's door, he cried out, a terrible, tormented sound.

"Melanie! I'm sorry!"

The words raised chills up and down her arms and back.

"Melanie! I'm sorry." This time, the words raised chills in her heart as well. Slimy, uncomfortable chills.

Why did he keep saying that? What had he done that he felt so badly about? And why wouldn't he talk about it?

He cried out again. Should she do something? Go to him? As Melanie stood frozen, Lexa stumbled out of their bedroom. She pushed past Melanie and pounded on Conner's door.

"Conner! Conner!"

He screamed again, so Lexa opened the door. At that point, Dr. Timberi limped up, wrapped in a bathrobe and leaning on his cane. Sadie came behind him.

"Excuse me, Melanie." Dr. Timberi rushed past her, following Lexa into the darkness of Conner's room.

Sadie looked at Melanie and gave her a shy smile before joining the others in the room. "He'll be okay, sweetie."

From inside the room, Lexa cried out, her cry blending with Conner's in tortured harmony.

"Lexa, what's wrong?" Dr. Timberi asked, loud enough that Melanie could hear it in the hallway.

"N-n-nothing. I'm fine," Lexa gasped.

Conner screamed again.

The torment in his voice made Melanie ache for him.

Yet part of her felt unsettled and alarmed. What had he done to her?

She remembered the letter in the piano bench. *I won't go into the details here, but in Conner's vision he did terrible things to you.*

And so, one more time, I'm going to warn you. Stay away from Conner Dell. One of these days, he'll hurt you.

Whatever Conner had done to bring such anguish into his voice, it must have been something bad.

Dr. Timberi's words came back into her mind. *It can lead to madness . . . It can turn even the brightest Lights into shadows and create monsters.*

What if—no.

Not Conner.

Except—

Her roiling stomach churned her concern for Conner into nausea.

189

Stop this! He needed compassion and understanding! She didn't even know what happened.

How much has Conner ever told you about what happened when he was our guest?

Of course, if he would just talk to her, then she would know. The fact that he wouldn't talk meant it must be really bad.

Melanie struggled to resist these thoughts. But that cold, slimy feeling wiggled and grew bigger inside. Why wouldn't he talk to anyone? Was he becoming a monster? Or just going crazy?

Or both?

Long after Conner's shouts ended, Melanie lay on the couch, brooding over these thoughts.

She turned over.

Lady Nightwing might have lied about him begging to become a Darkhand. That didn't sound like Conner. And if she'd lied about that, what else had she lied about?

She tossed. Still, Conner had acted in ways she didn't understand, and that scared her. Why wouldn't he talk to her? What about the shadows?

She turned again.

And if he'd hurt her in the Shadowbox, whatever he'd done, would he do that for real one of these days?

At some point, between tosses and turns, her body overwhelmed her mind and she fell asleep. But long before that time, a gap had grown between her and Conner.

CHAPTER 29.

NIGHT VISION

ALONE IN HER ROOM, LEXA KICKED HER covers off for the kabillionth time, kept awake now by much bigger worries than being left out or having friendly spats with Melanie. She didn't know if she'd ever sleep again as her mind kept replaying the vision that had come when she'd touched Conner.

Trying to wake him up had triggered a vision. A short flash, just a fragment, really. But enough to frighten her more than anything she'd experienced up until then.

Since Dauphin Island, she'd had dreams where Conner had been screaming with a hate-twisted face. And she'd seen Melanie sobbing and full of despair. But tonight she'd seen them both together.

Conner wasn't just screaming. He screamed at Melanie. It was like a movie with the sound turned down, so Lexa couldn't hear what he said, but his face reflected the awful ugliness of whatever he yelled. Melanie's face reflected it too. As Melanie sobbed, Lexa understood what the cliché phrase "a broken heart" meant. Each word Conner said seemed to slice her spirit down, cutting her into smaller and smaller bits.

And then Conner raised his hands and shot black fire out of his hands—

Lexa blinked her eyes, hoping to push away what she'd seen. The next part was too terrible to even think about.

It couldn't be true.

But her visions had always been right before. Lexa spent the rest of the night kicking her covers and praying that, just this once, she was wrong.

CHAPTER 30

CLIFF JUMPING

CONNER WOKE UP THE NEXT MORNING, unrested and unsettled. Last night his dreams had continually replayed what he'd done to Melanie. The sharks of guilt, shame, and fear came back, breaking through the wall and tearing into his soul.

Showering didn't wash away his feeling of uncleanness, and getting dressed didn't cover the emotional nakedness that came with shame. He wanted to disappear under the covers of the bed but forced himself to go down to breakfast.

Sadie had filled the table with bacon, warm biscuits, and steaming gravy, but Conner had no appetite. He poked at his breakfast while Lexa devoured her food and avoided looking at him. He didn't mind since he didn't feel like talking anyway. But when Melanie came down a few minutes later, she didn't say anything and seemed to keep her distance from him and Lexa. Had they had a fight?

Conner tried to catch Melanie's eye, but every time he looked at her, she looked away. And she didn't answer a private head-talk message he sent. That made his mood even worse, and tension filled the room like the gravy covering his plate.

No one said anything during the meal. Dr. Timberi tried to make conversation for a few minutes, but pretty soon he gave up, focusing instead on Sadie's fresh scrambled eggs.

After breakfast, Dr. Timberi pulled Conner aside. "Conner, something is clearly wrong. Please tell me what is troubling you."

Dr. Timberi cranked his famous Stare up to full power, and Conner felt like the cherubim were staring into his soul again. Then Dr. Timberi's expression changed. His eyes overflowed with understanding and kindness, silently coaxing Conner to tell him everything.

"Why don't we go outside, where we can talk privately." Dr. Timberi led him onto the back deck and down the stairs. As they walked down the grassy slope, a few of those baby cherubim/giant firefly things flew around him.

Conner opened his mouth, wanting to get it out—but something held him back. If he told Dr. Timberi all that had happened, he might get arrested for being a Darkhand. Even if that didn't happen, people would think about him differently. He hated the thought of watching Dr. Timberi's eyes reflect disappointment and disgust.

But he needed help. He couldn't keep on like this. Every instinct urged him to talk. To finally get this burden lifted.

But once he told, he couldn't take it back.

"Conner, most people talk far too much about themselves and their feelings. Generally speaking, a bit more restraint would serve us well. However, talking about traumatic experiences can be beneficial. When a problem lives unspoken in your mind, it grows larger and larger. Talking about a problem seems to limit and confine it, imposing boundaries. Beyond that, our worst fears are sometimes based on incorrect, or at least incomplete, understandings. A friend can point out faulty assumptions, helping us see more clearly."

Conner looked at Dr. Timberi, hesitating on the edge of the cliff. Should he jump? "Conner, tell me what is troubling you," Dr. Timberi said in a gentle voice.

Conner took a deep breath. No more punting. Time for a Hail Mary pass. Hopefully, Dr. Timberi wouldn't think badly about him. Or turn him in for being a Darkhand.

"Well," he started, "when I got kidnapped, the Blacks put a collar on me. I can't remember what they called it, but somehow it stopped me from using the Light."

"A refraction collar," Dr. Timberi said. "It keeps the wearer from using the Light."

Conner shuddered as he remembered the pain the collar caused. "Lady Nightwing's assistant, Mr. Stanley, came to pick me up from the Blacks. He took me through the Otherwhere, but some cherubim attacked him and he passed out. While he was unconscious, they asked me if I wanted to keep going to the Darkhands' base or go home. They said if I went to the base I could maybe help bring it down or something."

"What?" Dr. Timberi gasped. "Conner, I did not know this!"

Conner nodded. "I really wanted to go home. A lot. But I started thinking about my family—and Melanie—and I didn't want to be a coward. So I said I'd go. The cherubim said I'd need extra help, so they changed the collar so it would enhance the Light instead of blocking it."

Dr. Timberi's eyes grew very wide. "Remarkable," he murmured. "Go on."

"When I got there, they took me into Lady Nightwing's lab and she tried to get me to join them. I told her no, and I used the Light to blow up her lab and ruin some experiments. With the cherubim's collar, it was easy. But Lady Nightwing got really mad and took me to the Shadowbox."

Conner's throat tightened as it all rushed back to him. The claustrophobia. The overwhelming, soul-crushing Darkness. The heart-clenching, gut-twisting, raging panic. "Then, I—"

"Conner! Hey, Conner! Wow! This is so cool!"

Conner jerked his head back toward the house. Pilaf?

Pilaf stood on the deck, waving at Conner with both hands, staring at everything with wide, blinking eyes and a giant grin. Madame Cumberland stood next to him, beaming as always. Pilaf waved at Conner again and ran down the deck steps and across the grass toward him.

"Oh, for the love of Pete!" Dr. Timberi growled. "Conner, we'll need to continue this conversation later."

Conner couldn't believe how glad he was to see Pilaf. Pilaf made him laugh and forget about becoming a Darkhand. Apparently, Pilaf was the only other person under the age of forty who wasn't mad at Conner. For some reason, neither Melanie nor Lexa would even look at him. Of course, they didn't seem to look at each other either.

That might have been for the best, though. He didn't deserve Melanie, and he worried about what he'd done. Or would do. It was getting harder to keep the past and future straight in his mind.

CHAPTER 31

BLACK FIRE

LEXA COULDN'T HAVE BEEN HAPPIER TO SEE Pilaf. He was always nice and sweet and wouldn't leave her out the way Conner and Melanie had.

Pilaf explained that after he had cancelled out Light and Dark at the mall, Dr. Timberi had become worried that the Darkhands might try kidnapping him, so Madame Cumberland had talked to his mom and brought him to Mockingbird Cottage. They hoped the Magisterium would send someone to test him, but so far, they said they didn't have time to send anyone. So, for now, Pilaf would just hang out.

When Dr. Timberi got them together outside again, Lexa noticed that Melanie didn't sit next to Conner. She hadn't sat by him at breakfast, either. Hmmm. Interesting. In fact, she didn't even look at him—just kept her eyes straight ahead and focused on Dr. Timberi. Lexa looked over at Conner, whose flushed face and tense jaw shouted with frustration.

Hmmmm. What had happened? A fight? Oh honestly! Had she seriously missed their first fight?

Lexa started to think a message, asking Melanie for details, but paused. After what she'd seen in her vision, a fight might be the best thing.

She wondered again if she should talk to Dr. Timberi or at least warn Melanie. But what would they do to her brother? Bad future aside, he was still her brother, and she didn't want him thrown into some Magi prison.

Dr. Timberi tried to teach them to phase, which meant turning invisible. But no one did very well. Melanie did the very best: she got both arms to disappear. Lexa only managed to make her nose and left knee blink out for a minute, but at least she did something. Conner didn't even get his gateway open.

After a frustrating hour, Dr. Timberi gave up and hit them all with The Stare. "Something is clearly wrong today. The tension among you three is thick enough to choke on. However, I know enough about adolescents to know that you'll die many painful deaths before you'll discuss feelings you don't wish to share. So I won't waste my time asking you what's wrong." He sighed. "Perhaps some combat training will burn off some of the tension you obviously feel and release a little steam." No one said anything, although Lexa thought Conner did seem to perk up just a little. "Now, in combat, there are some basic techniques, tactics, and fundamental skills that everyone learns. However, each Magus develops his or her own particular combat style—yes, Pilaf?"

Pilaf, with a raised hand, bounced up and down like hail on a trampoline.

"Sorry to interrupt, but there's a lot I don't understand yet, and if you go on I'll probably just get more confused."

Dr. Timberi smiled. "Do you have specific questions, Pilaf?"

"Yes, sir. When you fight sometimes you just shoot a beam of Light—"

"That is the most basic attack," Dr. Timberi said. "It requires less energy but also has less intensity."

"And sometimes you make stuff out of Light, like an animal or weapon, and you use that instead."

"Attack Illuminations," Melanie muttered. "More powerful and concentrated than just plain Light but harder to keep going."

Lexa sighed. Of course, Melanie had to show how much she knew.

"And what about the sigils?" Pilaf squinted. "Sometimes you use them for messages, but I think I saw some being used in the fight."

Dr. Timberi smiled. "Very observant, Pilaf. A sigil is a piece of your soul. It can be a potent weapon, hitting your enemy with all the power of your spirit. Sigils also do what you want with no instruction. But they can be captured and damaged. A few months ago, Lexa's sigil went looking for Conner. It flew into something called a sigil trap, which yanked her body out of this Sanctuary, pulled it through the Otherwhere, and forcibly reunited her with the sigil that had been captured. Sigils can be tortured or even killed, which can cause great pain and death to the person.

"In combat, a sigil is like a sword. Powerful, even deadly in close quarters, but they also leave you vulnerable.

Attack Illuminations are more like bullets shot from a gun—potentially lethal, but out of your control once fired."

Pilaf nodded. "Okay, thanks for explaining that. One more question. If you shoot a Darkhand, does it kill them?"

"Not always. Again, think of a bullet. Unless a bullet hits a vital area, it will wound but not kill. A Darkhand's reaction to Light will depend on a myriad of variables: how powerful the Light is, how directly you hit the Darkhand, and how much Darkness is inside of that person. Normally you knock them unconscious and hopefully weaken their connection to the Darkness. But, yes, sometimes you will end up killing your adversary. That is something we do not take lightly. We only fight when the alternative is unacceptable, when we must protect our own lives or those of others. Magi never start fights, but they always finish them. Darkhands will fight to the death and show no mercy, so never allow yourself to be in a situation where you need it." The way he said that gave Lexa shivers.

Dr. Timberi continued. "Moving on now. One can also animate objects for use as weapons. We call this Tactical Telemanipulation." He flicked his baton and a cardboard figure of a person in a black hood appeared down in the yard. Another wave of his baton sent chairs and benches from all over the yard smashing into the poor, cardboard target. "Tactical Telemanipulation. A useful technique and one that does not require a tremendous amount of energy. But unless you score a direct hit, it is not very powerful."

Pilaf raised his hand again.

"Yes, Pilaf?"

"Conner told me about when they fought the Stalker. They basically filled pizzas with Light and then launched them at a high velocity over and over. The pizza didn't hurt him, but they became a delivery mechanism for the Light. Is that Tactical Telemanipulation?"

Dr. Timberi's eyes sparkled. "Excellent question, Pilaf! That is called Infusion, which occurs when an inanimate object is filled with Light, almost like a water balloon carries water. A more advanced form of Tactical Telemanipulation, Infusion is a more powerful attack and therefore requires more energy to execute."

"So is that the most powerful method of combat?" Pilaf didn't raise his hand. He just blinked out one question after another.

"The most deadly form of battle is a sigil duel. In this combat, a Magus faces off with a Darkhand, fighting directly through their sigil and phantumbra. It is hand-to-hand combat with the ability to destroy both soul and body. Does that bring you up to speed, Pilaf?"

"Yes, sir." Pilaf nodded. "Thanks."

"If you are interested, Pilaf, there is a collection of important works about Lightcraft up in the garret. Lexa can show you, if you like. Most of our combat techniques come from a fascinating book called *War with Light*, by the ancient Chinese Magus Chang Yi-Sen."

Lexa hoped Pilaf had stopped asking questions because Dr. Timberi did have a tendency to ramble a bit anyway, even without questions.

"In combat, the Darkhands often attempt an ambush and will fire at you from hiding places. The basic tactic to counter this is something we call grapeshot. In addition to allowing you to assess their strength, it removes their momentum."

Dr. Timberi pointed his baton in the air, and a cantaloupe-sized ball of gold Light shot out, arcing over the fruit trees before exploding in mid-air, sending hundreds of tadpole-sized Lights streaming down.

"Cool!" Pilaf yelled.

"That attack will not seriously harm a Darkhand, but it will flush them into the open. Incidentally, how could I make the attack more powerful?"

Pilaf blinked. "Instead of just having Light fall down, make them into attack Illuminations? Maybe snakes or something?"

"Very good, Pilaf!" Dr. Timberi pushed his baton in the air and the same thing happened—except this time, the cantaloupe-ball exploded into gold snakes dive-bombing the ground. "Since the image you choose shapes the impact and potency of the Light, it will be more serious for the Darkhand who gets hit. It also demanded far more energy from me."

Panting a little, Dr. Timberi sat down in a chair. "You all take a turn now." He waved his baton and three cardboard Darkhands appeared. "Shoot a large mass of Light up in the air at an angle. When it gets above your target area, visualize it breaking into smaller pieces."

Lexa and the others all got to their feet as Pilaf raised his hand again.

"Yes, Pilaf?"

"Sorry to interrupt again. All the grown-up Magi have things to shoot with—like your conductor's stick and Mrs.

Davis's paintbrush. How come the kids have to use their hands?" Lexa had wondered that herself.

"Another perceptive question. We call those objects cynosures, and they are given upon taking the oath that makes one an official Magus. A cynosure enhances one's existing skills and will focus power; it does not create those skills or generate that power. Thus, new Adepts learn without them. Now, please point your arms up at a forty-five-degree angle." He pulled his whistle out. "On my signal. One, two, three." He blew the whistle and a brass band played.

Lexa raised her arm, but nothing happened. She focused harder and got the same results—nothing at all. Tensing every muscle in her body, she tried again.

"Lexa, you are far too tense. You had this problem before with Translocation, I recall. Relax. Connect to your gateway, and allow the light to come."

Lexa closed her eyes and took a few deep breaths. Her gateway had been saying lines from her last play, but she thought she'd try something different today. She recited some of Maria's lines from *The Sound of Music*. After a few words, her arm jerked, spewing out a watermelon-sized glob of lopsided yellow Light, which hovered in the air before smashing on the ground like a rotten water balloon. Pilaf cheered for her, jumping up and down and clapping his hands.

"Hmmm." Dr. Timberi stroked his chin. She thought he might be hiding a smile. "Keep trying, Lexa. Now, Melanie, are the symbols stuck on the whiteboard again?"

Lexa didn't hear Melanie's response, but she didn't see either Conner or Melanie shooting anything. She felt just a bit smug that she could do it (well, sort of), and Conner and Melanie couldn't. Who was left out now?

With a few more volleys, Lexa managed to shape her rotten watermelon into something more like an obese volleyball. She also got it to sort of arc through the air before splatting. Getting the blob to a certain size, making it fly just right, and then having it break up—*waaaayyyyy* more complicated than it looked.

Angry mutters from Conner distracted her. His face burned red, and frustration had carved deep, frowning lines everywhere. He stabbed and chopped the air with his arm, but nothing happened. He did it again and still nothing happened.

Once more. Nothing. He clenched his right fist and hit the palm of his left hand hard enough that Lexa winced.

He looked about as mad as he had when he'd torn Geoffrey Anderson's locker door off a few months earlier. His building rage reminded Lexa of her vision last night right before he'd—

Conner shoved his hands forward into the air, and Lexa choked as thick, black flames shot out of Conner's fingers, blasting into the ground, consuming the Darkhand figures, and leaving a smoking crater.

WHAT LEXA SAW

As SULFUR CHOKED THE AIR, LEXA STARED at Melanie, forgetting their feud.

First, her vision, then Conner's angry face. And now stinky black fire? The only people who used that were—

"Conner, wait!" Dr. Timberi yelled as Conner ran down the steps, blurring into a blazing red comet and disappearing around the house.

Dr. Timberi sighed. "Never a dull moment with you three."

Pilaf opened his mouth, and Dr. Timberi added, "Sorry, Pilaf. You four." He held up his hand for silence and listened. "I have not heard the sound of a comet leaving the Sanctuary, so he must still be on the grounds. Excuse me, please. I think I had better go find him."

Dr. Timberi limped down the steps, walking around the corner house.

Pilaf looked at Melanie, then Lexa. "I'm guessing that's not good?"

"No, Pilaf, it's not good," Melanie said through shaking lips. "It means Conner's becoming a Darkhand." Sobs cut off her words.

"Conner?" Pilaf laughed and only stopped when he seemed to realize neither Lexa nor Melanie had laughed. He looked back and forth from each of them, blinking with a baffled expression. "Wait a minute. I know I miss social cues and don't usually recognize sarcasm and irony. But I really don't think you're joking."

"We're not," Lexa said.

"Conner?" Pilaf blinked so fast Lexa thought he might lose some eyelashes. "Seriously?"

"Yes, Pilaf. Seriously," Lexa said. The words felt heavy in her mouth. "It started over spring break. The Darkhands kidnapped him, and something happened while he was there. He hasn't been the same since."

"Well, I probably wouldn't be myself either," Pilaf said. "It could be post-traumatic stress disorder."

"No. It's more than that," Melanie said through her tears. "He hears shadows. And now he shoots black fire, which is what Darkhands do. And he wouldn't talk about what happened to him when he was captured."

Lexa couldn't bring herself to mention the vision she'd had, of what Conner had done, or would do, to Melanie. But it all fit. The heaviness got worse, almost crushing the air from her lungs.

Her brother was becoming a Darkhand.

Lexa felt a keen, piercing sadness much worse than if he had died. In fact, when he'd been kidnapped a few months ago, she'd been devastated, knowing he could die. She'd even cried—a rare action for her. But this felt way, way worse. Losing your brother to death was tragic. But losing him to evil and Darkness, knowing he would become a monster—

"Wait a minute." Pilaf's blinking approached light speed. "How do you know Conner hears shadows?"

"Because I was with him when he got attacked," Melanie sobbed. "I heard them."

Pilaf tilted his head. "But that means you heard them too. And you're not a Darkhand."

Lexa grabbed at the faint thread of hope Pilaf had thrown before tidal waves of doubt washed it away. Her vision proved something a lot worse about Conner than talking to shadows, although that did sound pretty bad.

"It's not just that." Melanie managed to stop the tears and speak. "I didn't want to say anything at first. But I think it's important now." Melanie walked into the house and came back a few minutes later with a piece of paper, which she handed to Lexa.

As Lexa read Lady Nightwing's words, she struggled with an overpowering urge to tear the letter up into pieces and shout that they were lies. She didn't want to believe it. A loud theeling told her it couldn't be true.

Except her vision had been so clear and she'd learned to trust her visions. And what she'd seen fit perfectly with this letter. Visions trumped theelings—seeing was believing.

Pilaf read the letter and flushed purplish-red. He threw it down on the ground and stamped his skinny, white chicken leg. "I don't believe it! Conner would never beg to be made a Darkhand. He always stands up for what's right, even if he has to fight people."

Lexa considered that for a minute. Pilaf had a point.

"And as far as hurting Melanie, I don't believe that either. Didn't he get kidnapped because he was trying to save your little sister? What's her name? Madi? Have you ever seen Conner hurt anyone, except when he was protecting someone weaker? This whole Kindling thing started when Conner got mad because Geoffrey was bullying me and he wanted to stop it. This letter sounds pretty sketchy to me. Anyway, why would one of the bad guys want to help you?"

Lexa appreciated Pilaf's loyalty to Conner, and the power in his voice surprised her. And if she hadn't seen the vision, she would have sided with him. But Pilaf needed to know the truth. They all had to accept the truth. Maybe they could still help Conner, but not if they didn't face reality. And they needed to protect Melanie.

"Melanie's right, Pilaf." Lexa could hardly squeeze words through the knot in her throat. "It's true. I saw it in a vision when I touched Conner's head the other night. Conner's going to kill Melanie."

The silence that followed Lexa's declaration was interrupted only when Dr. Timberi limped around the house, puffing with each breath. He didn't sound very good. "I did not see him, but I'm sure he hasn't left the Sanctuary. Perhaps—"

Silver Light flashed in the air, swirling into a rose bush. Madame Cumberland's voice filled the air. "Morgan, Melanie, I think you need to come quickly. Apparently there's been an attack on Madi."

ᛗADI

MELANIE SENSED THE BLOOD DRAINING from her face. She thought she'd cried all her tears earlier, but more of them found their way into her eyes. An attack on Madi? Her almost-second-grade sister?

"Is she all right?" Melanie asked.

"She's safe," Madame Cumberland's sigil replied. "I am going there now."

"I need to go see her," Melanie said.

"Me too!" Lexa shouted.

Dr. Timberi gave a tight, stressed smile. "We will be right there, Mona."

"I'll see you soon," she said as her sigil faded.

"What about Conner?" Pilaf asked.

"I very much fear Conner will have to wait," Dr. Timberi said.

"Maybe I'll stick around and try to find him," Pilaf said.

"Thank you, Pilaf. Please tell Conner not to worry

about what happened. We will return as soon as possible and sort it all out. Melanie, Lexa, please come with me." Dr. Timberi led them down the steps and opened the Shroud. He and Lexa walked in, followed by Melanie. As Melanie entered, a crackling sound behind caught her attention, and she looked over her shoulder.

From this vantage point, she saw Conner sitting on the roof within easy earshot of their conversation on deck. Red Light crackled, and Lady Nightwing's crumpled letter flew from the deck up into his hand.

As he read, his face crumpled like the paper. He looked up at Melanie, deep hurt staining his face.

Their eyes met. Melanie wanted to say something. She wanted to tell him she was sorry, assure him that she didn't believe the letter. But she couldn't. Her conflicting feelings hammered away at her, giving her a colossal headache.

"Melanie, we had better hurry." Dr. Timberi turned the key, and the curtains closed.

While Melanie seesawed between guilt about Conner and icy-hot worry for Madi, it seemed to take far longer than usual to get through the cherubim's inspection and then walk down the endless hall of curtains. When Dr. Timberi finally opened the curtain that led them onto Melanie's front lawn, anxiety propelled Melanie into the house.

Inside, her mom and dad stood over Madi, who lay on the floor, coloring a picture. Madame Cumberland knelt by Madi, talking about the picture she was drawing.

"Madi! Madi! Are you okay?" Melanie ran in and threw her arms around her. Madi seemed surprised.

"Hi, Melanie. I thought you weren't coming home until school started. Hey, did you hear about the shadow wolf I saw today?"

"What happened?" Melanie asked.

"What happened?" Her dad glared at Dr. Timberi. "What happened is that my seven-year-old is getting attacked! It's not enough to rope my seventh-grader into all this dangerous stuff!"

"Frank." Melanie recognized the warning look in her mother's eyes. "We've discussed this." Her dad snorted but closed his mouth. Melanie's mom took a breath, and Melanie could tell she was trying to stay calm. "Today Madi and I went to the mall. While we were there, well, Madi why don't you tell them what happened?"

Madi's eyes lit up. "We were looking for a new swimsuit for me, and right then a big wolf flew through the air. It looked like the dog that Conner made out of Light at Disney World except it was made out of shadows instead. It went past me and then stopped. It turned around and sniffed the air and came up to me. It seemed nice, so I reached out to touch it.

Melanie cringed. That sounded bad.

"What happened when you touched it?" Madame Cumberland asked in her softest voice.

"I saw a movie in my mind. Black fires. But then the wolf ran away from me like I hurt it or something. I felt bad. And then it jumped back into the air and disappeared."

Madame Cumberland and Dr. Timberi stared at each other. Melanie couldn't tell who seemed more bewildered.

"This is all your fault, Timberi!" Her dad jabbed his finger in Dr. Timberi's chest. Melanie remembered when

Dr. Timberi had punched him a few months ago. She hoped that didn't happen again.

Dr. Timberi grabbed the jabbing finger, speaking in the quiet voice his students recognized as being a danger sign. "Do not do that again, Frank." The two men glared at each other, and deep waves of anger flowed between them. Once again, Melanie wondered what her father had against Dr. Timberi.

Madame Cumberland stepped between them. "I don't know for sure what Madi saw, but it sounds like it's connected to these fires. Morgan, why don't we go discuss this?"

Dr. Timberi looked at Madame Cumberland. *Don't worry, Mona. I will not punch that loud-mouthed, bloviating fool in the face again.* He looked at Melanie and winced. *Forgive me, Melanie. I shouldn't have said that.*

"I think we'd best get back to the Sanctuary," Dr. Timberi said out loud. "But the fact that Madi saw a shadow-creature tonight as well as Conner's sigil back at Disney World, suggests to me that we need to get someone out to test her. Perhaps you can contact Notzange?"

Madame Cumberland nodded, and Dr. Timberi looked at Melanie and Lexa. "Let's be on our way. Now that we know Madi is fine, we should get back to Conner."

Melanie gave her parents each a hug, two to Madi, and then followed Dr. Timberi back into the Otherwhere.

·CHAPTER 34·

PAVLOV'S DOGS

ONCE THEY WERE INSIDE THE OTHERWHERE, Melanie looked at Dr. Timberi. "Has Madi Kindled?"

"No, Melanie. But, like Pilaf, she can apparently see Light and Dark."

"Is that because I'm a Magus?" Melanie asked. "Did it rub off on her?"

"Perhaps," Dr. Timberi said. "But generally this kind of thing happens if there is a family history of Kindling, not merely an isolated case."

In spite of the day's stress, Melanie laughed at that thought. "Well, I'm pretty sure we don't have a history of Magi in our family. Not with the way my dad's reacted to all this."

Dr. Timberi didn't seem to be listening. He frowned and tapped the tips of his fingers together. "What Madi saw when she touched that wolf suggests a clear a link between the phantumbra and the fires."

As soon as Dr. Timberi said "fires," Lexa jumped up and down. "Oh! Oh! I totally forgot my dreams. I mean, I'd have them and then forget in the morning. Anyways, I've had these dreams about shadow-wolves chasing the kids that got kidnapped, and the dream always ended in black flames."

In Melanie's head, the symbols on the whiteboard jumped and buzzed, almost leaping off. She jumped too, as everything became clear. "Pavlov's dogs!" she yelled.

"What and who?" Lexa asked.

Melanie forced herself to slow down and explain. "A scientist named Pavlov rang a bell before he fed his dogs. Eventually, he conditioned his dogs to drool every time they heard the bell."

"Gross!" Lexa squealed. "What does this have to do with dog spit?"

"Pavlov established that one could condition animals to respond in specific ways to certain stimuli," Dr. Timberi said. "Go on Melanie."

"What if the shadows are messages, not attacks? Signals. Like Pavlov's dogs. The people who get them—probably those kids who got kidnapped—are being conditioned to do certain things. Like start fires."

Dr. Timberi nodded. "So Lady Nightwing is controlling her victims remotely. That explains why this happens at night. She sends phantumbras to transmit messages when they're asleep."

"So is this like downloading a computer virus, but into the kids?" Lexa asked.

"Exactly," Dr. Timberi's skin had become gray-green. "She may have been doing this every night, perhaps multiple times. Who knows how far along this process is?"

"Wait," Lexa said. "If they do this at night, why did Madi bump into a phantumbra in broad daylight at the mall?" Lexa asked.

Dr. Timberi frowned for a moment. Then his eyes flew wide open. "Because I recently had the Adumbrators put detection nets up around their houses. The phantumbras can no longer get through."

Lexa jumped up and down again. "Remember during the fight after the movie, I saw Taylor in a uniform, like she worked somewhere in the mall?"

Melanie nodded. "That makes sense. Because the detection nets were up, Lady Nightwing sent the phantumbras somewhere else where they would find those kids. So that one was meant to find Taylor at the mall. But why would it come up to Madi?"

Dr. Timberi shrugged. "I do not know. Madi clearly sees things most people don't. I wonder if she might radiate some kind of awareness of Light and Dark that momentarily confused the phantumbra. When she touched it, perhaps it sensed she was not the right target and fled."

"But how are they setting the fires?" Lexa tugged at her ponytail. "I thought I remember someone saying that nothing showed up on the security cameras or anything."

"Autonomic!" Melanie shouted as the answer appeared on her whiteboard. "The fires were autonomic, remote autonomic responses. Lady Nightwing is having them do it remotely, maybe even in their sleep. That's why no cameras ever caught it."

"Brilliant," Dr. Timberi said. "Evil, despicable, criminal, and cruel. But brilliant. However, there is some good news. If those children learned how to use Darkness unconsciously, we ought to be able to neutralize the process by the same means. Sending sigils while they sleep will hopefully heal and stabilize them. I'll have the Magisterium get on that."

"What's the point of the fires?" Lexa asked.

"I do not know," Dr. Timberi said. "I assume the fires must be tests for something bigger."

Melanie looked at Dr. Timberi. "Aren't these phantumbras the same things that attacked Conner at Dauphin Island?"

"Most likely."

Melanie frowned. "What if that wasn't an attack? What if they were sending messages to download into him? Conner was kidnapped too, after all."

"But he's only had one phantumbra," Lexa said. "It seems like Taylor and the others have had a bunch."

A new surge of anxiety swept through Melanie. "Oh no. We've been in the Sanctuary. They can't go there." An even worse thought came now. Guilt and fear competed to see which could pummel her the hardest. "Plus, my Light was shielding him at Dauphin Island." She paused, not wanting to go into detail. "I don't think it is anymore."

Lexa looked panicked. "So that means there might be a whole bunch of phantumbras just floating around waiting to hit Conner as soon as he steps out of the Sanctuary?" Lexa stared at Dr. Timberi. "Are you sure he didn't leave the Sanctuary earlier?"

Dr. Timberi started to run through the Otherwhere. "Yes, but who knows what might have happened since then. We need to get back to Conner immediately."

When they arrived at Mockingbird Cottage, Pilaf ran out to meet them, his normal pale face faded a few shades paler. "He streamed away just after you all went into the Otherwhere," Pilaf said. "But first he wrote this note." Pilaf handed Lady Nightwing's letter to Dr. Timberi. They all took turns reading what Conner had written on the back.

> *Hey Everyone,*
> *Well, it should be pretty obvious that I'm becoming a Darkhand. I don't want to hurt anyone, so I'm going to go far away. Tell everybody hi and please remember the good stuff about me. Lexa, tell mom and dad I'll write to them when I can.*
> *Sincerely,*
> *Conner*

Dr. Timberi fired off a sigil. "I sent Conner an urgent message warning him about the phantumbras. I hope we are not too late. We must find him—but to do that, I need to understand all that is happening. I have a feeling you all know something I do not. It would be helpful to have all of the information." He pointed at Lady Nightwing's letter.

Melanie and Lexa told Dr. Timberi everything they knew. His voice grew very soft. "It would have been helpful to know all of this much sooner." He threw Lady Nightwing's letter in the air. As it fell, he slashed the air with his hand. Furious gold Light erupted around the paper, consuming it in seconds.

As the ashes floated to the floor, Melanie saw fire burning in his eyes.

"Tracking Magi is difficult. Unless he does sustained Lightcraft in the same location, it will be almost impossible to find Conner. Lexa, our only real chance is for you to use your gifts as a Seer. Try to see Conner, or anything else that might give us insight about his location."

"I'll try." Uncertainty tainted Lexa's voice. "But I've never done anything on purpose before. It just comes sometimes."

"Try, Lexa." Dr. Timberi gave her The Stare. "Your brother's life—and soul—may be at stake. If those phantumbras get him first . . ." His voice trailed off, chilling Melanie, whose insides felt like the ashen remains of Lady Nightwing's letter.

Lexa closed her eyes, squinting them tightly shut. Beams of yellow Light radiated out from her head in every direction, stretching out like a halo made of hundreds of antennae.

After a few minutes Lexa's eyes jerked open.

"Lexa, did you see Conner?" Dr. Timberi asked.

Her voice shook. "Yes. At the school."

"Good!" Dr. Timberi said. "The school is warded, so the phantumbras should not be able to get to him. If he went straight there—"

Lexa shook her head. She swallowed, and her voice sounded small. "He's trying to burn it down. With black fire."

"Quickly, then." Dr. Timberi's mouth pressed into a grim line. "I'd like to handle this without involving anyone else."

As Dr. Timberi rushed them through the Otherwhere, Melanie wondered if the cherubim would be mad if she threw up. The boiling nausea that came when she thought of Conner becoming a Darkhand grew worse as she considered the whole sorry mess.

What would Dr. Timberi do? Could he stop Conner? Would Conner fight? What if they had to stop him by force? Those thoughts churned the nausea even more.

When they came through the Shroud, they stood outside the school, which was encased by a bubble of Light.

"Wow! What's that big bubble?" Pilaf asked.

"The school is warded," Dr. Timberi said. "It is complicated, but basically, you cannot enter the school directly through the Otherwhere." He sent a sigil through the bubble, and a small opening appeared. "Magi can stream in through the shield, but this prevents the Darkhands from sneaking in through the Otherwhere. Unless, of course, they mount a full-out attack the way they did during the first battle Conner, Lexa, and Melanie witnessed a few months ago."

He led them through the opening, and they followed the sounds of sharp whistles and hisses around a corner. Conner stood next to the theater. Just outside the shield, blasts of black fire pummeled the shield, shot by an invisible attacker.

Conner held a red Illuminated fire hose, dousing the black flames with red Light from the hose, extinguishing the fire and protecting the shield. He hadn't seen them yet.

As Melanie tried to understand why Conner would

be fighting against Darkness, Dr. Timberi glared at Lexa, who winced and looked sheepish.

"Sorry," she squeaked. "My vision showed it from the outside looking in. It looked like Conner was shooting the fire, not putting it out."

Dr. Timberi's expression relaxed. "It's an easy mistake, Lexa. You are not the first Seer to miss an important nuance because of perspective. I need to speak with Conner. Perhaps the three of you could go wait across the street? In a rather unusual turn of events, it appears the monkey bars are free."

Feeling a little better but confused, Melanie followed Lexa and Pilaf through the shield and across the street to the park.

CONFESSION

As more black fire appeared, Conner smothered it with another blast of red Light. It felt good, sort of like a video game where you could randomly blow up aliens or something.

Another pop of black fire erupted, but before he could do anything, a fountain of gold Light rushed past him, extinguishing the flames.

Don't leave, Dr. Timberi said as Conner tensed, ready to stream away. *I know about everything—the note, the shadows. Listen to me, Conner. You are not a Darkhand.*

Conner turned to face him. "I shot black fire."

Dr. Timberi shrugged. "That is certainly unusual, but it doesn't make you a Darkhand. Conner, before we continue, let me ask you something urgent. Did you come here directly from the Sanctuary?"

Conner nodded. "Yeah. I didn't know where else to go."

Dr. Timberi sighed. "Good. We think that the

moment you step out of a shielded area, like the school or the Sanctuary, a pack of phantumbras will be waiting to attack you."

More black flames crashed against the shield. "How long have the flames been going on?" Dr. Timberi asked.

"It started a little while after I got here," Conner replied. "I came here after I left the Sanctuary 'cause I didn't really know where else to go. I figured maybe these flames were tied in with the other fires. But I don't see where they're coming from."

"Nor do I. We need to give that some thought later. However, while I appreciate your diligence in fighting the flames, I believe that the shield will protect the school. Please come sit with me." Dr. Timberi pointed to a bench on the courtyard.

Great. The moment he'd been dreading had finally come. Dr. Timberi sat down and fixed Conner with kind but piercing eyes. When he spoke, compassion sandwiched each word.

"Conner, a few months ago, you heroically sacrificed yourself so that a little girl could go home to her family. As a result, the Darkhands did something that continues to hurt you. If you tell me what happened, I can try to help."

Conner dropped his head. No one could help him now. He understood the reality of his future. Everyone did. He studied the dirt below, focusing on each rock and tiny ant. He kicked at the ground, digging a small trench before he looked up. Dr. Timberi didn't seem to be in a hurry. He just sat there with an encouraging smile he must have stolen from Madame Cumberland.

Conner didn't want to talk. On one hand, maybe they'd go easier on him if he confessed. On the other hand, it didn't matter anymore. Nothing really did. Mostly, he wanted the nagging, aching secret to stop gnawing at him.

"Well, where were did we get before?" he asked.

"You said that the cherubim gave you the choice to go to the Darkhand base or go home to safety. You courageously chose to go forward, and they altered the refraction collar so it enhanced Light instead of blocking it. Your resistance at the base made Lady Nightwing angry, and she put you in the Shadowbox."

No use delaying anymore. Conner took a deep breath and let his words spill out. "I wanted to fight her, but she told me that if I didn't obey her, she'd hurt all the kids she'd kidnapped. So I stopped fighting. She chained me inside the Shadowbox and then lowered it into a pool of water. The walls got clear so I could see outside in the water. Shadows swam around and called my name. I tried to ignore them, but then everything changed. I saw the Stalker hurting my family, and it seemed so real. I panicked and sent a sigil to stop him, but the shadows caught my sigil. They turned it dark, and I started to feel really weird inside.

"Then I sort of merged with the Stalker. It was his body, but somehow, I was inside. Like, I was him, but still me. Like in a dream. I know it doesn't make sense, but it seemed totally real.

"While we were combined like that, the scene changed, back to the night of the storm when the Stalker first came. All the dogs in the neighborhood were barking, and it annoyed me. I could sense their spirits. They glowed inside of them like little candles. The dogs made me mad, so I pinched their lights out. It was easy."

Conner's voice dried to a hoarse croak. He looked away from Dr. Timberi. "I felt their fear as they died. And I liked it. It made me feel excited." Saying that out loud, putting it into words, made him sick.

"A little dog was by my feet, looking up at me, almost like it was smiling. It was Melanie's dog, Cuddles. I pinched her light inside, but only a little. Cuddles started shaking and whining. I pinched just hard enough to make her shake, and then I let go. As soon as she could breathe, I'd do it again. It was funny to see her twitch."

The shame inside nearly suffocated Conner. He hated himself more than he could say.

"Melanie came over and started crying about Cuddles. She begged me to stop, but that made me want to do it even more. I forced her to watch while I finished Cuddles off. Slowly." Stinging, salty tears burned his eyes. "And I laughed."

He forced himself to keep going, to squeeze the rest of the truth out. "Melanie cried and I laughed and made fun of her. All of a sudden, I could see inside of her heart, and I understood her insecurities and deepest, worst fears. I knew what to say to really devastate her and make her feel like she was worse than nothing." Conner groaned, wishing he could burn the words he'd said out of his memory.

"I said bad things to her. Really bad. I don't mean just names or curse words. I figured out how to make her feel ugly and worthless and stupid, like no one had ever loved her or ever would. I made her hate herself. I killed her spirit just like I murdered her dog."

The words rolled out now, revealing how terrible he was. Conner prayed that he could just stop existing.

"The more I hurt her, the meaner I got. She cried and I just laughed. I enjoyed it. Finally, she grabbed my hands and begged me to stop." Conner's voice trailed off to a whisper. "I let her beg—and then—" He started to sob now. But not even an ocean of tears would wash away the evil awfulness of what he did next.

"I slapped her hard enough to turn her head. She grabbed my hands, but I shoved her down. Her head hit the floor and she stopped moving." Conner shuddered underneath his sobs, remembering the sound. "I killed her. I broke her heart and spirit, and then I killed her body."

Conner collapsed, shaking and sobbing, hating himself and what he'd become. Hating what he would do in the future. Lady Nightwing was right. He'd become a Darkhand. And now, his future was clear.

Strong fingers gripped his shoulder. "Conner, look at me," Dr. Timberi commanded.

Conner looked up, bracing himself for anger, shock, and disgust.

To his surprise, Conner saw a smiling, tear-stained face.

"Conner . . ." Dr. Timberi's voice cracked with emotion. "You are an exceptional young man, a son of whom any father would be so proud."

Confusion slapped him senseless, and it took a long time before Conner managed to say, "What?"

"Conner, listen to me. You need to understand something about the Shadowbox—"

Dr. Timberi? Melanie's voice cut in, throwing gallons

of lemon juice into Conner's raw spirit. *I'm really sorry to interrupt, but remember that girl, Taylor? She's over here at the park. She seems a little, um, strange. Lexa thinks it's important.*

Dr. Timberi sighed. "Always an interruption." *Melanie, please engage Taylor in conversation, and I'll come over as soon as I can.*

What do we say? Melanie asked.

Tell her you've come to help her make the shadows stop. Ask her if she'll please speak with me.

What if she says no? Melanie asked.

Then we'll figure something out. This is an improvisational operation. Keep your thoughts open, and I'll help you as best I can.

TAYLOR

LEXA LED MELANIE AND PILAF UP TO TAYLOR, who sat on a bench underneath a tree.

"Excuse me, um, Taylor?" She dressed her words in her politest voice.

Taylor jumped and blinked, looking around as if she were completely confused.

"Are you okay?" Lexa asked. Taylor just stared at her.

"I'm Lexa, and this is Melanie."

"And I'm Pilaf."

Taylor turned to Lexa. "You two were there. At that place. At the end, before they let us go. There was a boy with you." Her eyes seemed dull and lifeless.

Lexa nodded. "Yeah, we were. That boy is my brother, Conner. Um, Taylor, can we talk to you?"

Taylor shrugged. "Sure." Lexa sat next to her on the bench, and Melanie and Pilaf dropped on the grass across from them.

Taylor dropped her voice. "I've been wanting to talk

to somebody. My mom sent me to a therapist. They both think I'm crazy. But you were there, right? I'm not imagining it?"

"Yes." Lexa put on her sweetest, most sympathetic voice, trying to imitate Madame Cumberland. "And you're not crazy. We know some people who can help you."

"Doctors?" Taylor seemed unimpressed.

"Not exactly. More like—uh . . ."

Pilaf raised his hand. "If the people that kidnapped you are like the Sith, then the people we know are like the Jedi."

Lexa stifled a laugh. Nerdy, but accurate.

Taylor seemed interested. "You mean, they do magic stuff, but they're good?"

"Exactly," Lexa said.

Wow, Melanie said. *Think how hard it would be to Kindle and get kidnapped by the Darkhands, but not have anyone to talk to, no one to explain anything or help you through it.*

That thought hammered Lexa with great force. The loneliness of Taylor's situation tugged at her heart.

Melanie leaned forward. "Taylor, have you had any messages or anything? Maybe in your dreams or—"

Taylor jumped up and snarled. Rage transformed her face as she raised her hands and shot black fire at Melanie, who seemed too shocked to move as the flames rushed at her.

"Melanie!" Pilaf shoved her away from the fire's path. But the momentum of his shove took him into the incoming flames, which pounded into his chest. Pilaf gasped and crumpled to the ground.

"Pilaf!" Melanie screamed, crawling over to him. She threw up a shield around the two of them while she tried to revive him, but Lexa knew it wouldn't last long.

Dr. Timberi! she yelled.

Coming!

Lexa jumped up, putting herself between Taylor and Melanie, who huddled over Pilaf.

Taylor had dropped her hands and seemed almost asleep, as if she were in a trance. Lexa spoke in a calm voice, hoping to soothe her. "Taylor, it's okay. I know that they did bad stuff to you. But we can help you. These dreams—"

Taylor growled again and shot black fire at Lexa, who jumped in the air, streamed above Taylor's head, and landed behind her.

Don't say "dream," Melanie thought. *She's probably conditioned to freak out when people mention dreams.*

Taylor spun around to face Lexa, and while her back was turned, Melanie waved her fingers. A rock next to the bench flashed with pink Light and vanished, reappearing in the air above Taylor's head.

"Sorry, Taylor," Lexa said. "I know this really isn't your fault."

Melanie snapped, and the rock dropped, knocking Taylor out.

Nice, Mel!

Thanks.

Pilaf sat up, shaking his head and rubbing his chest. "Ouch."

Pilaf! Lexa ran over and hugged him. *You're alive! A hit like that almost killed Dr. Timberi a few months ago.*

"I'm fine." Pilaf sat up. "Just knocked the wind out of me. And I feel a little nauseous."

Get down! Dr. Timberi's thoughts rang into their heads. *Stay hidden!*

Lexa, Melanie, and Pilaf dropped down to the ground, hiding behind some shrubbery near the seesaws.

Peeking through the bushes, Lexa watched Dr. Timberi duck behind a car across the street from the park, just outside of the shield around the school. About a hundred yards away, four Darkhands sheltered behind some big landscaping boulders, shooting black fire and clouds of Darkness at him.

Stay hidden, Dr. Timberi said. *I don't know if they've seen you or not. I sent for the others and they should be here—*

He gasped as a bolt of darkness hit his shoulder, and he dropped to the ground.

Dr. Timberi! Lexa yelled.

Go help him, Lexa! Melanie shouted. *Stream over and we'll follow you.*

Lexa nodded and ran, jumping into the Lightstream. As she began to stream, a small breeze gusted, stirring up motion near a tree farther up the street. She saw ragged, black coattails blowing in the wind.

The Stalker was back.

ℓiġht aⲚd Ɖark

THE STALKER! MELANIE JUMPED AT LEXA'S warning and looked around, but before she saw him, Pilaf yanked her down to the ground. She hit the dirt as black fire flew overhead. She'd forgotten about Taylor, now awake and running toward them with a demonic-looking expression. Melanie sent a cloud of pink Illuminated wasps at Taylor, and then she and Pilaf ran toward the street again, Pilaf clutching his stomach.

As they ran, the Stalker stepped out and shot some kind of strange, pale fire. Right then, Taylor sped up and lunged for Pilaf. She jumped into the air, and her leap carried her straight into the Stalker's flames. As the weird flames collided with her, she fell down, stunned.

Melanie shot a pink piranha at the Stalker. It hit his hand, and he scowled and vanished.

Up to the curb now, Melanie looked across the street as Conner emerged from the shield around the school, running to help Dr. Timberi.

Melanie and Pilaf yelled at him to go back, but he didn't hear. As Conner left the protection of the shield, a loud static sound screeched in the air. A large wolf made out of shadows appeared, sailing for Conner.

Conner picked it off with red Light and it vanished. But more crackling sounds came, and soon the air seemed to be full of phantumbras. At least a dozen of them now snarled and flew at Conner.

Conner, stream away! Go back to the Sanctuary! Lexa yelled.

Conner ran up the sidewalk, the phantumbras chasing him. Melanie managed to shoot one of the monsters, and Dr. Timberi and Lexa each took one down as well.

Conner began to blur. He'd almost turned into comet form when one of the phantumbras pounced, catching his legs in its jaws. Conner stumbled, and another wolf pounced, followed by another. In spite of the shots of pink, gold, and yellow Light, six of them charged into Conner.

"NOOOOOOOOOOOOOO!" Melanie screamed and ran across the street, arriving at the same time as the others. Darkness and black flames flew all around her, but she didn't care.

The air around them seemed to explode as Madame Cumberland, Mrs. Grant, and Coach Jackson all streamed in, followed by Mrs. Davis, Mr. Miller, and Mr. Duffy.

For a moment, Melanie couldn't see. Flashes of Light and blasts of Darkness filled the air.

Conner pushed himself up on his hands and knees. His eyes had the same clouded look that Taylor's had earlier. He clambered to his feet and lurched around, looking wobbly, almost drunk. He took a step, then stumbled, falling right into the path of a sizzling ball of burning Darkness.

Melanie screamed, and everything seemed to decelerate into slow motion as Conner and the Darkness came closer to each other.

Conner didn't have Pilaf's unique abilities. He would die. Conner Dell would die. And his last memory of Melanie would be reading that note. She'd never be able to explain, apologize, or—

A massive wave of Light flooded out of her soul, rushing toward Conner.

Conner staggered backwards as the black fire slammed into him, but Melanie's pink Light hit him at the same time, and the two opposite forces made him spin.

Conner spun faster and faster, with tendrils of Light and Darkness whirling around him like hundreds of streamers. He began to float, rising higher and higher, becoming the center of a swirling vortex of Light and Dark.

About ten feet in the air, Conner stopped rotating. As he floated spread-eagled, the Light and Dark separated. The Light covered the right side of his body, ending in a giant, glowing ball around his right hand. The Darkness did the same on his left side, sizzling around his left hand.

Dr. Timberi stood up, shouting Conner's name. One of the Darkhands shot a large jet of black flame toward Dr. Timberi. But it jumped out of course, flying into Conner's left hand, followed by another blast of Darkness and another. Each new bit of Darkness the Darkhands shot did exactly the same thing, rushing toward Conner as if he were a magnet attracting metal shavings. Every bit of Darkness floating in the air made its way to Conner, joining the boiling mass in his left hand.

What's happening? What should we do? Lexa asked.

I don't know—but it looks like he's become a focal point for Darkness and Light, Dr. Timberi replied.

Sensing an advantage, the Magi fired at the Darkhands—but their Light did the same thing. Illuminations, sigils, and blasts of Light all flew out of their trajectories, leaping into the glowing cloud of Light in Conner's right hand.

When Conner had absorbed all the Light and Darkness in the air, the shield around the school started to spark and crackle. It flashed and wavered, and then the giant bubble of Light flowed to Conner as well.

Conner shook as Light and Dark pushed against each other, meeting in the middle of his body. Sparks snapped and strange bolts of dark lightning crackled in the air all around him. The Darkhands shouted and shot more Darkness. As Conner absorbed it, the Darkness in him visibly pushed the Light back, advancing toward his right side.

"Fire!" Dr. Timberi yelled, and the Magi all shot as much Light as they could manage. It too jumped into Conner, and for a few seconds the Light seemed to push the Darkness back, gaining a few inches.

I don't know what to do! Dr. Timberi said. *If we stop shooting Light, the Darkness will overtake him completely. But I don't know how much more of this his body can bear. I hope we're saving his soul, but I fear we'll kill him in the process.*

Conner twitched and jerked, sending flashes and splatters of Light and Dark everywhere. Each convulsion got worse, and the random blobs of Light and Dark grew bigger and more violent.

Pilaf, no! Madame Cumberland yelled as Pilaf ran toward Conner. Melanie watched in horror as Pilaf jumped up and grabbed Conner's left shoe. The Darkness around Conner vanished.

At the same moment, an enormous cloud of pink Light, the biggest one yet, rushed out of Melanie and leapt into Conner's chest.

It only lasted for a few seconds, but with Melanie Augmenting Conner's strength and Pilaf absorbing the Darkness, the Light covered Conner.

Pilaf fell to the ground, and Melanie staggered, grabbing Lexa for support. The world around her seemed pale and shaky. And it didn't stop moving.

Conner screamed and shoved his arms to the left, as if pushing back against an invisible wall. An immense, burning, blinding tidal wave of Light flew out of his hand and crashed over the screaming Darkhands. Light flashed, and no more screams came.

Free of both Light and Dark now, Conner dropped, hitting the street, still and motionless.

Melanie's dizziness accelerated as everything around her went crazy. Shouts and yells sounded far away, past the thick gauze that seemed to wrap her thoughts.

She felt so dizzy. So weak.

People ran past her, carrying a body.

A body.

Conner's body.

She opened her mouth to scream, but nothing came out and she fell down.

Strong arms grabbed her, and she saw bright lights, felt them inside her.

And then they were back on the front lawn at Mockingbird Cottage. Shouts and tears. Teachers leaning over Conner, yelling.

She couldn't move. She was too numb. And slow. So slow. And tired. Her brain seemed disconnected from the rest of her body.

Everything got blurry.

A small light appeared in the air above Conner, like a firefly. Another one came, then another. And another. Soon the air above him twinkled with colored lights as if strands of Christmas lights had learned to fly. More lights came. Lights of different colors and sizes—

Her mind struggled to find the word.

Lights poured in from every direction. A few flew past her. As they passed, she felt the gauze unwrapping. Her brain connected again. She felt exhausted. But at least she could think.

Lucents. That was what the Lights were. Baby cherubim.

They swirled around Conner's motionless body.

The Lucents moved in a slow circle at first, speeding up with each circuit. As they accelerated, Conner's body floated a few inches and then several feet off the ground.

His body rose from horizontal to vertical, and the Lucents swirled faster, surrounding Conner in a spinning column of Light that tinted his dark curls almost golden. His hair and clothing floated, bobbing as if he were underwater.

After several spins, Conner opened his eyes, staring straight up into the sky. Melanie wondered what he could see. A look of untainted, untamed joy blazed on his face. He looked like a kid on Christmas morning, mixed with someone who just got an "A" on a hard test, blended with the way you feel on the last day of school. It looked like he had never even known what sadness was.

Fatigue overwhelmed Melanie, and the world went black around her.

LUCENTS

CONNER FELT HIMSELF BEING LOWERED TO the ground like a baby in gentle hands. He looked up at the sky as the last strains of music faded.

Come back, please! he thought.

Next to him, Lexa's mouth moved, but he didn't really hear her words.

He looked at the Lucents, floating away. *Please come back?* He wanted to hear the music and see the colors and, most of all, feel the love and peace and warmth. Had that been heaven?

Lexa continued to talk. Like getting out of bed on a cold day, he forced himself away from the experience and focused on Lexa.

". . . so worried! Ohmygosh, are you okay? I was so worried!"

She engulfed him in a potentially suffocating hug, and he hugged her back.

"I'm fine. Seriously."

When Lexa finally let go, Dr. Timberi put an arm around his shoulder. "Conner, are you all right?"

He nodded. "Yes, sir." He looked around. Where was Melanie? Why didn't he see Melanie?

"Melanie is fine." Madame Cumberland walked out of the house. "She's exhausted. She used a lot of her Light to Augment your strength, probably more than she should have. But she'll be fine with some rest."

"What happened?" Lexa asked.

Conner paused, trying to clear his thoughts. "When I was in the ocean, remember how I said all these little lights saved me? Well, it was those things—"

"Lucents," Dr. Timberi said.

"Yeah. The baby cherubim."

"I don't feel very good," Pilaf croaked. He threw his hands over his mouth and ran into the house.

"Excuse me, everyone," Dr. Timberi said, "Can you please give me a few moments alone with Conner? We really must talk."

Everyone walked into the house, leaving Dr. Timberi and Conner alone on the front porch. In the silence, Conner became aware of the smell of flowers and the song of frogs and crickets.

"Conner, what just happened with the Lucents is extremely rare. In fact, everyone assumed that only happened in myths and legends. Did they speak to you?"

"Well, mostly I just felt things. Love and peace and Light. I heard singing—just like when I almost died. I think the main reason they came was to sort of repair me. My soul got pretty torn up in the Shadowbox, and they healed it." He looked up as a pair of bats flapped through the air above them.

"But they did try to tell me something. It's hard to say for sure because they don't speak in a language like we do. You know how the big cherubim speak thoughts in your head? Well, the babies communicate through images, not words."

"What were the images you saw?"

"Gates and doors and bridges. And flashes of Light and Dark over and over."

"Fascinating. Absolutely fascinating." Dr. Timberi nodded. "Now, to finish our earlier conversation. Do you understand what a Shadowbox does?"

"Turns you into a Darkhand?"

Dr. Timberi snorted. "A Shadowbox twists the truth of your soul, Conner. Imagine a fun house mirror that distorts your appearance. It makes tall, skinny people look short and fat. Or vice versa. It is not accurate. In fact, the Shadowbox gives you a reversed view of yourself, forcing you to watch yourself acting in a way completely contrary to your character. That is the torture of it. You see yourself doing things you find particularly revolting, believing them to be real. It is a lie, not a prophecy. It does not foretell the future in any way."

"It doesn't?"

"Not at all." Dr. Timberi pounded his cane for emphasis. "Now, consider what you saw. You were cruel to helpless animals and then you treated a young woman you love in a brutal, abusive way." Dr. Timberi's voice cracked. "In other words, Conner, your greatest fear is being cruel to those weaker than you, and you love and respect Melanie so much that causing her harm is the most terrible crime you can imagine. Your worst nightmares have revealed a singularly pure and gentle heart, and I could not be prouder of you."

In his mind, Conner repeated Dr. Timberi's words over and over. He must have repeated them a hundred times before he could even dare to wonder if it could be true. A tiny flicker of hope sparked inside the dark ashes of his heart.

"What about the black fire I shot? Magi don't do that. Plus I've been hearing shadows lately. If I'm not a Darkhand, what does that mean?"

Dr. Timberi shook his head. "I love the way you ask me these questions as if there's a simple answer I memorized from a textbook. Conner, I don't understand all of this—no one does. But let me assure you of something. You are no more a Darkhand than I am. There are some fundamentals in this conflict, laws that cannot be broken. Did you swear any oaths or make any promises?"

"No."

"Did you actually *do* anything—beyond having a traumatic, forced nightmare?"

"No, but—"

"Then how could you possibly be a Darkhand, Conner? What did you do that would have transformed you from a Magus into a Darkhand? Think clearly."

"But Lady Nightwing said—"

Dr. Timberi pounded the ground with his cane as his voice thundered, "Lady Nightwing abused you, Conner! And then, like most abusers, she told you it was your fault. That is an abominable lie commonly told by evil people. You are not a Darkhand. I say that with complete and total certainty. Something did happen to you in the

Shadowbox, Conner. Something we need to study and explore. But I repeat: you are not a Darkhand."

Conner felt like he had emotional whiplash. In the space of a few minutes, everything had flip-flopped one-hundred and eighty degrees. It sounded too good to be true.

"It is easy to believe the worst of yourself, isn't it?" Dr. Timberi said in a much softer voice. "And excruciatingly difficult to believe the best. But try. At least be open to it."

Conner nodded. He could try that. He'd trust Dr. Timberi and let it grow from there.

CHAPTER 39.

CAUSATION AND CORRELATION

MELANIE WOKE UP IN DARKNESS, UNAWARE for a few seconds of where she was.

Disoriented, she walked out of her room. Clinking noises led her to the kitchen, where Sadie heaped an enormous platter with fried chicken. She gave Melanie her shy smile. "You're up now! After sleeping for almost twenty-four hours, you must be famished. I'll have supper ready soon if you want to go out and sit a spell."

Melanie walked onto the deck. The sun bobbed along the top of the trees, flirting with the idea of setting. In the yard below, Pilaf judged a streaming contest between Lexa and Conner.

Watching Conner stream and run, laughing and smiling, tugged at her heart. The way he moved seemed almost poetic to her. How had Dr. Timberi described it? Like an otter swimming? Each movement so full of joy and life— Melanie choked on a sob. She missed him already. To think of Conner becoming a Darkhand, or going crazy—

"He's not a Darkhand, Melanie," Dr. Timberi said from his chair by the horloge.

She jumped, a bit startled. She hadn't noticed him.

"Sir?"

"Conner is not a Darkhand. Not even close." Dr. Timberi frowned. "Of all the evil things Lady Nightwing has done, the sheer cruelty of this episode may be one of her most vicious acts. The letter she sent you was a devilish masterpiece—everything from the Harvard address to the way she blended huge lies with a subtle twisting of the truth. It was brilliant."

"Why would she do that?"

"Perhaps to drive a wedge between two promising Adepts. Perhaps she realized Conner was not receiving her phantumbras and hoped to provoke a crisis that would get him out of the Sanctuary where he'd be more vulnerable. Perhaps she simply wanted to cause pain. Who knows?"

Melanie hesitated. She wanted to believe this. But—

Laughter echoed in the yard below as Conner and Lexa threw balls of Light at Pilaf, who jumped and grabbed them, making them disappear as soon as he made contact.

"You are quiet, Melanie. I suspect you do not entirely believe me but are too polite to say so."

"I want to believe you. I'm just confused. What about Lexa's vision? And the prophecy that Conner saw in the Shadowbox?"

"Let me clarify a few things. Conner ruined some of Lady Nightwing's experiments and she used the Shadowbox to punish him. It was torture, not initiation. She promised him that if he went in without fighting, she would not hurt the other children."

That did sound like the Conner she knew. The Conner who faced down bullies and gave himself up to save a seven-year-old girl.

"Now, the unpleasant truth is that in the Shadowbox, Conner saw himself hurting you in some ugly ways. And Lexa also saw that in her vision. I compared their accounts and they match exactly. However, Seers can have vivid visions of the past as well as the future. Additionally, Lexa seems to be able to touch someone and see things they are feeling deeply. The night Conner had a nightmare, Lexa tried to comfort him, and when she touched him, she saw it too. But it was a vision of the past, not the future. As we talked, Lexa acknowledged that. In fact, when she first read the letter, Lexa's theelings all shouted at her that it could not be true. But she got confused since the vision and theelings seemed to contradict each other."

This all made sense. Melanie had one more worry, though. "Are you sure he's not going crazy? Because you said the Shadowbox can cause madness."

Recognition, then regret, gleamed in Dr. Timberi's eyes. "Oh dear, Melanie. I fear I explained that badly." He paused. "When you asked me about the Shadowbox, I was distracted and distressed. What I said was true, but incomplete. The Shadowbox can cause madness. However, it is immediate, not gradual. If Conner had been driven insane by the experience, he would have emerged in that state already.

"There is one last piece to this puzzle that I did not explain. The Shadowbox gives the victim a view of himself that is completely opposite his true character. It forces him to believe he is doing the things he finds most repellent, most evil."

Understanding dawned on Melanie. "That means he'd never really hurt me."

"It means, my dear Melanie, that Conner would rather die than give you a moment's pain. Physical or emotional. The worst thing he can imagine is hurting you. Conner is neither mad nor evil. And he loves you with all the sweet awkwardness of his seventh-grade heart. That is a great gift, Melanie."

That realization overwhelmed her, filling her with excitement and a soaring joy. It also made her sad, tugging at each strand of her heartstrings. How must Conner have felt when she'd shunned him? When he'd seen that letter?

Tears sloshed into her eyes. She needed to make it up to him somehow.

"I feel really bad," Melanie said, when she could talk again. "I guess I jumped to some conclusions."

"Do not be hard on yourself. The conclusions both you and Lexa made were entirely logical. They simply happened to be wrong. We all do this sometimes, incorrectly seeing a result and reasoning backward. I assumed, for example, that the phantumbras were attacks. The thought that they were messages never entered my mind.

"Chickens and eggs, Melanie. Cause and effect. Causation and correlation. Sherlock Holmes observed that it is a capital mistake to theorize before possessing all the evidence. We never know what we don't know. We often see something without realizing our perspective is wrong."

He paused for a few seconds. "Now, please accept

a bit of advice from someone who has watched dozens and dozens of adolescent relationships pop like bubbles and ruin friendships. I said that Conner loved you, and he does. To the extent a thirteen-year-old can. Teenage romances are notoriously unstable. Protect your friendship with prudence. Be friends. Good friends. Affectionate friends. But leave it at that. If love is real, it will grow along with you until you are both mature enough for a durable relationship that will shelter and feed it."

Melanie nodded. Super embarrassing to hear that from a teacher, but she saw the wisdom of Dr. Timberi's words.

Down in the yard below, more laughter came as Lexa and Conner collided while streaming. Pilaf yelled something about a foul and heaped penalties on Conner, who laughed and streamed away, followed by a small cloud of Lucents.

"I need to talk to him," Melanie said. "But what will I say?"

Dr. Timberi smiled, a bit of sadness mingled in. "I don't know, Melanie. But you will."

"I have a few questions," Melanie said, ready to change the subject from awkward emotions to analysis. "How did he shoot the black fire? And if the Shadowbox usually causes insanity or evil, how did that not happen to Conner? And what happened yesterday with the Light and Dark?"

Dr. Timberi smiled. "I have been pondering those same questions since last night. When Conner chose to go to the Darkhand base—"

"Wait—excuse me. I'm sorry to interrupt. What did you say? He *chose* to do that?"

"Yes, Melanie. The cherubim told him he could be instrumental in destroying the evil there, but he had to go on his own volition. They offered to send him home if he'd prefer. He told me that he wanted to go home. But he thought about his family. And you. He didn't want to face you again, feeling he'd been a coward."

She tried to get her head around that new piece of data. Conner had the chance to go home, but chose to go ahead? Into Darkness and torture and who knew what else? The symbols on the whiteboard spun over and over, but Melanie still struggled to understand.

"When he chose to go forward, the cherubim gave him a necklace that enhanced his ability to use the Light, performing roughly the same function as an Augmentor. I suspect that is important. Another important fact is that during his encounter with the Lucents, Conner felt they were trying to tell him something by interspersing images of bridges and doors with Light and Dark."

Right then, Conner and Lexa streamed up. They each had a rope looped around their waists, and Pilaf rode behind them on roller skates, holding onto a rope with each hand.

Melanie didn't quite know what to say to Conner. He smiled at her—a shy, hesitant smile—and she smiled back.

He stood in a part of the deck evenly split between light from the house and darkness from the yard. A perfect boundary.

A boundary!

The symbols on Melanie's whiteboard popped now,

almost jumping off the board and into the air around her head. "I've got it!" She yelled. "Conner had that collar the cherubim filled with Light. The Shadowbox is like the gateway to Darkness. He went through that gateway, but he did it with the cherubim's Light. So the Light and Dark basically collided and turned him into a boundary between Light and Dark."

Dr. Timberi's eyes smiled. "Well done, Melanie! I believe you are right. An intersection where both Light and Dark connect, and is, in turn, connected to both Light and Dark."

Melanie wondered how long he'd known that. He didn't seem surprised. Had he been waiting for her to discover it on her own?

"Kind of like a penumbra," Lexa said. "It's sort of between light or dark. It's kind of—both."

"Well said, Lexa." Dr. Timberi nodded. "A human penumbra."

Pilaf raised his hand, bobbing up and down. "So, a Magus is like a magnet that attracts Light. Darkhands attract Darkness. Is Conner like a super-magnet that attracts both?"

"Exactly," Dr. Timberi said. "My guess is that being exposed to so much Light and Dark at the same time last night triggered something and essentially magnetized Conner until he attracted both of them. The two powers fought for dominance, but when you absorbed the Darkness and Melanie Augmented the Light, it gave the Light an edge.

"However, that much energy basically fried his circuits, and thus the Lucents came to heal him, just as they saved him from drowning. They seem to watch over you, Conner, perhaps because you accepted the mission when the cherubim sent you to face Lady Nightwing." Dr. Timberi shook his head. "Fascinating. Completely unprecedented."

Melanie scrunched her nose. "So, at Dauphin Island, all the shadow attacks on Conner might not have been attacks. The phantumbra was delivering messages from Lady Nightwing. But were the other shadows just responding to Conner since he became magnetic to them?"

"I believe so," Dr. Timberi said.

"What about that thing in the ocean?" Conner asked. "I mean, it wasn't just trying to play."

"You made it happen," Pilaf said.

"What?"

"You told me when you Kindled, the Light followed your thoughts, right?"

"Yeah."

"Remember what happened right before that shadow pulled you under?"

Conner frowned for a minute. "Yeah, I think so. I felt a fish brush my ankle and it sort of creeped me out. It got me thinking about what might be under there and—" Conner's eyes grew nearly as large as Pilaf's. "I joked about being dragged under by something. So, me being scared about something made it happen?"

"Uh-huh." Pilaf nodded. "It's the same thing as the Light following your thoughts when you Kindled. The shadows did the same thing. Being in the Shadowbox was the equivalent of Kindling, but for the Darkness."

Conner nodded. "I think you're right. I just

remembered that one time at Dauphin Island, after the Stalker came, the Shadows jumped up and I yelled at them to stop. And they did."

"So why did they stop coming at you?" Lexa asked. "Or at least take a break."

Dr. Timberi smiled. "Melanie."

"What?"

"As an Augmentor, Melanie can share her Light with others, supplementing their own. I imagine that at some point, she decided, consciously or not, that she did not want Conner to be harmed. This would have effectively surrounded Conner with a shield."

Melanie looked at the ground, hoping her blush did not show as much in the shadows. "Yes, that did happen. After Conner almost drowned."

"So your autonomic abilities with Lightcraft have basically been shielding Conner remotely. Remarkable. Additionally, once he came to the Sanctuary, the shadows were not able to follow."

Lexa tugged at her ponytail. "Soooo, Conner isn't a Darkhand. He's a Magi, but the shadows obey him?"

"It would seem so," Dr. Timberi said. "And if we are correct, then the implications are staggering."

Melanie scrunched her nose, trying to keep up with flying symbols on the whiteboard. "Could Conner use the Dark against the Darkhands?"

"Yes. I am only guessing, but imagine the chaos he could inflict on Umbra! He could command, maybe even destroy, the Darkness. The possibilities could, quite literally, change the world."

The silence around them rippled with excitement as

everyone thought through what Dr. Timberi had just said. Chills crisscrossed Melanie's skin.

"Conner," Dr. Timberi whispered. "Do you see the shadows at the other end of the deck?"

"Yes, sir."

"Reach out to them, just as you would reach out to the Light."

Conner stared at the shadows. Tension popped out all over his face.

Melanie watched, a feeling of electric anxiety in her chest.

"Relax," Dr. Timberi said.

Conner closed his eyes. He took a deep breath, then stretched his right hand out and wiggled his fingers.

Nothing happened.

Melanie let her breath back out. Oh well. It had been a nice thought—

Lexa squealed and pointed. The shadows on the other end of the deck began to shimmer. Gently at first, they bubbled and popped, and then jumped up, forming a bouquet of flowers which floated over to Melanie.

"Oh my," Dr. Timberi whispered. "This battle just changed. I think our side just split the atom." He smiled. "Now we must figure out how to build the bomb."

CHAPTER 40

THE RELIQUARIES

FOR LEXA, THE REST OF THE SUMMER seemed like one long, lazy day. Each morning Sadie stuffed them with an amazing breakfast and then Dr. Timberi trained them until lunchtime: streaming, phasing, combat, evasive maneuvers, and more. After lunch, they trained again until Dr. Timberi got hot and went inside to take a nap. While he napped, the Four Musketeers played horseshoes, croquet, and badminton, swam, and helped pick green beans, cucumbers, and tomatoes. After one of Sadie's spectacular Southern suppers, Dr. Timberi drilled them a little longer before stopping for the evening. They filled the nights with games like kick-the-can, hide-and-seek, or chasing Lucents. While they played, Dr. Timberi adumbrated, staring into the horloge for hours. Sometimes Melanie would join him.

A few minor irritations crept into their paradise. By the end of the summer, Melanie still couldn't stream, and Conner never got the grasp of phasing, although Lexa could do both very well. And, to Pilaf's growing frustration, the Magisterium never sent anyone out to test him, or Madi, for that matter. Madame Cumberland told them a lot of things were going on to keep the Magisterium busy.

The shadow attacks and fires stopped, and nothing seemed to be happening anywhere at all. Lexa thought that sounded like a good thing, but Dr. Timberi worried, feeling sure that the Darkhands were plotting something really big that distracted them from their normal activities.

Aside from these frustrations, everyone enjoyed themselves. Fights and feuds past, they laughed and worked and played and ate. Madame Cumberland, Mrs. Grant, Lee, and other Magi joined them often, streaming in and out, and summer passed too fast.

As fall drew nearer, Lexa often slipped away to prepare for *The Sound of Music* auditions. One morning, about a week before try-outs, she woke up early, too excited by her coming victory to sleep. She dressed and walked out onto the deck, planning to rehearse the title song in the quiet morning to get more in tune with the role.

Outside, she noticed a change: the hint of a chill and the scent of wood smoke sneaking through the air. She ran down the hill in the backyard, spinning her arms and singing until a summer thunderstorm split the sky, drowning the yard with buckets and buckets of water.

Lexa ran inside, planning to take refuge in the garret room. With everyone still asleep, she couldn't sing, but she planned to work on the subtext and emotional layers. She tiptoed up the stairs, hoping not to awaken anyone. She froze a few steps up as she heard voices.

"That must be why they have stopped all their activity," Dr. Timberi said. "They would spare no effort to apprehend him. He knows far too much."

"Don't get too excited, Morgan," Lee said. "This isn't confirmed yet. And I'm technically not authorized to tell you but, seeing how it's him. . . well, anyway, I better get back."

"Thank you, Lee."

Lexa backed down the stairs as she heard Lee's brisk footsteps coming toward her. "Morning, Dell." He nodded and walked past her without stopping.

"Hi, Lee."

As she climbed the stairs and entered the room, Lexa saw Dr. Timberi staring out the window. She paused, trying to decide what to do. He seemed preoccupied, so Lexa didn't want to disturb him. In the silence, all she could hear were the containers on the shelf, pulsing with Light and humming with energy.

After several seconds, he turned around, "Lexa, please feel free to do whatever you came up here to do. I was just leaving." Walking to the shelf, he shot a sigil into the gold box with the swans. The box flashed, shining brighter than the others. After a few seconds, the Light faded and the chest glowed and hummed like normal.

"Hey, Dr. Timberi, what are those things anyway? I keep meaning to ask you."

"They are called reliquaries, and they house our Last Sigils."

"You're not going to do sigils anymore?"

Dr. Timberi chuckled, warm and relaxed. "I hope to do sigils for many years to come. A Last Sigil is a regular sigil with a unique and special purpose. You have seen enough to understand that the lives of Magi are unpredictable. Each Magus knows that his or her next mission may be the last." He paused, and the stillness grew heavy. "A Last Sigil is a message you leave behind for your loved ones in case you do not come back."

"What if you're unconscious or locked up in a dark room like Notzange was?" Lexa asked.

"That is precisely the point. You organize your Last Sigil in advance, prior to facing danger, leaving it safely behind in its reliquary. These reliquaries hold the last sigils for all the Magi in this area. When a Magus dies, or is presumed dead, we hold a service called a Remembrance Ceremony. The friends and family of the deceased Magus gather to open the reliquary and hear the Last Sigil."

"But how does it work? If it's part of your soul and you die . . ."

"Your body dies, Lexa. Not your soul," Dr. Timberi said. "And since your sigil is a part of your soul, it lives on. However, because your body no longer anchors your soul to this world, a Last Sigil is quite weak. It speaks and then fades away, like smoke in the wind."

"That sounds really sad," Lexa said. "Watching it fade away, I mean."

"Yes," Dr. Timberi nodded. "That is a solemn moment. But it is also a great comfort to hear from someone you love one more time. Consequently, Magi take this seriously and update their Last Sigils frequently, especially before leaving for potentially dangerous missions."

Lexa stared at him. "Were you just updating your Last Sigil?"

Dr. Timberi's expression had changed. He seemed energized. Sure of something.

"Would you please excuse me, Lexa? I have an urgent errand."

"Where are you going?" she replied.

"To find something I lost." He walked down the stairs, his footsteps growing faster and faster. A minute or two later, Lexa saw a gold flash of Light and heard the whistling shriek of a comet leaving the grounds.

He didn't come back for the next week, and none of the adults would talk about where he had gone. Lexa began to worry, remembering her dream. The part about the fires and Conner and Melanie had all come true. Everything had happened, except the part about the Stalker and Dr. Timberi. She hoped he was okay.

As their last week at Mockingbird Cottage sprinted by, Lexa felt growing unease, and on the day they left Mockingbird Cottage, a powerful sadness ballooned inside of Lexa. She couldn't shake the feeling that something had ended.

For good.

ᴀUDITIONS

LEXA WOKE UP HOURS BEFORE HER ALARM
went off. Excitement and anticipation electrified her
brain, and she couldn't sleep. She showered and got ready
in her quiet house. After two nights home, she missed
Mockingbird Cottage more than she could say. School
would start in two days. But today, the only thing that
mattered was auditions. Assuming Dr. Timberi had come
back.

He wouldn't skip auditions, right? Not after all this
time.

She hadn't heard anything different, so she assumed
everything would go on as planned.

Lexa got ready and streamed over to the school. She
had signed up for the 9:00 audition time and didn't want
to be late.

It seemed strange for the school to be so empty and
quiet. Most of the lights had been turned off, and the
smell of floor wax and cleaning supplies had replaced the

familiar school-day jumble of scents: lotions, hand sanitizer, deodorant, and school lunch. Somehow, it felt like a tomb, and a shiver sneaked up and down her back a few times.

Shaking the gloom away, Lexa walked into the theater, feeling at home as soon as her toes tapped the stage floor. Surrounded by set pieces and props, the familiar, earthy smells soothed her: the sweet tang of paint, the mellow scent of lumber, and the warm darkness. A tiny thrill of excitement tingled down her back. To Lexa, the theater always seemed alive with the friendly ghosts of past productions and unlimited future possibilities.

Dr. Timberi stepped into a pool of light on the stage. "Hello, Lexa."

"Dr. Timberi! You're back." She ran and hugged him. He didn't flinch and even gave her the briefest of hugs back. Maybe she and Melanie had accomplished something.

Dr. Timberi smiled. "Are you ready?"

"Are you kidding? I've been ready since May!"

Dr. Timberi laughed and looked at the piano player. "Mrs. Wise, please give Lexa four bars of introduction."

Lexa opened her mouth and her voice rolled out, rich and full, her feelings linked in perfect harmony to the emotional layers of the song. She nailed her audition. Nailed it.

"Thank you, Lexa." No excitement was in his voice, no expression on his face, but she understood. He had to be professional and calm, especially with her. He couldn't show any Magi favoritism or anything. "I'd like you to come to call-backs tomorrow afternoon for Maria. Can you be there?"

She gulped down her excitement, keeping her voice professional and calm as well. "Sure. I'd be happy to come."

Waiting an entire twenty-four hours nearly murdered Lexa. She filled the time by practicing with a laserlike focus Conner called creepy. "Sheesh, Lex," he said, "it's like you're stalking this part."

But she ignored him. Twenty-four hours until call-backs. Approximately thirty hours until Dr. Timberi posted the cast list. Approximately thirty hours and a few minutes until the whole world would know about her great triumph. Then, all the sacrifices would be worth it. An entire summer of constant hard work rewarded.

Time trickled in a slow drip, a blurry blend of excitement and boredom. It felt like Christmas Eve for a little kid. Times a billion.

At call-backs, the finalists for smaller parts went first. Unable to focus or practice any more, Lexa paced the halls outside the theater while Dr. Timberi auditioned everyone from featured Nazis and singing nuns to the Captain's children.

Two or three forevers later, sometime in the afternoon, Dr. Timberi called the four finalists for Maria and the Captain. Lexa walked in to meet her theatrical destiny.

She passed Melanie, coming out of her call-back for some minor role. Melanie hugged her. *Good luck, Lexa!*

Warmth rushed through Lexa. What a supportive friend! Melanie would be a nun or something small, but she still focused on being excited for Lexa.

Thanks, Mel!

Good luck, Lex! Conner added, walking out behind Melanie.

Thanks!

Lexa swept into the theater and took a seat.

"Good luck, Lexa." Lily Martin sat next to her, smiling her *waayy* fakely-sweet smile.

"Thanks." Lexa forced herself to be nice. She'd have to rise above being petty and be gracious in victory. Lily would be bitterly disappointed.

"Good afternoon." Dr. Timberi walked onto the stage. "Please turn to the scene on page twenty-two. Lily, will you and Zach go first, please?"

Lily and Zach walked to the stage and acted their scene. They stumbled a few times on words, but overall, Lily surprised Lexa by doing a good job. Well, pretty good.

"Thank you." Dr. Timberi's unreadable expression seemed even more unreadable. "Lexa and Joey?"

Lexa strode to the stage, confidence surging in each step. She owned this scene.

As they read, Lexa did not merely act. She *became* Maria, channeling the character, energized by what she knew had to be a five-star performance.

"Thank you, Lexa and Joey." Dr. Timberi rubbed his eyes. He looked a little stressed and tired. Poor man. Casting a play must be hard. Lexa decided to give him an extra hug after the cast list was posted. It wouldn't be appropriate right now because Lily might think she lost the part because of favoritism or something.

After they switched partners and read a few more scenes, Dr. Timberi excused Zach and Joey but asked

Lexa and Lily to sing all of Maria's songs—which Lexa knew perfectly.

Two hours later, Dr. Timberi excused them with a heavy sigh as he rubbed his forehead. "Thank you both. I appreciate your time. I expect to post the cast list later this evening. I'll send out an email when it is posted."

Dr. Timberi's expression betrayed no clue about his thoughts. But Lexa knew. She nodded and left, humming "My Favorite Things" as she walked through the empty halls.

For just a moment, the silence of the school soaked up her excitement, and the creepy, tomblike feeling returned, bringing more shivers. Singing louder, she ran out to her mom's waiting car.

Later that night, Lexa had sprawled across her bed, analyzing Maria's lines, when her phone dinged, signaling the arrival of an email. She jumped up and grabbed the phone with trembling fingers.

> *Dear All,*
> *I have posted the cast list on the theater section of the school website. Let me thank everyone who tried out. With so many talented students, the casting proved quite difficult. I look forward to a wonderful production.*
> *Sincerely,*
> *Morgan Timberi*

Whooping and squealing, Lexa tore through the piles

in her room, searching for her laptop. The school website never worked well on her phone's small screen. Clothes, towels, and dirty socks flew as she hunted for her laptop. When she saw the case, she dove down, grabbed the computer, and flung it open. The signal bars for the wireless took forever to show up. When she finally had a signal, excitement made her fingers clumsy, and she mistyped her username and password at least twice before logging in to the school website and clicking the link to download the cast list.

The list opened, and she took a deep breath, trying to collect herself. She closed her eyes and tugged her ponytail. *Slow down, Lexa. Breathe.*

This was her great triumph. The first lead of her final year at Marion Academy. She needed to savor and relish every second.

Singing the title song seemed appropriate. A hush came into the room as she wrapped herself in the role. She bowed her head, clasping her hands together in a prayerful position. Chills paraded up and down her body as her soul reached out across the years and touched Maria's. She rehearsed the words to a short acceptance speech she'd prepared to send in a sigil to Dr. Timberi.

Ready now, she opened her eyes. Music swelled in her heart as she read the list.

CAST (In Order of Appearance)

MARIA . . . . Lily Martin

The music jarred into a dissonant crash as Lexa froze. She read it again. And again. With growing desperation she continued to read. But the letters didn't change.

As stunned disbelief changed to vague comprehension, Dr. Timberi seemed to reach inside of her, grab her guts, and twist, wrenching every vital organ in her body. LILY MARTIN? That talentless, unmemorized fake?

Sharp stabs of excruciating pain stole Lexa's breath and she had to muster every bit of her willpower to make her eyes and brain work. As she scanned down the list, a few other names stood out.

ROLFE. . . . . Conner Dell
LIESEL . . . . Melanie Stephens

It took three passes through the cast list to find her own name.

SISTER MARGARETTA . . . . .Lexa Dell

Flashes of fiery agony alternated with bursts of numbness as Lexa stared at the monitor. A nun? She was a nun? Pain flared, boiling the numbness into anger. Righteous fury coursed through her now. Dr. Timberi had stabbed her in the back. Humiliated her in front of the whole school. After all she'd done for him, all the kindness she'd shown him. With Magi like him, who needed Darkhands?

How dare he? How could he do this to her, of all people?

She needed to confront him and let him see what his cruelty had done. He ought to see the consequences of his actions and understand how badly he'd hurt her.

But how? How could she? An idea came to her.

She fired off a sigil to Dr. Timberi. A few minutes later, his swan appeared in her room, speaking in a tired voice. "Yes, Lexa?"

She kept her voice cold and formal. Distant, crisp, and clipped.

"Hello, Dr. Timberi, this is Lexa Dell. I was wondering if you could help me understand what I did wrong. I'm disappointed, of course, and want to know what I can do better next time, should I ever try out for another play."

Lexa nodded at her word choice and icy tone. That was a good start. It would let him know she was upset.

Dr. Timberi's sigil sighed. "Lexa, if you think that would be helpful, I'd be happy to talk with you. I think, however, that it might be best to speak in person—"

"Thank you." She filled her words with freezing disdain. "I'll be right there. Are you at the school?"

"Lexa, I think perhaps a good night's sleep—"

"I think it might be most helpful to me while everything is fresh." Lexa imitated the way her mom talked to customer service people. The sooner the better, so he could realize just how badly his actions had hurt her.

He paused. "Very well. I am at school finishing some work. I will wait."

"Thank you." *Conner?* She sent her thoughts next door to his room.

Hey, Lex. Are you okay? Sorry about—

I'm fine. I'm going over to the school to talk to Dr. Timberi about my audition. Will you let mom know in case she wonders where I am?

Uh, Lexa, are you sure that's a good idea? I mean, he's probably tired and you're maybe a little emotional and—

I'm fine! I just want to find out what I could have done better.

Whatever, Lexa. I can feel your thoughts and that's not what you're really thinking. You're upset and you want to make sure he knows it—

Lexa closed their connection and ran a few steps, streaming into a comet. It took her longer than usual. Probably because her heart lay bleeding in tiny little shreds. But she managed, arriving at the school a few minutes later.

"Lexa?" A pink unicorn appeared above the lockers and Melanie's gentle voice echoed through the hall. "I'm so sorry. I know you really wanted that part. But maybe you should take some time—"

"I'm fine!" Lexa snapped. "I just want to have a mature conversation with Dr. Timberi about why he gave my part to someone else."

"Lexa, I'm on my way to the school. My mom's getting the car, and Conner's streaming over. Please don't do anything till we get there."

Lexa brushed past the sigil, marching into the theater. A lump knotted itself in her throat as she walked onto the stage, which felt dead now, no longer alive with possibilities. The stage where she would not be Maria. The stage where she would not be the star. The stage where she would be Sister Third-Nun-from-the-Left.

Dr. Timberi stepped out from behind a curtain. "Hello, Lexa." He smiled, warm but unsure. She recognized the unspoken question in his eyes, felt concern radiating outward. Concern for her. For some reason, that infuriated her. Sure, *now* he cared how she felt. *Now* he cared what she thought—after ruining her eighth-grade year before it even started.

"I don't suppose you've been to your locker yet?" he asked.

Why in the world would she go to her locker when school didn't start until tomorrow? "No."

"I hope you will check it on your way out." He seemed anxious "I didn't realize we'd be talking tonight and assumed that would be the first place you'd go tomorrow."

Lexa struggled to maintain her even, icy tone. "Dr. Timberi, I was just wondering if you could tell me what I did wrong."

He paused before speaking, seeming to choose his words with great care. For some reason that annoyed her even more.

"Lexa, you didn't do anything wrong. To the contrary. You were well prepared and did a good job. Unfortunately, the part didn't quite fit you, or rather, it fit Lily better."

"So, she's better than me?"

"That's not what I said, Lexa."

"Then why did you give her my part?" Her voice rose, and she didn't try to restrain it.

"Lexa, a leading role is not a present I wrap up and give to a favored student. I have to find the students that fit the role most closely. It's not a matter of personal affection or even talent. Many talented people are not well-suited for specific roles."

"But I worked so hard! All summer! And Lily wasn't even memorized! How could you do this to me?"

"Lexa, I'm sincerely sorry you are hurt, but I think you are being a bit unfair."

She barked a bitter laugh. "I'm being unfair? *I'm* the one who's being unfair?"

"Yes, as a matter of fact, you are." Dr. Timberi's voice got tight, and Lexa sensed stormy emotion, although he kept his voice low and even. "You act as if you were entitled to this role and have been treated unfairly. That is not the case. You tried out for a role, but someone else was a better fit. That is painful but not a personal affront. You are turning this into an insult, as if you've been injured. That is simply not the case. Really, Lexa. I expected better of you."

She felt like she'd been slapped, kicked, stomped, then slapped again. He expected better of her?

His voice softened, and he smiled. "Lexa, not getting the roles you want is part of theater. It is part of life. I know it hurts, but that will pass. I am truly sorry for your disappointment. It will get better soon."

He paused and then opened his arms with awkward uncertainty, offering a hug. "I would hope we can still be friends."

Lexa sneered, allowing the jagged icicles in her heart to freeze her words. "I think you and I have different definitions of friendship." She spun around, striding off the stage with her head held high.

She walked through the backstage area and into the hall, almost bumping into Conner and Melanie.

"Lexa?" Melanie's voice walked on tiptoe, which annoyed Lexa. "How did your talk with Dr. Timberi go?"

Lexa sniffed but didn't say anything.

Melanie grabbed her arm. "Lexa, did you talk to him?"

Lexa twirled around, jerked her arm away, and glared

at her. "Yes! I talked to him and he said I'm not as good as Lily Martin."

"He said that?" Conner asked. "In those words?"

"It's what he meant! He's so mean! I can't believe he did that to me. And then he said he wanted to be friends! Seriously! After he publicly humiliates me and gives me a nothing-part, he wants to be friends. As if."

"Lexa, that's not fair." Melanie sounded more direct now, less tiptoey. "When you try out for a play, you know you might not get the part you want. It's happened to *some* of us for years now. You've had lots of leads and you'll probably have more."

"Yeah!" Conner added. "Do you have to get the lead every time? Anyway, it's not fair to be mad at Dr. Timberi. He's like a ref. He has to make the hard calls. He probably felt really bad about it. Think of it from his side—"

"I don't care! I don't care!" Lexa's frustration and hurt echoed through the empty halls. Deep down she knew she was being irrational. In fact, a large, throbbing theeling shouted at her to stop, but she ignored it. "After all I've done for him! It was unfair and cruel and he's not my friend. He's a mean, stupid jerk, and I hate him! I *hate* him!"

Melanie's eyes grew wide as she looked behind Lexa. Conner closed his eyes and shook his head.

A sinking feeling plunged down into Lexa's stomach, displacing some of her rage. She turned around, knowing already what she would see.

Dr. Timberi stood a few feet behind her. For a few, sprinting seconds, Lexa felt glad that he knew how badly he'd hurt her, that he understood how he'd made her feel.

Then she noticed the unhidden hurt flooding the eyes that stared back at her. Deep, disappointed hurt.

Shame turned her anger to ashes, and Lexa found herself unable to speak. As she stammered, trying to say something, the pain on Dr. Timberi's face hardened into a blank mask until no emotion was left.

When he spoke, his voice stayed neutral, but his whole body seemed to strain against deep emotion. "I apologize for interrupting what is clearly a private conversation. Good evening, Miss Dell." He spun around and walked back to his classroom, footsteps tapping a brisk march on the tile.

Lexa wanted to call out to him, but as the weight of what she had done became clear, words slipped away from her. She couldn't even think.

His words echoed in her head. *Good evening, Miss Dell.* Miss Dell. All summer it had been Lexa. Now they were back to Miss Dell.

Lexa, how could you? Melanie asked, tears welling up in her eyes. *You couldn't be excited for me or Conner or even Lily! You had to make this all about you and sulk and storm and then say that to Dr. Timberi. Do you have any idea how that must have made him feel, especially hearing it from you?*

Sparks of defiance crackled inside of Lexa. She felt bad, but she wouldn't give in to Melanie bullying her. *Yeah, whatever. He's a teacher. Like he cares what we think.*

Melanie stepped closer, rare fury building on her face. *Stop it! That's not true! He's not just a teacher. He's a lonely man with a sad past who's saved your life at least three times! Oh, Lexa! He just started accepting hugs and allowing himself to feel love again.*

Melanie took a deep breath, as if stifling a lot of things she wanted to say. *I'm sorry you're upset, Lexa. I've been there a lot myself when you were busy celebrating one more lead and I was in the chorus again. But what you did was so cruel and immature that I can't even stand to think about it.*

I'm embarrassed to be your brother right now, Conner growled. *You should have seen his face when you said that. Nice going, Lexa.*

Melanie looked at Conner. *We'd better go talk to him.*

And say what? Conner asked.

I don't know—but we should try.

As they walked toward Dr. Timberi's room, the tomb-like feeling of the empty school seemed heavier. More oppressive.

Alone now, Lexa remembered Dr. Timberi asking about her locker. She tugged the door open, and a crisp, beige envelope fell out, with "Lexa" written across it. Engulfed by a sinking feeling the size of China, she opened the envelope and pulled out a piece of paper filled with precise handwriting.

> *Dear Lexa,*
> *I just posted the cast list for* The Sound of Music. *In thirty-five years of directing, I have never had such a difficult casting decision.*
> *It is clear you prepared for your auditions in an admirable way. I could see how badly you wanted this role, and I wish I could have given it to you. I imagine you are bitterly disappointed—as am I.*
> *Lexa, you, Conner, and Melanie have become*

precious to me. Not having family of my own, you three have filled this gap.

You, especially, with your kind heart, fierce loyalty, and ready affection have soothed old wounds that have troubled me for a long time. This summer, I sensed your extra efforts to reach out to me, and I sincerely appreciated your kindness. In return, I wanted so badly to cast you in the role you wanted. I hoped to reward your hard work and bring a smile to your face as you have to mine.

On the first edition of the cast list, your name was at the top. But as I typed it, I knew it was wrong. It would not have been honest to give you that role. The fact that you wanted it, and that I wanted you to have it would not have been sufficient justification for denying the opportunity to the person who was obviously best suited. Casting you in that role would not have positioned you for success, and it would have broken trust with my students. Doing so would have wronged you, Lily, and myself. For, if a Magus does not have integrity, he has nothing.

And so, I trust in your professionalism and maturity, praying that you will not see this decision as a personal rejection. After the initial disappointment fades, I believe you will see the wisdom of this decision.

As much as I wish it were otherwise, I cannot in good conscience give you the lead. But I can offer you the position of assistant director/stage manager. As you know, this is a position of singular responsibility, and this person has my complete trust and authority.

Because I rely so heavily on the stage manager, it is imperative that it be someone I trust: someone who is intelligent, capable, and talented. And if she's like a daughter to me, so much the better.

I hope you will consider this, Lexa. In the meantime, please know that I am deeply proud and very fond of you.

Sincerely,
Morgan Timberi

Golden Light blazed outside, reflected in the hallway windows as Dr. Timberi streamed away. Lexa wanted to rush after him, to explain and apologize—but she couldn't. The lump in her throat had spread to her chest, pulling her down like lead tied to a hummingbird.

How could she have been so stupid? So thoughtless and—she sniffed. A sulfury smell filled the hall, followed by a loud crackle. She looked up to see black fire rushing down the hallway toward her.

·CHAPTER 42·

THE DUEL

ORRIED, CONNER FOLLOWED MELANIE out of Dr. Timberi's room. Dr. Timberi had been polite, but not his normal self.

I'm worried about him, Melanie said.

Me too, Conner replied. *I—*

A loud crackling noise followed by a familiar smell pulled Conner away from their conversation. He looked up in time to see Lexa throw herself to the ground, dodging a stream of black flames now heading for him and Melanie.

They dropped, rolling in the basic evasive pattern Dr. Timberi had taught them earlier. Mid-roll, Melanie paused and fired some spinning windmills of pink Light in the direction of the fire. Watching her in action, Conner felt fiery pinwheels spinning through his heart. In spite of the fact that she couldn't stream, Melanie had become an incredible fighter over the summer.

We need to get out of here! Lexa shouted from her position at the other end of the hall.

Brilliant deduction! Conner shouted back. *Any ideas?*

Melanie dodged another blast, returning fire with a fleet of buzzing pink hornets. *Just go, you two,* she said. *Stream away and get help! I'll be fine.* Melanie sent an exploding blast in the direction of the fire. *I'll—blast— be—blast—fine!* Two more blasts and the fire stopped.

No way! Conner and Lexa yelled in unison. *We're not leaving you.*

They ducked as two more Dark blobs hurtled toward them. *But we should get out of the open,* Conner added. *Come on, Lexa. Theater.*

Lexa shot down to their location. Conner and Lexa each linked an elbow with Melanie, streaming toward the theatre and towing her along with them. Melanie faced the other way, returning fire and covering their retreat. From the pink flashes reflecting in the hallway windows, Conner figured she was hitting the Darkhands with everything she could think of.

Towing Melanie slowed them down, so it wasn't true streaming, but within seconds, they stopped in the dark theater.

I just sent a sigil to Dr. Timberi, Melanie said.

"Duck!" Lexa yelled as three jets of black flame screamed through the air toward them. They dove behind some fake rocks.

As the fire rushed closer, an idea popped into Conner's mind. He jumped up and reached out to the Darkness in his mind. "Go away!" he commanded, throwing his hands up in the air.

Nothing happened—except that the sizzling flames rushed closer. He reached out again, connecting to the

Darkness, but it felt wild and strange. Not like the shadows on the deck.

"Move!" he yelled again, desperation fueling extra feeling. Inches away from him, the jet of black flames bent, following the line of his body and shooting up to the ceiling. Several stage lights fell to the floor, melting into clumps of steaming metal.

Conner dropped back down, panting. That had been a few centimeters away from being a really bad idea. He rubbed his forehead and realized his eyebrows had been singed.

Nice, Conner! Melanie yelled.

Can you control this Darkness, Conner? Lexa asked.

Sort of. But it's really hard. The Darkness they're using is way stronger than regular shadows.

I think I see someone over there. Lexa jumped up into the air, turned into a comet, and streamed offstage left.

A smoky cyclone appeared in the air near Conner and Melanie. "Hello, Conner." Lady Nightwing emerged sneering from the haze. She looked at Melanie and hissed in a loud, fake whisper. "I'd be careful around Conner if I were you—"

Melanie interrupted her with a herd of galloping pink scorpions, and Lady Nightwing dodged backward, tripping over Conner's outstretched foot and falling to the floor. Before she jumped back up, an Illuminated pink whip appeared in Melanie's hand. "I know all about that!" Melanie sliced the whip across Lady Nightwing's cheek, drawing an angry shriek. "And I know what it means, you devious, lying witch!"

Melanie flipped her whip back to lash out again, but

Lady Nightwing leaped up, changing into a cyclone. She whirled away, followed a few seconds later by two additional tornadoes, spewing thick, sulfurous smoke and flames, which filled the air.

As the smoke suffocated the oxygen, Melanie and Conner dropped to the ground trying to find air to breathe.

Come over stage left! Lexa shouted.

They army-crawled over and found Lexa sticking her head under a bed used in *Peter Pan*. The blankets and sheets hanging over the sides created a barrier that kept most of the smoke out.

Do you think we can take them? Lexa asked. *Three against three.*

Four! Dr. Timberi's voice thundered through their thoughts as a blazing gold comet circled the bed.

Dr. Timberi! Lexa yelled.

Hello, possums. Dr. Timberi's head joined theirs under the bed. *Sorry I'm late. There is another attack going on—a large force of Darkhands is after Pilaf. They must have figured out what he can do. The other Magi are there, so we're on our own. Happily, between the four of us, we can best these three handily.*

How did they get in? Lexa asked. *I thought the school was shielded.*

It was—until Conner blew the shield up a few weeks ago. Mr. Miller has been working to restore it, but that is a complicated operation. Since school was out, he didn't worry too much about it. Now, I think we should teach Lady Nightwing a lesson.

Oh yeah! Conner said.

They're hiding in the seats. Direct your fire there on my

mark. Remember, fight to win! Dr. Timber said. *If we lose,
they will show no mercy. Magi never start fights . . .*

Conner, Lexa, and Melanie all joined in: . . . *but they
always finish them!*

"Once more unto the breach, dear friends!" Dr.
Timberi stood up and belted "My Favorite Things." He
sang at full voice, vocal cords locked and loaded, vibrato
set to "kill," not "stun." A ball of gold light whistled out
of his baton, arcing up into the air over the auditorium,
where it exploded into dozens of gold snakes that plunged
back down to the earth. As the snakes descended, three
dark cyclones spun out of their hiding places behind the
seats.

Attack! Dr. Timberi shouted.

Melanie jumped up on the bed, shooting blasts of
pink Light at the cyclones. As she fired, Conner and Lexa
each grabbed a different end of the bed and ran clock-
wise, streaming into comets. As they streamed, the bed
spun faster and faster around the stage, a giant, colored
pinwheel, spattering the air with Light and scattering the
cyclones.

One of the Darkhands regrouped and managed a
surge of black fire, blasting the bed into confetti. The Trio
jumped away, finding shelter behind some bookshelves
from *My Fair Lady.*

Peeking out, Conner imagined an old machine gun
from his dad's World War II movies. An Illuminated red
version appeared in his hand, and he jumped out, strafing
the air with buzzing bullets of red Light.

Next to him, Melanie stared ahead, muttering pre-
algebra equations. Pink Light flashed backstage and with

a loud rattle, the contents of the scenery shop flew out. Now the cyclones had to avoid Conner's Illuminated bullets while dodging paint cans, wrenches, hammers, and several broken stage lights.

Melanie seemed especially focused on Lady Nightwing's comet, creating some kind of Lightcraft algorithm that pelted her with a repeating stream of projectiles.

Humming loudly, Lexa joined the barrage, sending glowing sound and light cables whipping through the air like massive attack snakes.

Keep going! Dr. Timberi yelled. *They can't maneuver.* The whirlwinds jerked and stopped, changing directions abruptly and often, with a frantic sort of feel, as if they couldn't navigate very well.

BAM! Melanie pegged Lady Nightwing's cyclone with a five-gallon bucket of black paint.

As Conner watched the spinning cyclones, he felt the whirling Darkness, sensing it in the same way he could feel the Light. The comets were powerful and superfast, and he knew he couldn't stop the Darkness. But he realized it wouldn't take much energy to shove part of the Darkness in a different direction. He reached out and gave a little mental kick at the bottom of a cyclone.

That kick ended up being like tripping a sprinter. A small nudge sent the cyclone tumbling away at a crazy angle, spinning out of control until a friendly wall intervened. The man dropped to the ground.

Without any warning, the two remaining cyclones stopped in mid-spin, shooting toward the stage, the Trio, and Dr. Timberi.

The suddenness of the attack threw them off guard,

and Conner hesitated for a moment. Melanie and Lexa did the same.

Don't stop! Dr. Timberi shouted. *They're changing tactics because we are winning!*

The whirlwinds raced toward them, closing the already narrow gap. Dr. Timberi wiggled the fingers on his left hand and bellowed "Climb Every Mountain." A wall of golden flames burst up from the stage floor in front of the tornadoes. Conner imagined the sound of squealing brakes as the cyclones skidded into a stop inches away from the flames. Whirling in reverse, they backed away, losing momentum in the process.

Melanie sent a stream of pink Light at a costume rack, and ten Light-infused nun costumes jumped into the air, flying at the two cyclones, which faded into Lady Nightwing and a tall man. As the nun costumes attacked, the two Darkhands countered with waves of black fire. While the Darkhands focused on the killer nun costumes, Lexa yelled like Tarzan, and dozens of ropes and cables whipped down from the ceiling. Lady Nightwing dropped to the ground and rolled away, but her companion didn't move fast enough. The cables twined around his wrists and ankles, yanking him up and lashing him to the grid above.

Dr. Timberi stepped forward as Lady Nightwing climbed to her feet. He flicked his baton and the swan sigil appeared, growing large and somehow threatening. "I challenge you to a duel, you vicious harridan," he growled. "You foul, fiendish, unhallowed termagant!"

Lady Nightwing glared at him but said nothing. Conner didn't think she looked very confident as she waved her arms in an intricate pattern. Streams of Darkness appeared, weaving into a large, familiar shadow-wolf.

Dr. Timberi slashed his baton and the swan lunged forward, pecking at the wolf's face. Lady Nightwing snarled and raised her hands, and the wolf reared up on its hind legs and pounced. The swan flew back, then darted forward and bit the wolf's nose. "Churlish, ratsbane harpy!" Dr. Timberi yelled.

The wolf snapped at the swan, missing its long neck by less than a feather. As the swan flapped away from the snapping teeth, it planted a series of sharp kicks on the wolf's snout.

"Dissembling, venomed, miscreated beast!" Dr. Timberi roared.

The wolf sprang at the swan, but the swan dodged to one side, swung its long neck, and clubbed the wolf with its head. The force of the blow sent the wolf rolling.

"I'll kill you!" Lady Nightwing screamed. "I'll kill you all!" She raised her left hand and a ball of smoldering black energy appeared in her fingers. With her right hand, she sent her wolf forward, then threw the Darkness at Dr. Timberi with her left.

Dr. Timberi jabbed his baton forward, and his swan crashed into her wolf. Extending the fingers of his left hand, he met the incoming Darkness with a flood of gold Light.

Light and Dark collided, pushing against each other halfway between them, sparking and humming, but not making any progress in either direction.

"Then kill me!" Dr. Timberi growled. "Kill me, and I will take you along." His voice grew soft and deadly.

"I will gratefully give my life to extinguish you from this world and send your stunted, twisted soul to the deepest abyss."

The Light exploded forward, pushing the Darkness away. Lady Nightwing jumped back, dodging the blast.

They dueled on, circling and shooting, dodging and ducking, controlling the swan and wolf with their right hands, shooting at each other with the left. The animals snapped and lunged, bit and clawed, while Light and Darkness collided all around, creating a raging, sizzling storm. Dr. Timberi kept up, but Conner thought his breathing seemed labored and his reflexes a little slow.

Guys, I'm worried about him, Melanie said. *He's been kind of weak this summer. Do you think he should be doing this?*

She closed her eyes, and a few seconds later, Conner saw a pink glow around Dr. Timberi, who looked younger, stronger, and very, very dangerous. *Thank you, Melanie,* he thought, before shouting, "Vile, unmuzzled, barbarous wretch! Die and sink to the blackest pit in perdition!"

With surprising speed, Dr. Timberi crossed his arms. His sigil charged Lady Nightwing, while a blinding blast of gold Light shot out of his baton, slamming into the wolf. As the wolf dissolved, Lady Nightwing gasped and staggered backwards. The swan soared straight up, turned a loop-de-loop, and dove back down, crashing into her chest.

Lady Nightwing's face froze in rage—and then, shuddering, she collapsed into a heap of black robes on the stage.

Taking deep, ragged breaths, Dr. Timberi limped over and glared at Lady Nightwing's unconscious form. He gripped his baton like a dagger and raised it high above him in the air.

Conner held his breath as Dr. Timberi's hand trembled in the air as gold sparks sizzled up and down the length of the baton.

The baton hung in the air for several eternities, continuously shaking and spitting gold sparks.

"I should," Dr. Timberi said. "But I cannot. Not like this." He lowered his hand. "Heaven forgive my weakness."

Dr. Timberi turned his back on Lady Nightwing and limped toward the Trio.

"Lexa, perhaps you can tie her up—"

But Lexa's shriek interrupted him. "Behind you!"

Two knives hummed through the air, spinning toward Dr. Timberi's back.

Still shaking with effort, Lady Nightwing had dragged herself up on one elbow. Her other arm was extended, and she flicked her wrist, sending two more knives.

Before any of them could move, sickly green Light flashed, swallowing the knives up. *Who did that?* Lexa asked

Dr. Timberi didn't say anything, but he tripped forward, looking stunned.

Lady Nightwing chanted, waving her arms back and forth. Dense, inky smoke billowed through the theater, filling the stage in seconds, removing all visibility.

In the darkness, strange screeching, grinding noises filled the stage, followed by shouts and screams. Then—silence.

"Morgan, stop!" Lady Nightwing's harsh voice cut through the smoke. "I have something you lost."

Dr. Timberi dropped his hands. "No." His voice was like a prayer. "Please, no."

"What's wrong?" Melanie asked.

Listen to me! He looked at them with urgent eyes. *Melanie, remember the key to the Otherwhere that hangs around my neck?*

Yes, but—

At my signal, Translocate the key to your hand. Keep your hand closed and do not let her see. Open a portal into the Otherwhere and tell the cherubim you request refuge. When they ask about using my key, say, "Nicole."

Across the theater, through the smoke, Lady Nightwing laughed, triumphant and full of gleeful malice. "Morgan?"

Where will you be? Lexa asked.

Just listen! You must go as soon as I tell you to. Melanie, do NOT translocate the key until I give the signal or she'll sense the Light being used. Do you understand?

Yes, but . . .

DO YOU UNDERSTAND?

Yes, Melanie said.

As the smoke cleared, two figures became visible across the stage. The Stalker knelt on the floor. Lady Nightwing stood behind him. Her chest rose and fell, working for each breath. One of her trembling hands grasped a fistful of the Stalker's hair. Her other hand held a knife shaking at his throat.

Lady Nightwing laughed again, her cold, metal-on-stone laugh. "If he dies now, his body will decay and rot. What about his soul?"

"What do you want?" Dr. Timberi asked. *Get ready, Melanie.*

Lady Nightwing laughed. "Surely you know."

"You cannot have my students." His voice rang like steel hitting steel.

Lady Nightwing yanked the Stalker's head back and moved the blade of the knife closer to his throat.

"Stop!" Dr. Timberi's shouted. "Not the children. But I will offer you something far more valuable."

Her hand froze. "I'm curious. You have ten seconds to make me more than that."

No! Melanie shouted. *You can't!* She started to cry.

Please, Melanie. Dr. Timberi's thoughts flowed soft and gentle. *You don't understand.* Aloud, he said. "I will surrender myself to you. On the condition that he and they go free."

"NO!" Conner and Lexa screamed out loud, not bothering with thoughts.

Silence! Dr. Timberi thundered. *Melanie, get ready. It will be soon.*

Lady Nightwing laughed again, harsher and more ragged. "You Magi are so pathetic. So predictable. You'll sacrifice yourself and then I'll just capture the kids anyway. But whatever you want." She snarled at him. "Swear the Magi's Oath that you are giving yourself up unconditionally. No tricks."

"Agreed. But first I will shield the children."

"Fine. But if I even think you're trying to trick me, he's dead."

Dr. Timberi held up his hands. *Now, Melanie! Quickly, while the shield distracts her!* Dr. Timberi's hands wove a bright bubble of golden Light around them. Melanie shut her eyes, and pink Light flashed in her closed hand.

I have it, she thought.

At my signal, open the Shroud, and then run. She will undoubtedly immobilize me and then come for you. The shield will not hold long, so do not delay. And please take him with you. He pointed to the Stalker.

What? all three of them asked at once.

Dr. Timberi stood up and faced Lady Nightwing. "Let him go."

"Swear the Oath."

Dr. Timberi shook his head. "Let him go first."

Lady Nightwing's laugh boiled like acid in Conner's heart. "Fine. But I don't want him turning on me." She raised the hand with the knife and brought the jeweled hilt smashing down on the Stalker's head. He collapsed into a heap.

Conner, go get him.

Why? Conner asked.

Please, Conner.

Confused and fearful, Conner crossed the stage. Drawing on his super-strength, he pulled the Stalker's unconscious body back to the bubble of Light.

Why are you giving yourself up for him? Lexa asked as Melanie sobbed. Conner cried as well, not caring who saw.

I love you, dear ones, Dr. Timberi cried too. *You know that, I hope. Do not delay. You cannot help me now. I'm using the Light to bind myself to Lady Nightwing's will. If you linger, you will be taken as well.*

"Swear the Oath," Lady Nightwing said.

Dr. Timberi moved forward, standing halfway between the Trio and Lady Nightwing.

"I, Morgan Timberi, surrender to Lady Nightwing. I allow her to take me as her prisoner, binding myself to this course with all the power of the Light within me." *Get ready to go. You'll have only a moment when she'll be distracted.*

Why are you doing this? We could beat her all together! Lexa shouted.

Bright gold Light flashed around Dr. Timberi, binding him in thick ropes as Lady Nightwing raised her hands. "Let's see if you really mean this." She jabbed her fingers forward, and bolts of Dark lightning lanced into Dr. Timberi, who cried out in pain and collapsed onto the floor.

"One more time to make sure this isn't a trick." Her eyes grew wide and wild. She raised her hands and shot more Dark lightning into him as Dr. Timberi screamed and rolled around on the floor.

As soon as she comes to me . . . Dr. Timberi gasped. Conner felt his thoughts struggle to stay together as waves of pain crashed over him.

Lady Nightwing strode over to him, her hands pulled back, ready to strike like coiled snakes.

Now! Dr. Timberi shouted.

Melanie turned the key in the air. The metal lit up in her hand as shimmery, silver curtains appeared. The Shroud parted, but no one moved, unwilling to leave him behind.

Please go! Don't let me die in vain.

The Trio stepped into the curtains.

Don't forget him! Please, Conner! I beg you!

Conner grumbled but reached down and grabbed the

Stalker. As he did, his eyes met Lady Nightwing's, who looked up and saw them leaving into the Otherwhere. She shrieked and sent a huge storm of Darkness toward them. Dr. Timberi's shield repelled her blast but faded and grew dim.

Why? Lexa screamed. *Why are you doing this?*

As the Shroud closed behind them, they heard Dr. Timberi's last words: *Tell my son I love him.*

For three beats of their pounding hearts, they heard shouts of rage and terrible cries of pain. Then the Shroud closed, severing them from Dr. Timberi.

The Last Sigil

MELANIE CRIED FOR TWO WEEKS. MADAME Cumberland and Mrs. Grant cried. Lexa's mom cried. Even Conner cried and didn't try to hide it.

Everyone cried except Lexa, who wanted to but couldn't. The tears didn't come.

Instead, stone-cold guilt and numbness too heavy for tears clenched her heart and squeezed her throat.

Maybe because everyone else was only sad.

Lexa was responsible.

Lexa prayed that Dr. Timberi would be found and rescued, hoping for a miracle even when Madame Cumberland explained that was not likely. Dr. Timberi had been too large an obstacle for too long, too fierce an enemy. The Darkhands would not let him live.

And it was Lexa's fault. She knew it.

Conner and Melanie knew it too, and they both blamed her. Conner hadn't spoken to Lexa for two weeks. Melanie was more subtle. She tried to be nice, but their conversations had been cool and distant, and Lexa saw the accusation in her eyes.

Alone in her room, Lexa sat on the bed, rereading the note Madame Cumberland had given her a few days ago. Reading it over and over had become a sort of penance she inflicted on herself, feeling new pain each time she read it.

Dated the day of their conversation about Last Sigils and written in familiar handwriting, it read:

> *Mona,*
>
> *I'm off to look for Timothy. Lee told me some things that convince me he may be trying to leave Umbra. I have no idea how long I'll be gone. Hopefully I will return, but I realize it is dangerous, and I suppose I may not.*
>
> *This morning, Lexa asked about Last Sigils. After explaining them and updating my own, it occurred to me that I might make a request as well. Should a Remembrance Ceremony become necessary for me, will you please say a few words? Following that, I'd like Lexa to sing "Simple Gifts." We sang it last year in choir, so Lexa should know the song. However, music can be found in my files. Hopefully, this note will not be read for a long time and by the time I die, Lexa will be a grandmother!*
>
> *Fondly,*
> *Morgan*

Lexa's head dropped—too ashamed to hold itself up. He wouldn't have requested that if he'd known what she would say to him.

"Lexa?" Her dad pushed the bedroom door open, and she threw herself into his tight hug—the hug that had always made things better. In the strength of her father's embrace, for just a minute or two, she felt protection and relief from the unrelenting guilt.

"Lexa, shouldn't you be getting ready for the service? I don't know much about Magi funerals, but you don't wear sweats do you?"

She dropped her head again. "I can't, Dad. I can't go sing at his Remembrance."

"Lexa, I know you're sad, but—"

"It's not that. I mean, I am sad. But it's worse." She felt so dead inside, crushed by the weight of the terrible thing she'd done. So far no one knew except Conner and Melanie. Maybe it was time to confide in someone. "It's my fault he's dead."

Her dad stared at her for a few seconds. "Do you want to explain that one to me? I thought some mad scientist–witch lady attacked him."

Lexa looked up at the ceiling, unable to meet his eyes while she explained. "When Dr. Timberi posted the cast list, I got really mad. He hurt my feelings and I wanted him to know it, and mostly, I wanted to hurt him too."

Speaking the words, describing her immaturity out loud, embarrassed her. "So I asked if we could talk about my audition, and he said yes. I was going to go and be really cold and distant so he'd know I was upset. I imagined him apologizing, and I had this big speech worked up about how bad he'd hurt me and why I could never forgive him." She stopped, overwhelmed by the weight of her drama queen pettiness. She yanked her ponytail.

"If I hadn't done all that and made him talk to me right then, he wouldn't have still been at the school. None of this would have happened." Her mouth felt like sawdust. "And if that's not bad enough, the last thing he heard me say was that I hated him."

She longed to dissolve in tears, to let them wash the ache away and melt the rock inside of her chest. But nothing came.

"Lexa, listen to me." Her dad put his hands on her shoulders and looked into her eyes. "This was not your fault. Period. No, don't argue. Just listen. Yes, it was self-indulgent and immature for you to go to the school to talk to Dr. Timberi. And yes, you reacted badly to the cast list. But that doesn't mean that everything that followed was your fault, or that you are responsible. You can't beat yourself up like that. You're thirteen, Lex. You're allowed to be immature sometimes.

"From what I understand, this Lady Nightwing is a brilliant maniac, and she probably would have found a way to get at Dr. Timberi eventually. It's her fault. Not yours." His voice became softer. "Let it go, Lex. Let it go. Focusing on guilt can be a form of selfishness. Dr. Timberi wanted you to sing at his funeral. If you want to honor him, you need to put your own feelings aside. You've got an important supporting role to play in Dr. Timberi's last scene. It's not about you."

That changed Lexa's perspective, or at least shifted it. The numbness and guilt still sat rocklike in her stomach, but she realized she could do the right thing in spite of the way she felt. She owed Dr. Timberi that much. "Thanks, Daddy." She gave him a hug. "I better get ready."

When she got to Mockingbird Cottage, the lump in her stomach had spread to her throat, where it sat, becoming a wooden knot that wouldn't leave. She stood on the deck, looking down. His chair sat empty in the corner.

Too many people had come to fit inside, so a large tent had been set up in the yard below. A cool breeze rustled through the leaves as the sun set over the trees. A fresh pang jabbed Lexa. He would have loved watching this sunset.

Lucents dotted the yard, as colorful as the different Magi robes worn by the people walking into the tent. The Stephenses and Dells stuck out in their suits, ties, and dresses. Mr. Stephens also stuck out because of the scowl on his face. Lexa wondered again why he seemed to hate Dr. Timberi so much. She also wondered how the cherubim had let him through the Otherwhere.

"Lexa?" Madame Cumberland emerged from the house in gleaming, silver robes. "It's almost time to start. Are you ready?"

Lexa swallowed, wondering if the tightness would allow her to sing.

"He loved you three so much." Madame Cumberland rubbed her back for a few seconds, bringing another pang as Lexa remembered the awkward way Dr. Timberi tapped her there. "And you were particularly special to Morgan, Lexa. He would be so happy that you were singing today." Madame Cumberland straightened Lexa's brand-new, bright yellow Magi robes and wrapped her arm around Lexa's shoulder. She led Lexa to the tent and up to a seat in the front row between Melanie and Pilaf. Conner sat on the other side of Melanie and didn't smile when Lexa sat down, but he didn't scowl either, which was progress. Melanie gave her a tight smile, trying to be nice. At least Pilaf's smile was genuine. He didn't seem to blame her.

"How's the Stalk—I mean, Timothy?" Melanie whispered to Madame Cumberland.

Madame Cumberland shook her head. "I don't know. The Magisterium has him in maximum security. Too many unanswered questions to let him roam freely. I tried to see him, but no luck. Lee smuggled him a message, though, and a pie I baked. We'll see what happens at his Tribunal. You all will be important witnesses—but we'll talk about that later."

Madame Cumberland walked to the front of the tent, and Lexa looked at the carved chest resting on a table, remembering the day she'd found the reliquaries and learned about Last Sigils. That seemed like such a happy, far away time.

The tent grew silent, and Madame Cumberland smiled at the crowd, a smile full of warmth and sadness, as bittersweet and beautiful as a golden autumn day. "Thank you all for being here today. Morgan would have been so pleased." She paused and took a breath. "You all know the story of Morgan's tragedy. But not everyone knows the happiness that attended his final months, and that seems like the right story to tell today.

"A few months ago at our school, a miracle happened, something so rare it's almost unheard of: a triple Kindling. Three wonderful students Kindled at the same time. Morgan was tasked with serving as their Guide, given the job of teaching them Lightcraft.

"He jumped in with gusto, training them with all

of his energy. And as he did, another miracle happened. Morgan had built many walls around himself over the years. Those walls protected him from pain, but they also kept out joy and life and love. He maintained his walls with a formal stiffness and reserve he rarely relaxed. But as he worked with these three, their exuberance, energy, and honest, innocent affection made those walls come tumbling down.

"Morgan began to smile and laugh again, and he came to love those students with all of his oversized heart, even accepting hugs toward the end."

That thought sent an exacto-knife of pain through Lexa, slicing through the numbness into fresh, new layers of misery.

Madame Cumberland beamed at the Trio. "Because of these students, Morgan's last few months have been the happiest I've seen him since before he lost Nicole and Timothy."

Melanie started to cry, muffling her mouth with her hands to keep it soft. Lexa heard Conner sniff as well. But out of the corner of her eye, she also saw Mr. Stephens cover his face, his shoulders shaking. What in the world?

"We miss Morgan." Tears rolled down Madame Cumberland's face, but her smile got bigger. "We will miss him, but we rejoice that his last days were happy! And we rejoice that Timothy is back. Loss is a part of love. Death is a part of life. And once we accept that, we are free to be grateful for tender mercies, for love and friends and family."

Madame Cumberland nodded at Lexa, and she walked to the front of the tent. For a brief, scary moment, she got lost in the crowd looking up at her. It included men and women of all ages, representing different races and nationalities.

Lexa opened her mouth and took a deep breath, trying to make the swelling in her throat relax.

"'Tis the gift to be simple, 'tis the gift to be free
'Tis the gift to come down where we ought to be,
And when we find ourselves in the place just right,
'Twill be in the valley of love and delight."

She hoped Dr. Timberi was someplace where he could find the love he'd lost. That thought made the knot in Lexa's throat unravel into trembling sighs. The sighs grew into shaking sobs, and those sobs seemed to unlock something, because warm moisture rushed to her eyes and everything looked blurry.

Once the tears started, Lexa's grief and guilt fueled more and more of them, and her lungs surrendered to the earthquake of sobs rolling out from the epicenter in her core. Unable to finish, she stood there, sobbing and sobbing. Now, after all she'd done, she was ruining Dr. Timberi's funeral.

Conner jumped up. He walked over, and Lexa felt a comforting weight on her shoulders as he draped his arm over her. He opened his mouth, and his strong voice filled the tent, an octave too low like always.

"When true simplicity is gained,
To bow and to bend we will not be ashamed . . ."

The tears running down his face made his voice crack as well. But they soldiered on, crying at full volume.

Melanie joined them now, standing on the other side

of Lexa, holding her hand. Between Conner and Melanie, Lexa felt safe and secure, and they pushed on together. Occasionally, one of them managed to sing a word or two between all the tears and sobs.

"And when we find ourselves in the place just right,
'Twill be in the valley of love and delight."

They finished the song, huddling together in a three-way hug, bawling like babies as their tears mingled, washing away bitterness, healing old wounds, and knitting them together.

With sparkling eyes, Madame Cumberland raised her pointer stick and sent silver Light swirling toward Dr. Timberi's reliquary. Blinking over and over, Mrs. Grant flicked her red pen and blue stars joined the silver swirls. Sniffing loudly, Lee tapped his belt buckle, mingling dusty brown Light with the blue and silver. One by one, the gathered Magi stood, waving their cynosures and sending streams of colored Light twining and twisting around the carved chest. The box flashed with a rainbow of colors, the lid flew open, and a golden swan soared out.

"Welcome, dear friends!" Dr. Timberi's voice rang out strong and clear. "I hope you are well and happy. Whatever circumstances brought you to receive my Last Sigil, please accept my thanks.

"To my colleagues at Marion Academy: these last years have been a joy as we taught together in the day and fulfilled Sodality business at night. Mona, I am especially indebted to you. You kept me in the Sodality when I almost left, and your wise counsel to become a teacher filled a terrible hole in my life. Your friendship has been a great treasure these past years."

Lexa noticed Mrs. Grant whispering to her parents and the Stephenses—she must be doing a play-by-play since they couldn't see it.

"Hortense, it is no secret that you and I had our differences over the years. Last time we met, I spoke harsh words in angry tones. Forgive me, please, as I forgive you. In my death, may we please find peace."

Hortense let out an almost ghostly wail as she began to sob.

"As I organize this sigil, there are hints that my son Timothy may be trying to leave the Darkhands. I ask you, my friends, to follow up on these rumors and leads. If there is any chance of reclaiming him, please, I beg of you, take it! Tell him I loved him, and assure him that even though I'm gone, I will find a way to come and whisper that love into his heart. I do not know the rules of the place I go, but surely they cannot part loved ones forever. And if they do, you all know that I've never been very good at following rules."

Muted chuckles sounded among the sniffs and sobs.

"Finally, my Four Musketeers—Lexa, Conner, Melanie, and, most recently, Pilaf. Oh, possums! How can I tell you what you've meant to me? You will never know how much your energy, humor, and affection have done for me. You gave me a reason to live and laugh again. You reopened my heart to love and my soul to life.

"In your first adventure as Magi a few months ago, you bravely fought physical battles with Darkhands. This summer, I watched you fight different battles. These battles took place in your hearts and minds as you fought self-doubt, jealousy, insecurity, and other demons.

"You four are closely linked, with unusually complementary gifts. I believe the Light must be working to bring about some great thing through you. Consequently, we must assume that the Dark will oppose that plan and purpose. What better way to do that than by sowing discord and hurt feelings among you?

"We talked this summer about penumbras—blurry areas between Darkness and Light, neither totally illuminated or fully shadowed. I suppose that each of us is a penumbra in our own way—mixtures of dark and light. Every Magus is in constant conflict with Darkness, but especially the Darkness lurking in his or her own heart. Be wise and generous. Do not allow internal feuds to sever your connection from the Light and especially from each other."

The swan paused. "There is so much to say, but I have never liked long meetings. Do not mourn me, for I lived a full life, and I knew love. Love of a wonderful woman, love of a tiny son. Love of dear friends, and love of my students. Each of those loves is a majestic mystery, and each has been worth any pain. Forgive me of my shortcomings and remember me kindly as I go to sing in the cherubim's choir."

His voice went silent.

Lexa grabbed her ponytail and steeled herself to watch. She'd been dreading the moment the sigil would fade and he would be gone. Forever. That thought depressed her beyond anything she could express.

The swan sigil flashed, then flapped it's golden wings. The assembled Magi gasped, because it did not fade. Instead, it sailed into the air, executed a loop-de-loop, and dove straight for Lexa.

Warm shivers cascaded through her as the sigil connected, passing into her soul. Lexa yelped in surprise as a sliver of Dr. Timberi's consciousness came to life inside of her, filling her with love and acceptance and pushing away her guilt and regret. In a deep, undoubtable way, she knew he'd forgiven her.

As hope and light surged through her, she smiled for the first time in two weeks.

And then, she heard a voice. A faint and ragged whisper. *Lexa, help me, please.* She froze for half of a heartbeat.

Was she making it up? Hearing things?

Lexa, find me, please.

No. She wasn't making it up. The strongest theeling she'd ever had erupted inside of her. She didn't know whether to laugh or cry, so her voice bungee-jumped between laughter and tears.

"He's alive!" she yelled. "He's alive!"

As she spoke the words, she knew they were true. She knew with total certainty.

"Dr. Timberi's alive!"

Acknowledgments

SO MANY PEOPLE DESERVE MY GRATITUDE. Friends, colleagues, students, and readers alike have contributed to the creation of this book. To all those who helped in any way, I am deeply grateful. While I have benefitted from the kindness of many, there are some who have made particularly noteworthy contributions, and so I offer my public thanks to:

My family, for constant support, patience, and help.

Zach for his great ideas.

My boss, Ian Craig, for his kind support.

Lucy, John, Riley, Margaret, and Emma for helping me hear the words.

Leah, who grew from a bright student into a talented and valued collaborator.

Patrick, Lauren, Mary Winston, Margaret, Capucine, Emma, Lucinda, Vickle, and Lillian, who loaned their faces to my characters and sacrificed a holiday.

About the Author

BRADEN BELL LIVES WITH HIS FAMILY ON a quiet, wooded lot in Tennessee. He teaches music and theatre at a small private school and enjoys reading, gardening, and long walks with the dog. Braden loves interacting with readers. You can contact him at www.bradenbell.com.